Judge tongue
betw

'I' up for
air. He said it again as she stripped off her clothes.
But he did not resist when she pulled him down onto
the bed.

The situation was unreal. Shaw had never been
unfaithful before but he was about to betray his wife
with one of the town's most respectable citizens –
who was obviously sick in the head.

Except that she didn't look sick as she straddled his
hips. She looked, he thought as he gazed up at her –
the blonde hair dancing, the eyes closed, the mouth an
O of ecstasy – she looked quite out of this world . . .

Look out for other titles in the Sex Files series:

File 2: The Forbidden Zone – Nick Li
File 3: Unnatural Blonde – John Desoto
File 4: Double Exposure – S. M. Horowitz

THE SEX FILES
FILE 1

Beyond Limits

Carl K. Mariner

HEADLINE DELTA

Copyright © 1997 Carl K. Mariner

The right of Carl K. Mariner to be identified as the Author of the Work has been asserted by him in accordance with the Copyright, Designs and Patents Act 1988.

First published in 1997
by HEADLINE BOOK PUBLISHING

A HEADLINE DELTA paperback

10 9 8 7 6 5 4 3 2 1

All rights reserved. No part of this publication may be reproduced, stored in a retrieval system, or transmitted, in any form or by any means without the prior written permission of the publisher, nor be otherwise circulated in any form of binding or cover other than that in which it is published and without a similar condition being imposed on the subsequent purchaser.

All characters in this publication are fictitious and any resemblance to real persons, living or dead, is purely coincidental.

ISBN 0 7472 5718 3

Typeset by
Letterpart Limited, Reigate, Surrey

Printed and bound in Great Britain by
Cox & Wyman Ltd, Reading, Berks.

HEADLINE BOOK PUBLISHING
A division of Hodder Headline PLC
338 Euston Road
London NW1 3BH

Beyond Limits

ONE

QUANTOCK, PENNSYLVANIA. SEPTEMBER 19TH. 10.30 AM.

Chris Shaw was scheduling a round of golf on the phone with a buddy when he heard the commotion in the outer office.

'I don't care who you are but you're not going in without an appointment.' That was Rita, she was better than any Doberman for personal protection – though she did have a tendency to spill unnecessary blood. 'Mr Shaw is a very busy man and—'

Chris put down the phone and was on the point of calling Rita to heel when the door flew open and a slim blonde in a business suit burst into his office. He recognised her at once. You'd have to be a recluse in Quantock not to spot its most celebrated local resident, Judge Stacey Pine.

'Are you Shaw?' she demanded.

'Guilty,' he replied with a grin. Rita rolled her eyes to heaven and slammed the door shut behind the visitor.

'I'm told you're the best real-estate agent around. I want to see some properties.'

Fantastic! Shaw's pulse began to race with excitement. Now was the chance to shift one of the fancy-priced houses that had been sitting on his books for months. *Play it cool*, he told himself.

'Won't you take a seat, Judge.'

'Call me Stacey, for Christ's sake' and she gripped his hand firmly and looked into his eyes like a politician on the stump. Which of course was what she had been till she'd won the election.

'I don't have time for the civilities,' she went on. 'Show me something now.'

Chris was thrown for a second. Judge Pine had a reputation for cutting the crap. Obviously it was well earned.

'There's a couple of marvellous houses out in Northwood,' he said. 'One with a basement gym and a sauna and the other has the most wonderful atrium which—'

'No.' Pine was looking impatient already. Her fingers were twitching on the handle of her briefcase. To be honest she looked a little harassed. A lock of ash-blonde hair hung loose and she tucked it behind her ear as she spoke. 'I need a place here in town. Something smart but not pretentious. There must be something close, surely?'

'Sure thing,' said Shaw, picking a bunch of keys from his desk drawer. Inspiration had struck. 'There's a great apartment on J Street. The owners are in Europe. You'll love it.'

As he followed her out of the door Chris admired her ass – even the dull grey serge of her skirt couldn't conceal its contours. But what really put a spring in his step was the prospect of selling the O'Rourke place. The commission on that would fund the winter ski trip that Maxine was already nagging him about.

'We'll take my car,' he said.

It was a clear fall morning. The leaves on the maples on J Street had not yet begun to turn. The sun flooded the master bedroom of the O'Rourke apartment with a tree-green light as Shaw made his pitch.

'And over here we have a built-in closet you could hold a cocktail party in. Would you look at that? There's enough hanging space to keep Imelda Marcos happy.'

But Pine did not appear to be listening, her wide thin lips did not so much as twitch at his joke – which had never failed to raise a laugh yet.

She turned her back on him and pulled the white lace coverlet down the bed.

'The bed's made up?' It was the first thing she'd said since they'd entered the apartment. 'I thought the owners had gone to Europe.'

'Well, Mr O'Rourke comes back once in a while. To tell the truth I think he needs a break from his wife. I know the feeling.'

He caught a look from her stern grey eyes. 'Hey, I'm sorry. I guess that was pretty sexist. Maybe she needs a break from him.'

But the gaze had swept past him out into the blaze of light from the window, an unblinking stare that he found unnerving. Her fall of ash-blonde hair hung like a curtain around her face, the cheekbones sharp, the nose long and straight. She was an imposing woman and a damned beautiful one too, he had to admit, even in that dull grey suit with a cameo brooch at her throat like someone's grandmother.

'You got great views here,' he said, unnerved by her silence. 'We're almost at the top of the hill and you got a clear view over the city down to the south—'

'Hand me my briefcase,' she cut in, her voice controlled but firm. The kind of voice, he guessed, that Judge Pine used in court. He obeyed at once. To tell the truth, she scared the hell out of him.

As he passed over the case he noticed her hands were shaking. She seemed to fumble with the zipper. 'Are you all right?' he asked.

'I think I'll sit,' she said and slid onto the bed. Her whole body was quaking violently now.

'You're not well,' Shaw said. 'I'll drive you to a doctor.'

'*No!*' She seized his hand. Her grip was firm and hot, her fingers burning into him.

'Thank God,' she said and pulled him towards her. He sat down heavily beside her, taken by surprise. She wasn't shivering any more but she was breathing hard. He was very conscious of the heat and smell of her, a powerful late-night *tête-à-tête* kind of scent that he did not associate with a brisk career woman like Judge Pine.

'I owe you an apology, Chris.'

This was weird. Gripping his hand tight, she was pressing it to the side of her face.

'How do you mean?'

Her breathing slowed and her lips curled into a smile. 'I didn't come here to view the apartment. I'm sorry.'

'So?' Alarm bells were ringing. This was some kind of funny set-up. The woman was a flake and a time-waster but it was hard to be angry. Not with those wide grey eyes boring into his and the back of his hand on the silk of her cheek.

'Read this,' she said, producing a single sheet of paper from her case with her free hand. He took it. It seemed to be a legal disclaimer of some kind.

'It says that I'm of sound mind and take full responsibility for my actions. Also that I am in good health and suffering from no infectious diseases as of nine-thirty this morning. Keep it. It's for your peace of mind.'

'But why . . . ?' Shaw tried to stand but she held onto his hand and threw herself into his arms, pressing him down onto the bed. For a slim woman she seemed remarkably strong.

'Judge Pine!' Shaw protested.

'Kiss me!'

Her lips were on his, forcing her tongue between them. He let her.

'I'm married,' he said when they came up for air.

He said it again when she stood up and shrugged off her jacket. He muttered it to himself like a mantra as she stepped out of her skirt and stood there fiddling with the brooch at her throat. But he made no attempt to get up or prevent her from stripping in front of him. The situation was unreal. Shaw had never been unfaithful before but he was about to betray his wife with an elected officer of the court who was obviously sick in the head.

Except that she didn't look sick – not any more. Not now she had his cock in her hand and was straddling him, her lean smooth thighs on either side of his hips as she pressed the glans of his sex into the fork of her body and sank down. She looked, he thought as he gazed at her above him – the thick blonde hair now wild and dancing, the eyes closed, the mouth an O of ecstasy – she looked *possessed*. And when he lifted his hands to stroke her small jiggling breasts and felt the nipples like hot pebbles against his palm, she cried out in excitement. Never had he made so little effort with a woman before to such startling effect.

After she'd finished with him, riding him to a blazing climax that left him dazed, she simply pulled on her suit and blouse and walked out, leaving her underwear behind her on the floor.

By the time Shaw reached the street, Judge Stacey Pine had vanished into the autumn air.

TWO

BUREAU HEADQUARTERS, WASHINGTON DC. SEPTEMBER 26TH. 11.45 AM.

Stone stared into the dregs of his coffee. 'I'm seriously disappointed in you, Hannah. You've let me down.'

Hannah did not reply – he could understand Stone's point of view.

'It's bad enough for an agent to compromise himself with the subject of an investigation but this' – Stone held up a small audio cassette – 'is a major embarrassment for the department.'

'Yes, sir.'

'I can only presume that your brain was in your dick when you entered Mrs Costaine's apartment. Didn't it occur to you that the place was wired?'

'No, sir.'

The truth was that Hannah hadn't thought Martina Costaine a significant player in the complex criminal activities of the late Ethan Costaine. Certainly not significant enough to have her bedroom bugged. Not that the possibility had been at the forefront of his mind at the time.

Stone breathed a heavy sigh and dropped the cassette into the trash. 'All I can say, Agent Hannah, is that I hope she was worth it.'

Hannah didn't respond to that either. Though he could have said plenty.

'Would you mind coming in with me, Mr Hannah? Just to

check the apartment. I get nervous at night now Ethan's not here.'

They were sitting in Hannah's car outside the Costaine building. It was an awkward situation. The Bureau vetoed socialising with suspects but, in Hannah's experience, sometimes that was the only way to get to the truth. And though he hadn't gone out of his way to accost the glamorous Mrs Costaine at the museum fund-raiser, he'd done nothing to avoid her in the bar afterwards.

He had no idea who'd escorted her to the Shapiro Grand. His own date had to leave before dessert because her daughter had a cold – which was the price you paid for asking your sister. In the circumstances, driving home the almond-eyed and mildly intoxicated Widow Costaine could be termed a civic duty.

There were a lot of rooms to check in the Widow's penthouse apartment. He did it conscientiously. She found him in the bedroom.

'All seems OK, Mrs Costaine. I'll bid you goodnight.'

She considered him with interest, cornering him with his back to the midnight-blue brocade drapes that covered the vast picture window. She wore a sequinned sheath and no underwear – Hannah would have put money on it. Pinpoints of light sparkled on the curve of her hips, the sweep of her thighs and on the half cups that concealed – just – the tips of her breasts. Her dark hair was pinned in an elaborate confection that exposed the slender stem of her neck. Her black eyes twinkled with mischief as she took a step towards him.

The Merry Widow was a retired porno-movie actress from Puerto Rico whose best performances, so the Bureau's records revealed, had been suppressed by her late husband. It was not entirely a surprise to Hannah that she still liked to put on a show in private.

'My maid is staying with her mother,' she said, presenting her back to him. 'Help me with my hair please, Agent Hannah.'

It was the moment of truth. He could have left without touching her and, in the cold light of day, that would have been the sensible thing to do. But it was past midnight and there was a hunger in his loins that had to be fed. Her sumptuous *café au lait* skin was inches from his fingers as he began to extract the pins from her blue-black locks. As the gleaming hair tumbled across her shoulders she leaned back against him and pushed the soft cushion of her buttocks into his crotch.

He dropped the pins. She squirmed her ass into him and his body responded. He couldn't help it. Right then the Bureau and the Costaine investigation could have gone up in smoke for all he cared.

Martina reached behind her back and squeezed his cock beneath his trousers.

'What's this?' she murmured. 'Are you carrying a concealed weapon, Special Agent?'

'Don't worry, I've got a permit.'

He found the zipper on her dress and the hiss of its descent was echoed by the sound of her opening his fly. Her tits spilled into his hands, weighty and full, with points like cherry pits. She had her fingers on his cock by now and, for a moment, they stood glued together, exploring each other's intimate flesh like horny teenagers.

She turned her head to be kissed and he swivelled her round to embrace her properly. Her mouth was cool somehow, her lips shy at first then soft and melting and he realised she was playing with him a little. He liked that. He slithered the tight dress down, over the violin curve of her hips. She shimmied out of it, kicking the garment off her foot, all ten-thousand-bucks worth of it. He held her at arm's length to get a good look at what lay underneath. It turned out he'd been wrong, she *was* wearing underwear – a G-string brief with a heart-shaped pussy pouch that barely covered her mound. With her hair loose and her big breasts billowing she looked like a wet dream made flesh.

She burst out laughing, sending her tits into a delicious tremble.

'You look pretty funny like that,' she said and he realised he was still fully clothed, in his tuxedo no less – with his penis sticking out of his pants at full stretch.

'Let me help you, baby,' she said, her fingers reaching for his tie.

Maybe it was the way she laughed or the sight of himself in a cheval mirror looking like a bedroom klutz. More likely it was the sway of those big breasts as she stood there all but naked in front of him. Whatever it was, he picked her up and threw her onto the bed.

As he pulled his clothes off she slipped her panties down her legs and spread them wide. She had the nudest pussy he had ever seen, depilated to perfection, the pink folds of her labia like the intricate whorl of an unfurling rose.

He got on his knees and kissed her there.

'Don't stop,' she said after a moment and he didn't, tracing the perimeter of her delta with a feather-light touch. Her knees rose and her legs moved further apart. He slid his hands beneath her and gripped the cheeks of her ass. She felt soft yet solid as she relaxed into his grip, settling back to take her pleasure.

'Ooh,' she breathed as he ran his tongue the length of her slit and 'ooh' again as he pushed the tip into her vagina. She was wet in there, eager for him, but he withdrew to lap her gently then blow a whisper of breath across her clit.

'Fuck me,' she moaned.

'Not yet.'

'Yes, yes. Come on!'

He wanted to bring her to orgasm with his mouth but the excitement in her voice was too much. He crawled over her and she kissed him hungrily.

'Put it in,' she hissed but he made her do it, her fingers trembling as she pressed the purple head of his glans between the velvet folds of her pussy lips and then into the honeyed warmth beyond. Her eyes danced as he began thrusting.

It took barely a minute but they both came, with a shout from him and a long-drawn-out moan from her that ended in a sigh. It sounded rehearsed and Hannah reckoned that, one way or another, it had been. Not that he cared. He aimed to give her plenty more practice before the night was over.

★ ★ ★

And he did. The proof was on the audio cassette now nestling beside a styrofoam coffee cup and a Snickers wrapper in Stone's trash can. Hannah had no illusions that that was the only copy, edited versions would be circulating the Bureau from now till Christmas. He felt a complete fool.

'I'm reassigning you.' Stone said. 'My assessment is that you're not a team player, Hannah. You don't stick to the game plan. From now on you're off Costaine. I'm putting you on something where you can follow your instincts. But don't – repeat don't – fuck this one up.'

Hannah took a deep breath. 'Thanks, Jeffrey. I won't let you down.' Stone might be a pain-in-the-ass pen-pusher but it had to be said. He owed him.

Stone gave him a tight little smile – possibly the first Hannah had ever seen on his lips – and then slapped the desk with his open palm.

'OK, let's move on. Next up is a missing person. Felice Cody, thirty-four, single, lives on her own in Maxwell, Virginia. Her sister reported her missing yesterday – she could have been gone for three or four days. Find out what's happened to her.'

'Why are we involved?'

By way of an answer, Stone took a buff folder from his drawer and tossed it onto the desk in front of him. It landed with a thunk.

'Take a look at the file.'

Hannah picked it up. It was thick.

'What the hell does this woman do?'

'She's a research biologist, working for the military. What she does in her laboratory I cannot tell you because I don't have that kind of clearance – and neither do you. What she does in her spare time is write books about flying saucers and little green men kidnapping the President.'

'Hey!' Hannah was leafing through the file. 'This is F S Cody. She had a bestseller with *Starlight of the Gods*.'

'You see, I knew this job was right for you. You're on her wavelength already. Or should I say astral plane?'

'I keep an open mind, Stone. Her book blew me away.'

'Should be published as fiction, if you ask me.'

'Most of this stuff here looks like letters asking her not to go into print.'

'Yeah and an essay in response telling the Army to go fuck itself. She must be a hell of a scientist. Otherwise I don't know how she gets away with it.'

'Maybe she hasn't.'

Stone fixed Hannah with a hard gleam from behind his rimless spectacles. 'How do you mean?'

'I mean, from the look of this the most obvious people who'd want Cody out of the way are her employers. Maybe she's no longer so useful. Maybe she made so much money from the last book she told them to stuff the job.'

'Don't jump to conclusions, Hannah. If you read on you'll see that the latest thinking is to leave her alone. She's wacky but valuable. And we need to know what's happened to her.'

Hannah turned to the last page. There was a black-and-white print of Felice Cody at a bookshop signing session. She wore heavy-rimmed spectacles and a shapeless dress that looked like a mailbag. Her mousy-brown hair was scraped back off her forehead and speared through with a wooden barrette.

'Nice bone structure,' said Hannah.

Stone's face creased into a frown.

'Don't panic,' said Hannah, getting to his feet. 'She's not my type.'

THREE

TRANSCRIPT OF TORK JACKSON INTERVIEW. ATTENDING OFFICERS CHARLES AND JOHNSON, NJPD.

CHARLES: How old are you, TJ?

TJ: Eighteen.

C: And you are a student at Maybury High in Maybury, New Jersey?

TJ: Yes.

JOHNSON: You want to tell us what happened on Monday this week?

TJ: Sure. Miss Simons asked me to stay in class during the lunch recess. She said she wanted to discuss my progress.

J: Miss Simons is Madeleine Simons, your English teacher, right?

TJ: Right.

C: Go on.

TJ: Well, she started out talking about my grades which, I admit, aren't good and I thought she was going to chew my ass. Of course, you could say she did just that.

J: Very funny.

C: Get on with it.

TJ: OK. As I say, I thought she was mad at me because her lips were all pursed up and thin and her hands were shaking. I've seen her when she's worked up about something and she looked like that now. But suddenly she's talking about the football game on the weekend and I'm like, what the fuck is going on? Sorry, am I not supposed to say that?

J: Tell it in your own words, TJ, you're not in school now.

TJ: OK. So, she goes on about the football game and how well I played, which is true – I rushed for ninety yards and scored two touchdowns—

J: Yeah, we heard. You told us already.

TJ: Did I? Anyhow, Miss Simons comes on like she's some big-deal football fan which is rich since she's spent two years telling me being a jock is no guarantee of nothing and unless I study my entire life will go down the tubes. Then she starts saying how she's always had this special feeling for me and what a privilege it's been for her to watch me grow into a young man with a future and all kinds of stuff. She says she knows she gives me a hard time about studying but that's because she cares about me. When she says this I don't know where to look.

C: You were embarrassed?

TJ: You're not kidding. Miss Simons is this very cool scientific type and it's like the students are just machines to her. There's nothing *personal* about her, you know? For her to come out with all this is amazing. Then she starts asking me if being a football star makes me popular with the girls and I'm thrown way off track. She's got up from her desk now and come round to the side where I'm sitting and she kind of perches her ass on the edge of the desk so she's right in front of me. And she begins talking about, er, sex.

J: Sex?

TJ: Well, she calls it 'personal relationships' like it's some study subject but when she asks me if I'm friendly with Theresa Freni I know what she's really asking is, am I boffing her?

C: How do you know?

TJ: Because her voice kind of drops, so she's all breathy, and I notice she's squeezing her thighs together under her skirt. I mean, I can't help it. She's about three feet in front of me, wearing this flowery dress and squirming against the desk. Anyhow, I play dumb and say that Theresa is a real hard worker with the cheerleaders and an inspiration to us guys on the field. 'I bet she is,' says Miss Simons, 'she's got legs like a Broadway showgirl. What's it like to get between them?'

J: And what was your reply?

TJ: I didn't say it was a life-threatening experience, which is actually the truth because her brothers are connected. Anyhow, now Miss Simons is pulling her skirt up from the waist, inch by inch. 'How do you think I'd look as a cheerleader?' she asks. 'Have I got the legs for it?' Man, I nearly fell off my chair. She was quite a sight.

J: What do you mean?

TJ: Well, I'd never looked at her as a woman before, if you know what I mean. She must be almost my mother's age and she's such a bitch. I thought she was sexless, we all did. But here she is, just inches in front of me, raising her skirt ever so slowly, and her legs are smooth and firm and creamy. And she gets the hem almost to the top of her thighs which are all bare and shiny and she smiles at me. I'd never seen her smile before. I didn't think she could. It was like there was a different woman in her skin. A real warm, flesh-and-blood female. Then she pulls the skirt right up to her waist and she's buck naked underneath.

C: Really?

TJ: Damn right. And she's damn fucking gorgeous too. Her belly's kind of domed, just a little, and it slopes down into a black bush trimmed all neat. And down the middle is this groove and her pussy lips are on show, all pink and cute. I think I'm in a dream. I just stare at her until she says, 'Do you give head, Torquil?' and she grabs my hair with one hand and pulls my face into her crotch. I don't say anything – I can't. I just wrap my arms round her hips and dive in there. She's as sweet as a cantaloupe and juicy like one too. Christ, just thinking about it makes my throat dry up. Do you mind if I have a drink of water or something?

J: I guess we could all use one.

C: Here you go, TJ.

TJ: You guys are enjoying this, aren't you?

J: It's more fun than talking to your average punk. Just so

long as you're not stringing us along.

TJ: It's what happened, I swear. I'm just sorry Miss Simons has gone.

C: I bet you are. So, what happened next?

TJ: All the while I'm licking her out, she's got hold of my hair, pushing my face into her pussy, rubbing herself against me. And she's talking to me in this whisper, saying all kinds of horny things.

J: Like?

TJ: Like, I dunno, like the hot things you do when you're on the edge. 'Use your tongue, lick my clit, make me come then fuck me on the desk. I want your cock. You can put it in my cunt.' I know it sounds stupid now but it had me going. I mean, this was *Miss Simons*. I still can't get over it.

C: And did you have intercourse with her on the desk?

TJ: Yes, sir. After she came on my face she bent over the desk and I put it in her from behind.

J: Just like that?

TJ: Well, we kissed first. We kissed a lot, actually and I put my hands inside her blouse and she took my dick out of my pants. Her tits were humungous, just fabulous. And she looked at my cock with that serious look of hers and stuck the end of it in her mouth. I nearly shot off down her throat.

J: Did she say anything?

TJ: She said she'd really like to suck me off but she'd prefer my come up her cunt. Those were the words she used. Then she bent over the desk with her skirt up and her ass sticking out. She was quite big there, her cheeks all round and white. I lived in fear of her for years and I never realised she had such a beautiful ass.

J: And she said nothing else?

TJ: She said, 'Hurry up,' that's all. Then when we were doing it on the desk the banging started at the door.

C: What banging?

TJ: Like someone thumping on it with their fist and shouting. Miss Simons didn't seem to care. She said, 'Don't you dare stop, keep fucking. I'm going to come.'

And she did. She screamed and I came too. Then the door burst open and Associate Principal James and Miss Foggerty came in and they made me leave the room.

C: And you haven't seen Miss Simons since?

TJ: No. I tried calling her that night but there was no reply. Then I went round there and met some of your guys. I wish I'd of known she was going away. I'd of gone with her.

J: That's some story, TJ.

C: The last of the red-hot lovers.

TJ: Don't make fun of me. I got Miss Simons all wrong. I just hope she's OK. I really miss her.

TRANSCRIPT ENDS.

FOUR

MAXWELL, VIRGINIA. SEPTEMBER 27TH. 2.00 PM.

'I can't imagine why Felice needs so much security,' said the woman beside Hannah as she sorted through a large ring of keys in the hallway of Felice Cody's building. 'I mean,' she went on, 'it's not as if it's that bad a neighbourhood.'

Hannah could think of a few good reasons why a military scientist obsessed with the paranormal might want added protection but he didn't voice them. He just admired the bolt of honey-blonde hair that fell down Brigitte Behr's back and the purse of her pouting lips as she extricated another key from the ring and pushed it into one of the locks on the steel-plated door.

The missing woman's sister had insisted on accompanying Hannah and he was glad she had – and not only for her skill in cracking the safe of Cody's home. There was no avoiding the fact that Felice's younger married sister was a stunner.

She turned to Hannah as the heavy door yielded at last and favoured him with a dazzling grin of triumph. 'There we are, Mr Hannah. Now I only have to disarm the alarm system.'

He followed her inside and watched as she tapped a code number into the control pad on the wall behind the door.

'I'm sorry to put you to this trouble, Mrs Behr, considering that you've been through all this with the police department.'

She put her hand on his arm. The smile was gone and her hazel eyes were luminous. 'Please, Mr Hannah, I love my sister and I'm worried sick about her. How can this be trouble?'

She quickly pulled her hand back and added briskly. 'Anyhow, I've got to come over and feed the cats.'

Hannah took in the long dark hallway lined with toppling bookshelves and stacked packing cases. Three pairs of green eyes stared back at him out of the murk.

'Cats? How many has she got?'

'Six. I don't understand how she could bear to leave them. Something terrible must have happened to her, Mr Hannah.'

'We'll find her, Mrs Behr. Here, take my handkerchief.'

'It's OK, I'm not going to cry – I'm going to make coffee. Let me know when you're through.'

She left Hannah standing in the gloomy corridor, the cats following her as she went into the kitchen. Hannah tried a door to the right – a broom closet, mostly full of old magazines and yellowing piles of newspapers. The boxes in the hall also contained years of back issues. He delved into a pile – *The Paranormal, Out There!, Fortean Times* - the case was full of arcane and lovingly collected material. It made sense: F S Cody, bestselling author and archivist of the unexplained, lived and breathed her subject.

Further down, Hannah found a living room and a study, both overflowing with books and papers. Cody wasn't completely obsessed with paranormal phenomena, he discovered. CDs of Beethoven, Mahler and Wagner were piled on shelves next to reference works on cats and gardening. She had a sizeable collection of books on architecture and painting, not much of it modern. She had a distinct preference for the Renaissance, that was obvious. Aside from textbooks and a library of biology titles there was the usual canon of English lit and a lot of science fiction. A wall of shelves was given over to popular science, including her own work. He saw German and Japanese editions of her best-known book, *Starlight of the Gods*.

None of this was a surprise to Hannah – except for three pocket-size paperbacks tucked away on a bottom shelf. *Dungeon of Desire, Three Weeks On Her Knees* and *Slut Heaven* were the last things he expected to find. All three looked new. They also, from the condition of the spines and the turned-down marker pages, looked as if they'd been thoroughly read. He replaced them and moved on.

The bedroom was a haven from the untidy mustiness elsewhere. Sunlight streamed in from high windows onto a lace-covered bed. The floor was carpeted in thick-pile plum and the walls were sparely furnished with Matisse prints. At the foot of the bed stood a large slim-line television set and VCR. Hannah grinned. In common with most of the bourgeois population of the Western world, it seemed Felice liked to lie in bed and watch TV.

He went into the adjoining bathroom. It too was plush and clean and comfortable. Here there was no clutter, not even a toothbrush. He wasn't surprised. The police report had noted that some clothes and essential toiletries were missing.

He opened the mirrored cabinet above the sink. The usual stuff was there – pain-reliever, suntan lotion, fancy shampoos, dental floss. And a pack of Trojans.

Now that was interesting. There had been no mention in the file or in Stone's briefing of a man in Felice Cody's life. On the contrary, she was referred to as 'single' – in the sense of 'sexually inactive'. Hannah chuckled as he turned the condom packet over in his fingers. Nobody, in his experience, was completely sexless and this woman – though she looked like she was dead from the waist down – was obviously no exception.

This changed things. Suppose Felice had suddenly acquired a boyfriend – one who read soft-porn paperbacks, for example? Might she simply not have taken off with him? It was strange, of course, that she hadn't told her sister but there could be any number of reasons why not. The cats worried him, though. Surely no cat-lover would leave without making arrangements for their care? Maybe there was a neighbour in the building who helped out, one whom Brigitte didn't know about.

Hannah returned to the bedroom and examined the contents of an antique desk. There wasn't much. Letters from France from '*ta cousine, Rénée*' – a relative obviously;

and some photographs of blurry views – Felice looking weather-beaten sipping beer in a garden – holiday mementoes. He turned to the bedside table. There was nothing helpful amongst the pins and dusty dimes unless you counted a half-squeezed tube of KY jelly – which Hannah did. There was also, lying flat in the drawer, a half-pint of bourbon.

Under the bed he found a magazine. The bed itself was very low and he guessed the police officers who had already been through the room had simply missed it. He wondered what they would have thought had they turned up the copy of *Hustler* – the most recent issue, he noticed. On the assumption they were male they would certainly have flicked through it. Then they would have discovered the envelope tucked between its lurid pages and his enquiry would have had a more informed start.

One thing was clear to Hannah as he shuffled the deck of Polaroid images – Felice did not just have one boyfriend, she had several. There were a couple of beer-bellied middle-aged guys, one with tattoos, the other with a chest-rug of hair but the rest – he had to hand it to the so-called sexually inactive Felice – were young and hung.

The photographs, there were about a dozen, revealed a parade of naked guys ready for action. Most had goofy grins as well as erections – as if just before the main event the object of their lust had produced a camera and said, 'Smile.' One or two looked pissed off about it. A moody blond boy with hair down to his shoulders held a cock like a baseball bat in his fist. There was a murderous glint in his eye as he glowered at the camera and Hannah wondered how Felice had appreciated his attentions a few seconds later. He'd bet she'd loved it.

The last photograph was of the lady herself. Hannah almost didn't recognise her but the high cheekbones and oval eyes were the same. Otherwise she was unrecognisable. Of course in the other photographs he'd seen of F S Cody, she'd been wearing more than a garterbelt and a big smile. And of all the photos he'd now seen of this elusive woman there was no doubt in Hannah's mind in which she seemed the most alive. The conventional view of Felice Cody was way off-beam – the woman was a fox.

However, she was a missing fox and this new information did not make Hannah feel easier about her safety. If she was in the habit of having promiscuous sex with rough trade anything could have happened to her.

Hannah lay back on the bed. From the Polaroids it was obvious that this room had seen plenty of action. He looked around and there, smack in the centre of his vision, was the TV and VCR. He examined them more closely this time. They were expensive models he hadn't seen before. Beside the VCR was a pile of unmarked video cassettes. He could imagine what they contained. In all probability Felice and her studs had not been lying in bed watching *The Sound of Music*. He switched on and pushed a cassette into the machine.

It came on in the middle of the action. The scene appeared to be a garage or a workshop. In the background was a bench with tools and there were tyres and bits of car bodywork. In the foreground was a mattress where a man and woman were getting down to business. The man lay on his back, naked but for a sweat-tracked T-shirt. He was leaning up on his elbows watching the woman's head as it bobbed up and down on his groin. 'That's it, baby,' he was saying, 'nice and easy now. Take it right down your throat.'

The woman was wearing black panties stretched tight over a broad but shapely ass as she knelt over the guy. Her butt loomed large in the camera's view and a hand came out of nowhere and pulled the panties down over her rear. 'Yeah,' came an off-screen grunt, probably the cameraman, 'let the viewers see what you got.'

The woman acknowledged her sudden nudity by shimmying her ass; her buttocks were big and creamy in the lens. The divide between was deep and shadowy and a crop of thick brown pussy hair poked into view at its base. Her head bobbed more urgently now and Hannah could see she had a hand busy in there as well. The guy began to groan and thrust his pelvis up into her and the camera moved round to capture the climax of the action. From this angle the dangling white globe of the woman's right tit was fully visible, swelling and then elongating as it buffeted against the man's knees.

Hannah was riveted. It wasn't clear whether this was Felice in action, though he had his suspicions. He had a hard-on he could use to chop wood but that was pardonable – he was only doing his job after all. It was his duty to keep looking.

'Ugh!' went the guy on the mattress, now lying back with his eyes closed. His loins were thrusting upwards into the woman's mouth and she took all she could, jacking his shaft at the same time. Suddenly he erupted into her, his ass pounding the mattress as he threshed in orgasm. He carried on jerking even after it was over, his movements dwindling and his body twitching.

The woman pulled the loose hair away from her face and looked up, her breasts shivering, her wet lips drawn back in a happy smile. 'Who's next?' she said.

'Oh my God,' said a voice from behind Hannah. 'That's Felice.'

Hannah zapped the off-button and turned to see Brigitte frozen in the door frame.

'How much did you see?' he asked.

'Enough.' She stepped unsteadily into the room and sank onto the bed.

'Did you know about your sister's boyfriends, Mrs Behr?'

She laughed, though it wasn't a happy sound. 'She never had any. She was dumped by a man when she was at college and she's had no relationships since.'

'How about casual boyfriends? Not relationships as such but—'

'Fucks, that's what you mean, isn't it? Speak plainly, please, there's no point in being polite.'

'I understand you must be upset, Mrs Behr.'

'For God's sake, do you have to call me Mrs Behr all the time? To answer your question, "upset" does not cover it. I always felt sorry for my sister when it came to sex and it looks like my pity was misplaced. What else have you found?'

Hannah showed her the Polaroid photographs. She turned

them over slowly, studying each one.

'Do you know any of these guys?'

'Never seen them before. Though, in some cases, I rather wish I had.'

Hannah had withheld the shot of Felice but she snatched it from him and looked at it for a long time.

'I don't understand,' she said. 'We had a conversation only two months ago when she told me she hated the thought of being in bed with anybody. Man or woman. In any case, she said, she was too damn busy for sex.'

'So this' – Hannah pointed to the photos – 'is a new development, in your opinion?'

'Yes,' she said. 'That television's new, too, and the VCR. I've never seen them before.'

Her big eyes looked soulful and unhappy.

'I'm sorry, Brigitte,' he said.

'Put on another video,' she said. 'Let's see what else my shy sister got up to.'

He did as he was told. They watched in silence.

Framed on screen was a bed – the bed they were sitting on. Felice came into view and began to strip. She unbuttoned a long dark skirt and an apricot blouse with a swirly pattern. She threw them out of shot and posed in stockings, suspenders and a black lacework bra through which gleamed the white skin of her breast. She was clumsy and gauche. Hannah was embarrassed for her and her sister by his side. He was also massively erect.

Felice unhooked her bra and her tits spilled into the open. The orbs were solid and heavy, the discs of her areolae ridged and swollen. When she bent over to yank her panties down her thighs the big breasts swung forward like hanging fruit. Without ceremony she lay back on the bed and spread her legs. Her pussy lips gaped in the vee of her brown bush like a smiling pink mouth and she rubbed herself there, her other hand at an engorged nipple. The woman's desire was palpable.

A man came into the frame. He was naked and he approached the bed from behind the camera. His buns were tight and white in contrast to his broad bronzed shoulders.

He knelt on the bed beside Felice and covered one soft tit in his hand. As he lowered his head to hers, Hannah recognised the blond boy from the Polaroid.

They kissed wetly, Felice exploring between his thighs as he turned towards her. Brigitte shifted her position on the bed as the boy's cock came into view. It was only semi-erect but even so the shaft filled Felice's grasp and hung down beyond her wrist. Felice began to pump it, slipping the foreskin back over the flaming red knob.

There had been no movement of the camera and Hannah concluded that it was fixed on a tripod. There seemed to be just the two of them in the room and so far they'd not said a word. The only sound had been of bodies slithering on sheets and the obscene slick of hand on genitals. Now the blond boy whispered in Felice's ear and she giggled. 'Must I?' she said in a low breathy voice. 'Please, Howard. Don't make me.'

But she didn't sound distressed and she was moving to his directions, up onto her hands and knees, with her ass facing the camera. It was an uncompromising rear, square and meaty with tautly curving buttocks and a mysterious divide between. Whatever it was Howard was going to do to it, Hannah wanted to do it too.

The blond's big hands were on her cheeks now, spreading them to reveal her crack, from the dimple of her rosebud to the hanging purse of her brown-fringed pussy. He had a tube in his hand – Hannah recognised it – and he squeezed a long swirl of clear jelly into the open fissure. As he began to work the lubricant into Felice's anus it was obvious what was going to happen next.

Hannah turned to Brigitte. She was as white as the bed linen. 'Have you seen enough?' he said.

She shook her head. 'I don't believe this,' she said.

Howard's cock was at full stretch now, like a big white wand with a crimson head. He rubbed a gobbet of jelly along the barrel and positioned himself in the open vee of the woman's back-thrust thighs. The moment of penetration was obscured by the boy's tight white buttocks but, as they pressed in, Felice gave a jolt and a cry. The pair held still for a moment and then Howard began to thrust forward again. 'Ooh baby,' he said as he hit bottom. Then he pulled back and turned her ass so the camera could see his pole half buried in the mouth of her most secret orifice.

'That's it,' said Brigitte and reached for the off-button.

Hannah looked at her. She was shivering like a leaf in a storm. Her huge eyes latched onto him. 'I wish Felice kept liquor,' she said. 'I need a real drink.'

Hannah fetched a tooth glass from the bathroom and the bourbon from the bedside cabinet. She stared at the bottle in surprise and then shrugged.

'She didn't used to drink. But then there's a lot she didn't used to do.'

She downed the shot in one and held the glass out for another.

'Won't you join me?' she said.

Hannah shook his head.

'Not when you're working, I suppose. Though it's a funny kind of work, watching a woman get her ass fucked.' The obscenity sounded doubly crude on her full pink lips.

She took another slug and began to weep. Hannah searched for his handkerchief, then remembered he'd already given it to her.

'Oh for God's sake,' she said through her tears, 'put your arms round me, or don't you do that on duty either?'

Hannah hugged her to him on the edge of the bed. She circled his chest beneath his jacket and continued to sob for a moment. He could feel the heat of her body through the cotton of his shirt. Her fine blonde hair was in his face like spun gold and she smelt of something subtle and expensive. Her body was shaking and he realised he was shaking too, quivering with the kind of pent-up sensual tension that he could not, would not give in to. Against his belly his cock thrummed like a tuning fork. She nuzzled harder against him and, as the pair of them fell backwards onto the bed, he said silently to himself, *This is not my fault!*

Her lips were hot against his neck, then on his chin. Her bourbon-scented breath blew across his lips as she said, 'Don't tell me you don't kiss on duty either.' Then she licked the corners of his mouth with her sly cat-like tongue.

That did it. He rolled her over and kissed her hard, squeezing her slender torso to him, letting his hands roam where they had been itching to go ever since she had come up to him outside the building barely two hours earlier. He pulled her skirt up to her hips and plucked at her tiny panties with his fingers. She helped him drag them down her smooth thighs and kicked them free, all the while sucking on his tongue. As he bared her pussy and her top leg swung over his thigh, their hands clashed as they both clawed at his trousers. He thought how ridiculous the pair of them would look if they were they being filmed like Felice and her blond lover. Would a camera, he wondered, capture any of the incredible excitement he felt as he moved over Brigitte and her small fingers pushed his hugeness into the silky yielding softness between her honey-sweet thighs?

'Oh, oh, oh,' she moaned in his ear as their loins pressed together, her legs wrapped around his back, their connection like an electrical circuit of sudden and uncontrollable desire. It took barely a minute. The pair of them blew a fuse at the same time.

Afterwards she went to sleep in his arms and he held her tight, breathing in the scent of her long blonde locks as he pondered the riddle of the missing woman who had caused him once more to step out of line.

FIVE

TRANSCRIPT OF PHONE CONVERSATION BETWEEN AL AND
BENJY LEWIS, SEPTEMBER 24TH. AUTHORISED WIRETAP
RE: ONGOING DRUGS SURVEILLANCE OF SUSPECT AL LEWIS.

BENJY: Hey, Al, how are ya? Where you bin?

AL: Ssh, little brother, you know you don't ask me that.

B: I bin callin you. When you comin over? There's somethin I gotta tell ya.

A: I can't come over right now. I'm waitin for someone.

B: Bet you got a woman there. You got a one-track mind when it comes to pussy.

A: Hey, who's talkin? *You* got the mind, I got the dick. You don't need no thinkin, you need action.

B: I got it. That's what I wanted to tell you about.

A: Really? Let me guess – it's that waitress at Apple Pie, right? I told you she's worth checkin out.

B: No, Al. It's someone from work.

A: From that fancy bank in Manhattan? I suppose it's one of those part-timers who takes out the trash.

B: *No*, man. One of the execs from the top floor.

A: You shittin me? What's her name?

B: Kate Karlsen. Senior fund manager. Big wheel in the organisation.

A: And she's steppin out with a boy from the mailroom? You're dreamin, Benjy.

B: Well, we ain't exactly steppin out but I porked her last week. Wild but weird, man. That's why I was callin. You're the only one I can talk to.

A: Shoot then, bro. I can't wait.

B: Right. It's the end of the day, gone eight, and I'm on late with Aaron and Mouse. They's in the back sortin the last batch of mail for the mornin when Miss Karlsen comes in. I thought she had a late package, cos she often does. Though she's a big deal she's no snotty bitch. She's real polite to me and all the other guys and you want to do things for her, you know?

A: What's this female like?

B: Tall, slim-line, brown eyes, black hair cut in one of those short styles so it shows off her little white neck.

A: So she's cute?

B: In her own way, sure. She's always got shadows under her eyes though and she wears these skirts down past her knees like she's eighty. But when she smiles there's this little gap between her front teeth that I really like.

A: Sounds like you've had your eye on this babe for a while.

B: There's somethin about her, Al. Every hour of the day she's up there workin but those fat slobs on the sixteenth are always bad-mouthin her. I hear 'em in the restroom and in the elevator. They call her Miss Chaste Manhattan – ha ha. I feel sorry for her.

A: So when she comes in the mailroom last week you decide to do her the big favour?

B: Not exactly. What happens is, she says, 'Are you alone, Benjy?' and I tell her about the other guys in the back. 'Get them in here,' she tells me so I do. She wedges the door shut and puts this big black purse of hers on the counter. Then she says, 'Do you guys like women?' so we all say yeah. 'And money?' and we go, 'You bet.' We're all grinnin away cos this is better than work though we haven't a clue what she's up to. She's not grinnin though and I see her fingers are shakin as she opens up her bag and pulls out a fistful of notes. 'There's five hundred dollars each,' she says, 'if you'll show me a good time.'

A: Are you makin this up?

B: Why would I make it up? I'm not that desperate.

A: You're always desperate, Benjy. You never get no pussy unless I lay it on for you.

B: Well, this time I did, asshole. Do you want to hear about it or not?

A: Of course I do. Look, I'm sorry. I didn't mean to put you down. I just wanted to make sure you wasn't shootin me a line.

B: OK. So, anyway, we're standin there as she counts out fifteen one-hundred-dollar bills and gives us five each. We're so blown away we don't even say thanks. 'Come on,' she says. 'Take your pants off. Let me see what I'm payin for.' We just stand there like statues and I'm thinkin did I hear right? Suddenly Mouse starts gigglin in that stupid way of his and Miss Karlsen smacks him round the mouth. That shuts him up real quick. 'Get your dick out, fat guy,' she says, 'or give me my money back.'

A: So, did he?

B: He never had his hand on that many hunnerds before, he weren't gonna let go. He drops his pants and she puts her hand in his shorts and pulls his cock out. I wouldn't of paid ten cents for it myself. It's like a little sausage hanging down, all pink and hairless. But she don't seem to mind. She gets on her knees and puts it in her mouth. Me and Aaron are just frozen to the spot, watchin her lips and hands go to work on him, then she's suckin real hard, her cheeks goin in and out. And when she takes it out Mouse is more of a Moose, if you know what I mean. He's got this big angry horn on, all wet with her suckin.

A: Bet you had a boner too.

B: Fit to bust my pants. Especially when Aaron gets behind her and puts his hand up her skirt. 'Oh please,' she goes and wiggles her ass back at him. He yanks on that skirt, pulls it right up to her waist and she's got these little pink panties with flowers round the waist and they're stretched tight across her butt. Aaron gets his fingers in there and pulls the strip between her legs to one side and then we're lookin right at her pussy. Man, that's some sight. She's got this neat little forest between her legs, black as the hair on her head, and in the middle is her pussy, all pink and wet and poutin like it's beggin to be plugged.

A: So you plug it.

B: Aaron does. I haven't seen him get his joint out but there it is, big and veiny with the top kind of purple where he don't have no foreskin. He just spits on the end of it and sticks it in her. And when he does it she goes, '*That's what I want*,' and pushes her ass back at him. I tell you, Al, that's the horniest thing I ever saw – Miss Karlsen from the sixteenth floor on her hands and knees in the mailroom gettin it at both ends.

A: Sounds poetic the way you put it, baby brother. When did you get your turn?

B: Well, they don't take long. Aaron pops first and Mouse shoots off into her mouth about a second later. I have my cock out already, kind of lettin it cool a bit cos I don't want to go off early. And Miss Karlsen comes over to me and grabs it. 'Your turn, Benjy,' she says. 'Fuck me with that big pretty dick.' So I sit her on the counter and pull her panties off and unbutton her blouse. It's difficult because it's got tiny pearl buttons all the way up but she helps me and then I get her bra off and I see these little apples under there with big red points. Man, they're delicious I cram them into my mouth, one after the other. 'Oooh, oooh,' she's goin and tuggin at my shirt so when she gets her legs round my waist and slides off the counter onto my cock those points are diggin into my chest. I don't reckon Aaron and Mouse have done more than get her engine started cos she's bouncing on my joint as I carry her around the room. Like Jack Nicholson in *Five Easy Pieces*, you know, when he's porkin that little blonde with the boobs. I watched that once when I was blasted and since then I've always wanted to pork and walk. And now I'm carryin Miss Karlsen round on my dick, with those sharp little titties scratchin my chest and her tight round butt in my hands and my fingers right up her crack. And just when I think I can't hold her up any more she starts gettin out of control and we end up on the floor with her still jerkin on my belly and my cock going fizz like shook-up champagne. It has to be the most fan-fucking-tastic fuck of my life, I swear.

A: Wow!

B: Don't tell me you're impressed, brother.

A: Benjy, I am sincerely impressed. When can I meet her?

B: I wish I knew. As I'm lying in a heap on the floor she gets up, grabs her clothes and walks out the door. Mouse is standing there with a hard-on like a night-stick but she just shoves him out of the way. He's been moanin ever since that he's the only one not to screw her properly. Some people ain't hardly ever satisfied.

A: How was she the next day?

B: She didn't show. Hasn't been seen for a week. The top floor are having a shit-fit because she's knee-deep in all this mucho important business. Hey, we miss her in the mailroom too.

A: No kiddin.

B: Sure you don't want to come over, Al? I'm gonna go pick up some Chinese and rent *Five Easy Pieces*.

SIX

BUREAU HEADQUARTERS. SEPTEMBER 30TH. 4.10 PM.

Hannah could read Stone like a book. As he reported what he had discovered at Felice Cody's apartment, he could see the alarm on Stone's face turn to something like satisfaction. The alarm he put down to his own involvement – after Costaine, Stone did not trust Hannah with a sexual agenda. The satisfaction was more worrying. Like Hannah, Stone must have drawn the conclusion that if Cody was mixing with rough trade then it was likely her disappearance was not voluntary. Hannah knew Stone to be a decent man – for an anally retentive bureaucrat. If Stone welcomed the notion that Cody might turn up dead then someone else must have been leaning on him. It made Hannah even more determined to find Cody – alive.

'Come on, Jeff,' he said. 'What's the real scam? What was Cody working on?'

Stone spread his hands. 'I don't know – and I honestly don't think it's relevant.'

Hannah studied Stone's broad, ruddy face, the light bouncing off the high shiny dome of his forehead. He believed him. The look that signified satisfaction had gone, replaced by standard-issue anxiety.

'The point is,' Stone continued, 'this woman has spent fifteen years at the cutting edge of military research. She's a walking repository of invaluable information. If she's dead, she's dead – we close the file. But if she's taking horizontal meetings with half the neighbourhood who knows what she might say? The consequences for the nation could be grave.

It could also be seriously embarrassing for us.'

Hannah suppressed a grin. It was funny how often the prospect of embarrassment caused Stone anguish.

'In that case,' he said, 'I'd better find her quick. But I need help. A talk with a psychiatrist or sex therapist. There must be one of our people with that kind of training.'

Stone looked puzzled. 'So?'

'So I need to know what happens when a woman who's lived like a nun all her life goes off the rails. This is a thirty-four-year-old professional virgin who's turned into a nymphomaniac overnight. Why? More important, what next? Is this some recognised syndrome? Is she going to have a mental breakdown or get into the *Guinness Book of Sex Records* or what? Someone here must have an idea.'

Stone sighed and tapped a number into the phone. 'I didn't want to have to do this,' he said and spoke into the receiver. 'Jarvis, this is Stone. I'm on my way down.' He stood up. 'Let's go.'

'What's going on?' said Hannah as he followed Stone out of his office to the elevator.

As the metal box began to descend Stone said, 'You want help, I'm giving you help. Just watch your step, Hannah, that's all I ask.'

'What's that supposed to mean?'

'I'm taking you to see Special Agent Jarvis.'

'I'm none the wiser.'

Stone said nothing. As the elevator halted, he pushed past Hannah and led the way down a gloomy basement corridor.

Hannah was annoyed. 'Who the hell is he anyway?'

Stone turned suddenly and thrust his red face into Hannah's. 'Listen up, Hannah, and listen good. *He* is a she. Bonny Jarvis, twenty-eight, five-six with auburn hair, blue eyes and a full set of curves. Just the kind of partner you've been itching to team up with. But let me give you a word of advice. There's not one active sex chromosome in her entire body. She's got ice-water in her veins and a circuit board for a heart. That's why she's the keeper of the Sex Files.'

'What the fuck are they?' said Hannah but he was talking

to the wall. Stone had turned on his heels and disappeared through the door at the end of the corridor.

Jarvis's office was lined with filing cabinets and banks of computers and image-enhancing machinery. The long room hummed with the sound of electrical equipment. It was without natural light and the strip lights cast a fluorescent glow across metal and grey plastic.

In this artificial environment, the physical allure of Bonny Jarvis was like a blow to Hannah's ribs. Her milky blue eyes and rich red hair were startling and those full curving lips were made for better than sucking on a pencil. But her jaw was firm, like her handshake, and the flare of her nostrils suggested a woman of determination. Jarvis was more than just a pretty face, Hannah could tell. She was more like a challenge.

She did not look pleased to see Stone and Hannah. She looked even less pleased when Stone explained the reason for it. However, she listened politely to Hannah after Stone had left.

Hannah ran through the circumstances of Cody's disappearance as concisely as he could. He did not make a great job of it. Jarvis's steady blue-eyed stare was unnerving.

When he'd finished she said nothing, just swung round on her chair and began to work the keyboard of the desktop computer. A few seconds later the printer began to whirr and disgorged a sheet of paper. She plucked it from the out-tray and handed it to Hannah. It contained three names.

'Pine, Simons and Karlsen,' he read. 'What's this? Your stock analyst?'

For a second there was a ghost of a smile on her lips. 'You wanted precedents,' she said. 'You just got 'em.'

'These are women like Cody, right?'

'Right. Look here.'

Hannah pulled his chair up beside Jarvis as she turned back to the computer screen. He tried to ignore the smell of her – citrus and something sweet, cinnamon maybe – and the heat of her arm through the cotton of her shirt as she brushed against him. He concentrated on the screen. The image of a woman with ash-blonde hair in a high-buttoned blouse stared out at him.

'Judge Stacey Pine, forty-two, resident of Quantock, Penn.' Jarvis's voice was low and firm. 'Former assistant DA, then associate of Jackson, Teller, the big-deal law firm in the area. Elected Her Honour six months back and making a pretty good fist of it. Radcliffe graduate, top of her year, *very* smart cookie. Single, no known significant relationships with men *or* women. It was the only strike against her in the election. Her opponent made a big play of his wife and kids and implied Pine was a dyke. She denied it and blew him away with the voters.'

'And has she – er – adopted a promiscuous lifestyle.'

'You could say that. We have statements from a shoe-store clerk, a bank teller, two taxi-drivers and three pizza-delivery boys that between August 12th and September 18th she invited them into her house for the purpose of sexual intercourse.'

'And did they go?'

'All except the second taxi-driver. He thought it was set-up – besides his male lover was giving him a hard time for working late. He passed on Pine. The others bit her arm off. We have corroborating statements from the super in her building and the people in her office. There were men in her apartment at all times of the day and night – noise, laughter, loud music, all that stuff. And she'd turn up late, she missed two court dates and a pre-trial conference. Her assistant was worried some reporter would get wind of what was going on. Then she vanished.'

'When?'

'She seduced a real-estate man on September 19th as he was showing her an apartment. Then she walked out and hasn't been seen or heard of since.'

'And the others?'

Jarvis called their photos onto the screen: a bespectacled brown-haired woman with a crimped mouth and a power-suited brunette wearing a frown – Madeleine Simons, a schoolteacher at a New Jersey high school and Kate Karlsen, senior fund-manager for Rikard-Huysmann on Wall Street.

Neither of them looked like sex on wheels, to Hannah's eye. But he wasn't fooled – he'd seen Felice Cody in action.

Jarvis summarised. 'Basically, it's the same story as Pine and your woman, Cody. These are successful, hard-working citizens with responsible jobs and spotless reputations. And they've suddenly run wild, propositioning anything in long pants. According to everyone who knows them, this behaviour is completely out of character.'

'And they're both missing?'

'Vanished into thin air.'

'Leaving a trail of exhausted pizza-delivery boys in their wake.'

Jarvis glared at Hannah. 'You may find this difficult but I'd appreciate it if you'd keep your dirty-pecker sense of humour zipped up.'

The smile froze on Hannah's lips. 'Excuse *me*,' he said but the sarcasm seemed to slip by her.

'Where are Cody's tapes?' she said.

'Her sister gave them to me. I've got one in my briefcase.'

'Let me see it.'

Hannah handed it over and was shocked to see Jarvis march to a VCR in the corner and slip it into the jaws of the machine. The television above it fizzed into life. Hannah was in turmoil. Was he meant to sit quietly and watch *Partytime with Felice Cody* next to this refrigerated ball-breaker? A ball-breaker whose swollen right breast strained clearly against her uniform shirt as she bent forward to adjust the contrast on the set. Hannah took a deep breath and prepared himself for the ordeal ahead.

They plunged straight into the garage tape, the one Hannah had first discovered. It began at the point where Brigitte had surprised him in the bedroom. There was Felice with her spunk-happy grin offering to take on all-comers. A guy in a grease-monkey overall came forward and hefted her dangling breasts. She fished his cock out and rubbed the thick brown shaft against her cheek. Jarvis freeze-framed the picture.

'Look—' she pointed with a pencil to the wall behind the happy couple. 'There's a calendar. If I take a print off this we might get an idea of the date.' She played with her remote control and a printer hummed.

'This is a first-class machine,' she said. 'I can get reasonable images off lousy stock and enhance them on screen if necessary.'

'Right,' said Hannah. He wasn't hot on technical stuff.

'Let's move on,' she said and the picture jerked into life.

Felice pulled the guy's balls out of his coveralls and cupped them in her fingers. A big man, naked and erect, came into shot from the other side and knelt behind Felice. He put his hand on her hips and said, 'Let me in, sugar.'

Hannah freeze-framed again and printed. 'We should take a close look at these guys' faces. Something might turn up.'

The picture was running again. Felice was on all fours and the second man was fingering the cleft of her ass. His penis was red and angry, sawing the air in impatience. The first man climaxed over Felice's fingers, his juice splattering her breasts. 'Oh shit,' he said, 'I didn't mean to do that.'

Hannah swallowed hard. 'We could just go down to Resolution Motorwear in Maxwell. I bet these fellows have still got smiles on their faces.'

'That's where this is?' He had her attention. Hannah tried not to let his eyes stray to the sight of the big guy inserting his tool into Felice's back-thrust vagina.

'She takes her car there for servicing. No pun intended. I found her records.'

The big guy was really letting Felice have it, bulling his cock into her, his belly going slap-slap on the cheeks of her ass, her tits dancing beneath her bent-over body. The camera closed in on her face. Her eyes were shut and her teeth bit down on her lower lip.

'Yeah, Hoss, yeah,' came the voices of the by-standers.

'Fuck the tits off the horny bitch,' said another.

Hannah shot a glance at Jarvis. She was writing on a pad. She could have been taking down revision notes.

'Oh yeah! Lookit that!'

'Hose her down, Hoss!'

'Cream her ass!'

The camera had moved to the side. The big guy had

pulled out to pump his seed over Felice's bottom. The spunk rained down on her big white cheeks, now quivering and jumping with her excitement. She rolled over onto her back, her eyes blazing. 'More!' she breathed, her legs scissoring wide. 'I'm not through yet, you dirty bastards!'

Then the screen clicked to snow. Maybe, thought Hannah, the cameraman had decided to step into the breach. Whatever, he was relieved. Watching such naked passion next to Jarvis was hard work in every sense.

'Interesting,' she said.

Hannah could think of many words to describe what they had just watched. 'Interesting' was not one of them.

'How so?' he said.

'She looked feverish. She was sweating and her hands were shaking. Like she was in the grip of some force that had taken her over.'

'It's called lust, Jarvis.'

He thought she was going to shoot him down like before. Instead she looked puzzled.

'Is it?' she said. 'It seemed – more extreme. Like she couldn't control herself.'

'Jarvis, that's what the sex impulse does to people. It makes them lose control.'

'Oh. Well, I suppose you'd know all about that.'

Hannah grinned. At least there was one area in which he might have more expertise than her. He'd be happy to fill in some gaps in her knowledge, however. He took a chance.

'Look, Jarvis, let's get out of here. We need to work out where this thing is going. Let's go to a bar and brainstorm. Or have dinner. My treat.'

She laughed but it wasn't a pleasant sound, more like a bark of contempt.

'Get this, Hannah, I'm going nowhere off-duty with a man like you. Not now, not ever. As far as I'm concerned our relationship is strictly professional.'

Hannah was pissed. 'For God's sake, Jarvis, I'm only trying to be friendly in the interests of our *working* relationship. You don't even know me.'

She squared up to him, her nipples pointing at his chest

like twin pistols beneath her shirt. She looked magnificently sexy – but obviously she didn't feel it.

'I know enough about you, Hannah. I know that you're a smart agent. I also know you're an unscrupulous sleazeball with the integrity of a cockroach.'

Hannah was stunned. 'Come on, Jarvis, we only met an hour ago. How can you know *anything* about me?'

'I'll give you one clue – Martina Costaine. That tape we just watched is not the only X-rated recording that's come across my desk today.'

Jarvis's milky blue eyes bored into his, her pupils frosty with anger.

'Now, get out, Hannah. You're lousing up my office.'

Hannah went.

SEVEN

JARVIS'S APARTMENT. 6.30 PM.

Bonny Jarvis stood under the shower for longer than usual. She wanted to wash away the memory of the Cody video – the pictures were still flickering in her head. She saw hairy, sweaty men with thick red-tipped penises, laughing as they manhandled the woman's nude body. Heard the first man moan as he came off too soon. Heard the big man grunt as he thrust his great cudgel into Cody's vagina. Saw the spunk shoot all over Cody's back and buttocks.

And, most vivid of all, she saw how Felice Cody loved it. How her eyes sparkled as she gave those brutes the freedom of her opulent body and then demanded more. *More*, for God's sake!

The shower wasn't working as Jarvis intended. She turned the dial to full-on cold and cursed. As a rule, her job – her specialty area of weird sexual behaviour – was not a problem. On the contrary, she loved it. She toiled at the archive known as the Sex Files with a scientist's fascination. And, like a scientist, she kept her feelings detached from the subject under inquiry. So why, today, did she feel different?

She knew the answer to that: Hannah. She shouldn't have listened to the tape that Kirsten had given her that morning. Kirsten of the flashing black eyes and swinging hips. Sex wasn't a subject of scientific inquiry to Kirsten – her life was one hands-on experiment. She was always trying to fix Jarvis up with some guy. To her, the Hannah tape was just a joke.

But not to Jarvis. Somehow the grunt and grind of Hannah in bed with Martina Costaine had penetrated her defences. The sound of bare limbs sliding on sheets, the woman's mounting cries of excitement, the man's teasing remarks and then his moans too when he got serious, these things had made an impression. And, at the end, when Martina spelt out in detail what she wanted Hannah to do and then caught fire when he did it – that really got to Jarvis.

So, for Stone to walk into her office with Hannah and order – in effect – her cooperation on the Cody disappearance had stunned her. Then came the video, whose obscene images still played on the screen in her head. Christ! Hannah must never find out just how he pushed her buttons.

Jarvis dried herself quickly and shoved some frozen lasagne in the microwave. She knew she had to eat, behave normally, get her mind in thinking gear. She regretted being so downright ferocious with Hannah but lines had to be drawn fast with a snake like that. At least now she'd warned him off, those deep brown eyes would not be straying in her direction. She'd point him at Kirsten – they deserved each other.

She ate fast, straight from the tinfoil tray and washed it down with flat Coke. This was not the time for a gourmet meal.

She took her coffee into her bedroom. It was more of a study really. Her desk and computer took up more space than her single bed. She'd had half the wardrobe taken out to make bookshelves. No one, excepting her mother and the carpenter, had ever been in her bedroom apart from herself. Well, there was one other. But the identity of that person was classified. Like her work.

She booted up the computer and clicked onto the Net. She surfed at random, starting as she often did with the *Washington Post* and then following a news story which caught her eye about a missing woman. It had no relevance, as she knew it wouldn't. This woman was married with three children and worked as a part-time machine operator in a garment factory. She wasn't smart, successful or single. Her profile didn't fit.

Cody had a home page, Jarvis got into that and explored the links. There were a million of them, some science- and medicine-based, others to do with the fringe paranormal. Jarvis followed them doggedly but they seemed too way-out to connect with the other women. It was frustrating. She knew that the real link – the one that bound Pine and Simons and Karlsen and Cody – was out there somewhere but it was a needle-in-a-haystack job. The fact that the answer might be on the Net didn't necessarily help. The network was too vast and the service-provider too damn slow. After fifteen minutes waiting for a no-show download she got up to make more coffee.

The phone rang.

'Bonny.' The voice was like gravel, instantly recognisable. Her stomach contracted.

'Don't call me that.'

'Why not? It's your name, isn't it?'

'No one calls me that except my family. And you aren't family.'

'But we are *special* friends, aren't we, Bonny?'

'Drop dead, Lovelace.'

'You might try and sound just a little pleased to hear from me.'

'Anything to do with you revolts me.'

The voice laughed, a chesty rattle.

'In that case, I take it you can't meet me tonight.'

Jarvis did not reply. This was a development she did not want. On the other hand, it might be what she needed.

'When and where?' she said.

'Basquervilles—'

'Oh please, not that hellhole!'

'– in an hour.'

The line shut down.

Jarvis looked at the dead receiver in her hand and slammed it back into the cradle. Then she switched off the kettle and poured herself a vodka instead. She was going to need it.

Basquervilles was sleaze city – a clip joint where guys looked at strippers and waitresses did whatever was required to separate the dicks from their dollars, right there at the table.

It was just the kind of place Jarvis loathed. That was why Lovelace made her go there.

He was in his usual corner, at the back of the room and furthest from the stage – which was the only good thing about the whole business. Except that Lovelace operated on the inside track. That was why Jarvis played along and swallowed her pride. So she could also swallow the crumbs of information that he tossed her way. Tonight they'd better be good. She was in no mood to take shit though she feared she'd have to.

'I got you a drink,' he said. 'Trenton Valley spring water with a twist of lime, right?'

'You drink it,' she snapped. And said to the waitress as she sat, 'Bring me a vodka tonic, no ice.'

Lovelace smiled. At least she thought he did but there was little to discern of his face in the gloom. The gaudy blue-and-pink lights of the stage hardly penetrated this corner. He was just a presence, a large one, his bulk looming over her even as they sat. But his eyes shone out of the dark, like chips of stone.

'So what have you got?' she said when her drink arrived.

'What's the rush? Let's enjoy the show. That girl up there's an artist.'

Jarvis forced herself to look at the stage where a leggy blonde was wearing a snake.

'Cut it out, Lovelace. She's a degenerate with a habit to feed. Like all the other whores in here.'

He chuckled.

'She's doing what has to be done, Agent Jarvis. You're no different. Why else are you here?'

'I don't prostitute myself.'

He laughed again. God, how she hated that chesty rattle.

'OK, have it your own way. Would you like another drink before you put your hand on my cock?'

'Fuck you.'

'No need to get upset. Though I must admit your spirited resistance to the inevitable adds a piquancy to our meetings that I relish.'

'You're full of shit, Lovelace.'

'Such pretty lips and yet so foul-mouthed. In the old days you'd be made to wash it out with soap and water. Perhaps you should rinse it with something else.'

He grasped her hand and pulled it towards him. His hand was huge and hairy, like a bear's paw, and his grip was like iron. She was powerless to resist as he thrust it beneath the table. It met bare flesh. His fly was open and his erect penis speared upwards from his belly.

The organ was huge: a rock-hard column of flesh, hot to the touch. He pressed her hand against it.

'I won't,' she said.

'Then why did you come? You know the rules, Bonny.'

And so she did. She took a deep breath and curled her fingers around the shaft of his cock, it was so broad she could hardly circle it. He released his grip on her hand.

'That's better. I believe you've got magic fingers.'

'You know I hate you, don't you, Lovelace?'

'Sure. That's what makes this fun. Do you think you could stroke me just a little harder?'

'You disgust me.'

'I know. Ooh, that's nice. Perhaps I'll call you Jerk-Off Jarvis. You do it better than anyone I know.'

Beneath the table Jarvis's fingers rose and fell on the solid column of flesh in her grasp. She squeezed the great shaft from root to tip, slipping the thick foreskin back and forth across the bulging glans. His breathing came harder and she speeded up. She wanted this thing over. She wanted the pay-off.

But it wasn't going to be that easy.

'Hey, Candy.'

At his words, Jarvis tried to pull her hand away but he had her by the wrist.

'Candy, c'mere,' he called to the waitress who shimmied over at once, her cocktail dress riding high on her plump thighs.

'Can I help you, sir?'

'Take a look at this,' said Lovelace, pushing the table away so the girl could see Jarvis's hand caught in the act of jacking his erect penis.

Candy didn't even blink. 'My, that looks like fun,' she said in a voice of Texas honey. 'That's a hell of a doodle you got hold of there, sister.'

Lovelace held out a bundle of bills that Candy magicked out of his hand in an instant. She sat on the other side of Lovelace and said, 'Need some help?'

He tugged at the shoulder strap of the girl's dress and slipped it over her tanned shoulder. 'My girlfriend's a bit shy,' he said, 'but I know she'd like to see your tits.'

'Why, sure.' Candy dropped the other strap and pulled the dress down to her waist. Her huge breasts thrust out from her chest, pink and bare. Jarvis tried not to stare at them but they could hardly be overlooked. Her face was blazing and she wished she was anywhere but where she was.

Jarvis could understand Candy's appeal for the average horny guy. Her bleached blonde hair was in bunches and her mouth pouted in a sexy sulk. But her eyes were like a taxi-meter, clicking off the dollars on the clock as Lovelace pawed her big tits, lifting one, then the other, so the soft flesh bounced and swayed. The girl giggled and pushed her melons into his hand.

'My girlfriend doesn't like me to touch her body,' he said.

'Really?' Candy's eyes were circles of wonder.

'She won't let me fuck her either. Says my dick's too big.'

'You can't get a dick too big,' said Candy. 'Not too big for me anyhow.'

'But she will use her mouth on me, won't you, honey?'

Jarvis gazed at Lovelace in horror. Sick as this scenario was, she knew it was going to get sicker. She speeded up her hand on his cock. If she could just get him to come quick . . .

'Come on, Bonny,' ordered Lovelace. 'Show Candy how you make a fellow happy.'

'You bastard.'

'Hurry up.'

'No!'

'Is everything OK?' There was concern on Candy's pretty face. 'I thought we were all having a good time.'

'We are.' Lovelace put his arm round the girl's shoulders.

'Bonny here likes to be persuaded.'

'I won't do it!' hissed Jarvis.

'Stop being so selfish, my dear. I know lots of women who wouldn't be so prudish. Like Stacey Pine. But she's not here, of course.'

'What?'

'The same goes for Madeleine Simons and Kate Karlsen and Felice Cody. The way they are now, they'd probably pay for the pleasure of sucking my dick.'

'What do you know about these women?'

'On your knees – or I tell you nothing.'

It was probably the most humiliating thing Jarvis had ever done, fellating Lovelace's great horse-cock in a strip club, watched by a bare-breasted whore. She'd often wondered how far she'd go to get a lead. Now she knew.

His tool was enormous, so big she had to stretch her mouth to its widest to accommodate the swollen glans. She could barely get more than the head inside. It was like swallowing a billiard ball.

'Atta girl,' whooped Candy as Jarvis sucked and worked on the shaft with her fingers. The big limb was rigid like a branch and slippery like a bar of wet soap – it was as if he had come already but his excitement was such he would not go down. She wondered if he'd ever go down. Her jaw was aching already.

Lovelace had his hand on her neck. He had pulled the hair back from her face so Candy could see her lips taking him in.

'Yeah, yeah!' squeaked Candy. 'Suck that dick for me, sister.'

Then the big machine began to throb in her hands and the knob seemed to swell even larger, forcing her jaw further apart. As his juice hit the back of her throat he held her fast, filling her mouth with his thick seed.

She swallowed every drop. She had no choice.

Jarvis took her time in the restroom. She sat in a stall and blocked out the sounds around her, trying to stop herself shaking. She'd been in more dangerous places. She'd been in fear of her life. She'd faced death and survived. But this, she told herself, had to be the worst day of her life.

When she got back to the table Lovelace had gone. Panic gripped her. Had she been through all that for *nothing*?

'Are you OK?'

Candy was at her side, a glass in her hand.

'Here – it's on the house.'

The vodka cut through the lingering taste of the big man's come and Jarvis drank it in one hit.

'I don't know what you see in him, sister – he's a pig.'

'He's a dead pig.'

'That bad, huh? This might change your mind. Might be some cash, if you're lucky.'

Candy handed her an envelope and Jarvis snatched it in relief. She waited till she was outside before she opened it. Inside were two keys, both labelled 'Karlsen'.

She went home, threw some clothes into a bag and headed for the airport.

EIGHT

HANNAH'S APARTMENT. 7.30 PM.

Hannah had just closed the door behind him when the entry-phone buzzed. He was so out of breath he could hardly talk into the receiver.

'Hannah? Are you there?'

'Yeah. Who is it?'

'Brigitte.'

Cody's sister. He'd forgotten all about their afternoon together. Now he remembered. Vividly.

'Come on up, Brigitte.'

He just had time to splash his face with water and grab a towel. The sweat was still running down his back and his T-shirt and shorts were stuck to his body. It had been a serious run and he needed to recover. Right now he could do without visitors.

He heard the rumble of the elevator from the hall and opened the apartment door. Brigitte Behr stepped inside. She wore a caramel cashmere sweater that was moulded to her breasts. Her golden hair was tied in a knot that showed off the white stem of her neck. She looked expensive and delectable and clean – which was more than he was.

'I'm sorry, Brigitte. You've caught me straight off a work-out.'

'I know. I saw you come back. I was waiting for you in my car.'

Hannah ushered her into the living room and cleared the couch of Sunday's newspapers so she could sit. She didn't.

'I heard from Felice. She sent me a postcard.'

Hannah took the card from her hand. It was one of those Magic Eye patterns that gave you a headache while you tried to scan its secret image. Hannah could never work them out.

'I thought this craze was over.'

'It is, but Felice still likes them. She bought a stack a couple of years back.'

A bead of sweat plopped onto the green-and-turquoise image and Hannah mopped his face. He turned the card over.

The message read: 'Darling B, I'm running wild for a few days out West. Clarice from down the hall will look after the cats but can you stop in sometime and see she's doing it right? I'll be in touch. Be good, won't you? Love F. PS Just found this in my purse. Forgot to post it. Bet you haven't even missed me!' It was postmarked Long Grove, Illinois, September 27th.

'So she was in Chicago last Friday,' said Hannah. 'That's hardly "out West". Has she got friends there?'

Brigitte shrugged. Hannah wondered what she was wearing beneath that sweater. Not much, he imagined.

'Felice doesn't have friends. She's got contacts – about a zillion. UFO freaks and conspiracy theorists – you know. All those people who read her books. As far as I know they're on the end of the phone or sending her e-mail. She keeps herself kind of aloof.'

Hannah grinned. The Felice he'd seen could hardly be described as 'aloof'.

Brigitte picked up on his expression. 'Yeah, right. What do I know? I thought she was Mother Theresa but it turns out she's the Whore of Babylon. God, it makes me so *mad*.'

'It's OK, Brigitte. This card is good. It indicates she's not in danger. She'll probably turn up soon.'

'Oh, it's not *that*.' Her pretty face scowled at him. Hannah fought the urge to laugh – she looked so intense. He was pleased she'd turned up. He could feel the knot of anger in his stomach, placed there by that ball-breaker Jarvis, slowly beginning to unravel.

Brigitte was getting into her stride.

'It's the way she always acts with me. Like she's my moral

guardian. She's five years older than I am and she never lets me forget it. It's on that card – 'be good, won't you?' Hey come on, Felice, get off my case. Who are you to tell me to be good? What's so funny, Hannah?'

'The way you look like you want to kill me. I'm not Felice. I'm a guy who's been pounding the trail around Rock Creek for an hour and I'm sweaty and grungy and in need of a beer. Do you mind if we continue this conversation while I sit in the tub?'

Brigitte's fierce expression softened and she took a step towards him. 'Isn't that an unconventional proposal for a Special Agent to make?'

'I'm off duty now, Brigitte, and I don't give a shit.'

He pulled his wet vest over his head and reached for the towel. She stopped him and placed her small hand on the damp tangle of hair on his sternum.

'You'll mess up your nice sweater,' he said.

'Right.'

She pulled it off in one smooth sweep of her slim bronzed arms and threw it on the floor next to his T-shirt. Sure enough, she was nude beneath it. The pink crinkled points of her breasts skittered over his skin as she stepped in close and slid her arms around his waist.

'Before you get in the bath,' she said, 'can we do something real dirty?'

Hannah took the lobe of one ear between his lips.

'Mmm?' he murmured and bit gently.

She squirmed in his arms, the heat of her small breasts against his ribs.

'I want to do what Felice did. On the tape.'

'What was that?' He was nuzzling the crook of her neck, hugging her to him. He guessed her request but wanted to hear her say it.

'Do it to me from behind. Please.'

'From behind?' He ran his tongue along the line of her pretty pointed jaw.

'Yes.' Her big hazel eyes bored directly into his. 'Fuck me in the ass. Like he did it to her. Will you do that to me? Now?'

He kissed her hard. She almost swallowed his tongue.

He kicked off his remaining clothes and fetched cream from the bathroom. She was naked in his bedroom. He made her lie face down and placed a pillow beneath her hips so her ass stuck up in the air. It was round and white and cute. He hoped he wouldn't shoot off with excitement before he was lodged fast within its secret depths.

As her creamed her asshole, smoothing the jelly on slowly, savouring the pleasure to come, she talked.

'I always looked up to Felice. She was smarter than me. Prettier too when I was just a kid and she had boyfriends and went to parties. Then her fiancé dumped her after college and she had this personality change. Gave men up for good and most of her friends, became a real work-junkie. Mmm, that's nice what you're doing to me.'

'You've got a fabulous ass. Let me kiss it.' He lowered his lips to the silky cheeks. She giggled and pushed her rear back into his face.

'When she gave up guys it was like she didn't approve of me having any fun. None of my boyfriends were ever good enough, according to her. She was worse than my mother. She didn't speak to me for six months after I married Glen. And, two years back, when she found out I'd had an affair she really put me through it. She didn't lecture Glen though – not that it would have done much good. Just in case you're wondering, he's out fucking his girlfriend right now.'

Hannah said nothing, this was dangerous ground. Besides his mouth was full.

'God, Hannah, I want you in me now – I can't wait much longer.'

Neither could he. He knelt in the vee of her back-spread thighs and creamed the head and shaft of his tool. It twitched and jumped in his hands like a creature with a mind of its own. He'd never felt so big.

He pushed his fingers into her anus, one, then two. They slipped in easily. He took them out and quickly pressed the blunt head of his glans to her entrance.

'Oh,' she moaned and thrust back against him so suddenly that the tiny ring of flesh expanded and gripped him, sucking him in as he drove forwards on a liquid glide that took him right up her incredible ass in one shove.

'Ooooh!' she cried, whether in pain or pleasure he wasn't sure but there was no way he could retreat now as her rear passage sucked and squeezed his trembling prick like a voracious mouth.

He pinned the soft cushions of her buttocks to the bed and held her close and tight. For a moment they were still, with just their heartbeats drumming and that sly fluttering of her ass-mouth around his cock. She turned her head on the pillow and kissed him awkwardly. Her hair had come loose and one round hazelnut eye stared exultantly at him through a forest of blonde tendrils.

'Are you OK?' he asked.

'I'm so full,' she breathed. 'I've never felt like this before.'

'Shall I stop?'

'Don't you dare!'

He slipped a hand beneath her hips to seek out her pussy. It was sticky and hot.

'Yes, yes,' she muttered as he played with her long, loose lips.

He explored her cleft slowly from the join of their bodies at the rear up to the hood of flesh that concealed her clit.

'Oh God!' she moaned as he found the little button and she bucked her hips with surprising strength, lifting him up and down as she jammed her cunt against his fingers.

That did it, Hannah could hold back no longer. He speared his tool in and out of her, thrusting to the very depths of her sweet behind as she moaned and cried in orgasm beneath him. As he did so, into his head flashed the stony face of Jarvis that afternoon as she watched Felice getting hers on-screen.

How would Jarvis regard this particular scene? he wondered – his unwashed body covering the perfumed bucking blonde, his fingers diddling her twitching crack and his penis buried to the hilt in her insatiable ass.

'Take that, you frigid bitch!' he muttered as he emptied his balls into the shuddering dancing body beneath him.

He wasn't talking to Brigitte.

NINE

WASHINGTON-NEW YORK CITY. 10.00 PM.

Jarvis cursed as the young guy took the vacant place next to her on the shuttle to New York. He was tall and rangy with a lock of blue-black hair that he kept flicking out of his eyes. He wore a casually rumpled designer suit and a glint in his pearly blue eyes. She didn't know his name but she knew how to spell it – 'Trouble'.

'Hi, there,' he said as he folded his long limbs into the seat. 'I'm Greg.'

Jarvis said nothing and lowered her eyes to the in-flight magazine – not that she had any intention of reading it. She tried to focus on the Cody/Karlsen question but she could feel the guy's eyes crawling all over her.

'That's OK,' said Greg. 'I can understand that a beautiful woman like you wouldn't want to share her name with her travelling companion.'

She turned to him. Maybe she could nip this in the bud.

'Look, it's not personal but I never talk to people on planes.'

'Like you're not talking to me now, you mean?' He was grinning from ear to ear.

Jarvis gazed out of the window across the tarmac. The plane doors were closed and the engines were getting louder. They would be off soon. She couldn't wait. She wanted to get to Karlsen's apartment quickly to test a hunch. If she were right, the keys Lovelace had given her might just unlock the whole case.

A stewardess was intoning the safety procedure.

'You can ignore this bit,' said Greg. 'I'll put the life jacket on you if we get into trouble. Every cloud has a silver lining, that's my motto.'

'Shut the fuck up, creep.'

Jarvis hadn't meant to lose her cool – at least not until she had to. They hadn't even taken off yet.

Greg chuckled. She knew his kind. If he wasn't going to get into her pants he could at least get under her skin.

'Hey, you're the fiery sort – I could tell from the red hair.'

'I'm sorry. I've had a bad day. I'd really appreciate it if you left me alone.' Jarvis put as much sincerity into it as she could, meeting his gaze head on.

His face moved close to hers. She could smell his breath – minty, not unpleasant.

'Apology accepted. I can see I was wrong about you.'

'What do you mean?' Damn – she hadn't meant to give him an opening.

'Well, at first I put you in my top five babes of the season but now I see you're the best-looking bachelorette I've seen all year. You *are* a bachelorette, aren't you?'

His grinning, leering smile was inches from her lips. He thought he was getting somewhere at last.

'See?' he continued. 'You're not denying it, are you? So listen up, you'll be thrilled, I'm upgrading you from a nine to a nine and a half.'

Jarvis tried to control the rage within her. This guy was asking for it.

'I can't give you a perfect ten yet, of course. We'll need to do the nude inspection first. I'm stopping over in Manhattan tonight. We could order up a late supper and get down to it. What do you say? You never did tell me your name, did you, honey?'

Jarvis took his left hand, a grim smile now edging her lips. If she wanted any peace she had no option. And she was going to enjoy it.

She separated out his little finger and began to bend it.

'Since you ask, Mr Greg Fuckwit, my name's Special Agent Jarvis and you're in deep shit.'

'Hey!' The grin had disappeared from his face and he

tried to yank his hand from her grasp but she had it fast. 'Don't! You're hurting me!'

'That's the idea, Greg.' She jerked the finger out of its socket and his body spasmed in the seat. A squeal of pain burst from his lips but was muffled by the roar of the jet as it thundered down the runway. He tried to rise but he was restrained by his seatbelt. She squeezed harder and noted the tears pooling in his baby-blues. He lashed at her with his free hand and she caught it in hers.

'Listen,' she hissed into his ear. 'If you hit me I'll charge you with assault. I have witnesses all around who will back me up. Then I shall take your personal details and make sure the local police department is aware of your habit of harassing lone females. Do you think your family and friends would be amused to know you made indecent suggestions to a law-enforcement officer? How about your employer? Or your wife? Believe me, you sexist pig, I can make life very unpleasant indeed.'

'Oh Christ.' He was keening in pain. Jarvis tightened her grip.

'I'm sorry, I'm sorry,' he moaned. He looked like a whipped schoolkid.

'Just be grateful it's not your dick I'm holding,' said Jarvis into his ear. 'I might just pull it off.'

She let him go and he cradled his wounded hand in his armpit. He scrabbled in his pocket for a paper tissue and dabbed the tears from his face.

'You didn't have to do that,' he muttered as the plane stopped climbing and the seatbelt sign went out. He lurched to his feet and stumbled down the aisle to the restroom.

Jarvis closed her eyes and tried to enjoy her hard-won peace. Maybe she shouldn't have been so mean, she thought. Maybe the man she'd really wanted to hurt had just humiliated her beneath a table in a strip joint. Lovelace had stepped on her and so she'd stepped on Greg. Too bad. She'd always played hardball – as any man who crossed her would find out.

★ ★ ★

Karlsen lived in a service apartment in the East 60s. Downstairs there was a marble reception area with a scarlet-and-gold carpet. A pot-bellied guy in uniform on the desk gave Jarvis a considered once-over.

'We had a bunch of you people through here last week. Guess Katie's pretty important to get the Bureau out.'

'Katie?'

'Miss Karlsen asked me to call her that. She was real nice. I hope nothin' bad's happened to her.'

'Did she seem OK to you before she disappeared?'

'Yes and no. She started stayin' out late which wasn't like her. Her dresses got shorter too, if you know what I mean. Mind you, she had terrific legs. I told your people all this stuff a million times.'

Jarvis turned for the bank of elevators.

'Hey,' called Pot Belly, ' you want her mail? I bin keepin' it. Maybe there's clues or somethin'.'

She returned to the desk and waited impatiently for him to fetch Karlsen's stuff. Sometimes it seemed that every damn thing in the world slowed her down.

Jarvis admired Karlsen's apartment. It was luxuriously furnished, like some ritzy hotel. The art on the wall was striking. Avant-garde but not frightening. Bold but decorative. And there was a lot of greenery – big plants with scarlet flowers and a screen of climbers growing in the light from the east-facing window which looked towards the river. Jarvis liked that. Plants were the only living things she could tolerate in her own apartment.

The first thing she did was water them. The heating had been left on high and there was cracked earth in the tubs. It made Jarvis feel better to see the soil turn black with moisture as she gave the plants a drink.

She dumped her coat and the packages Pot Belly had given her in the bedroom. It was a cosy room with thick-pile peach carpets and wall-to-wall closets. She peeked into one – it was bulging with clothes, mostly suits and sensible skirts. But the floor was covered with shoes, some clumpy and old but most brand new. She picked up a pair of three-inch spike stilettos with scarcely scuffed soles and some spaghetti-strapped slingbacks in pink leather. This was not old-maid footwear. Fancy that.

Jarvis had been intending to check into a hotel but there seemed no point. Besides, it was now midnight, who's to say there would be any time for sleep?

Of the two keys Lovelace had given her, one was for the apartment door. The other, smaller one she'd recognised at once. It fitted a computer.

The machine was in a well-appointed den. She unlocked it and booted up. Doubtless someone had already hunted around Karlsen's files but she didn't intend to go that route. Casing a financier's worksheets and accounts was not her area of expertise. Her approach was simpler – and more fun.

She clicked into the Web browser for access to the Internet and then held her breath as she moved the arrow of the mouse to the icon for Personal Favourites. Yes! There was a string of listings. It would take her a few hours no doubt to sort through them but at least here were Karlsen's private areas of interest laid out for her to examine. This was not a needle-in-haystack job. Karlsen had bookmarked every one of these sites for a revisit. That had to mean something. Maybe it would provide the essential clue they were missing so far. Jarvis was banking on it.

By three-thirty in the morning Jarvis had blown out her theory. The sites she had visited shed no light on what had happened to Kate Karlsen or where she was now. Not, she thought as she made herself another pot of coffee in the kitchen, that it had been a waste of time. She had learned a lot about the missing woman. She had spent a couple of hours in her skin, viewing her interests and obsessions. Now Kate was no longer just a case – she had come alive.

The fact was that her tastes were pretty close to Jarvis's own. There was music, for one thing. Church music, that was a surprise. Jarvis didn't know anybody else who liked the English cathedral music of Thomas Tallis and William Byrd but Karlsen did. Gregorian chant, too. She'd hunted down sites all over the Internet and booked them. Then there was gardening – Japanese designs for Buddhist temples and bonzai techniques. Jarvis was interested in all of that stuff. And the movies of Rainer Werner Fassbinder, the buildings of Mies van der Rohe and the songs of k d lang. By the time she'd noted these things Jarvis felt that she and Kate were pretty much on the same wavelength

Of course there were other areas where they didn't overlap. Karlsen dabbled in a lot of personal growth and alternative medicine: meditation, crystal-healing and colonic irrigation didn't hold much appeal for Jarvis. 'Get real, Kate,' she muttered as she found herself staring at the home page of the third Tarot-teller in a row.

She was getting tired now, there was an ache across her shoulder blades and a pain behind her left eye which said, 'Quit, you fool, and go to bed.' But she was wired up, caffeine was powering her system. There had to be more to find – and she knew where she had to look.

Under 'home entertainment' Karlsen had listed a string of sites with labels like 'Freddy's Bare-All Page' and 'Cum Shots'. Jarvis had been avoiding these obvious porno stop-offs. Now she began to work her way through them.

There were no surprises. Karlsen, it seemed, had frolicked in the sea of sex on the Net with gusto. She had downloaded hundreds of obscene images, mostly of guys sporting enormous hard-ons, shooting their wads over women with obvious tit-jobs. Quite a few were gay sites, with guys in leather and fetish apparel, buggering and fist-fucking each other. Jarvis began to feel ill. She'd had her dick quota for the day, she thought. Except, of course, it was now some four hours into a new one.

She tried to view the images objectively. As far as it was possible to tell, Karlsen had only begun to visit these pages in the past couple of months. 'Harvey's Hard-on Home Page', for example, said it had been updated September 9th and there were others with similar legends, all falling in August/September. It didn't prove that Karlsen hadn't visited in the distant past but it certainly suggested she'd been busy in the near present.

Jarvis closed off the screen, frustrated beyond measure, and headed for the bedroom. She threw her clothes off and pulled on a floor-length nightdress that was too warm for the stuffy apartment. She didn't care. It was the kind of nightwear her mother used to buy her when she was a kid and it made her feel secure.

She brushed her teeth and used the bathroom. She found clean sheets in a closet and replaced the old ones on the bed – God knows what might have taken place on those. She sank into the bed and, reaching for the light, her hand snagged Karlsen's mail which she'd dumped in haste on the bedside table. She knew it could wait till morning but that was not her style.

Most of it was of no interest – junk solicitations, promotional offers and a dentist bill. That left two packages, one long and lightweight, the other squat and heavy.

The first package contained a pair of high boots as supple as rubber. Jarvis caressed the material with her fingers. This was not your regular footwear. These boots were made from the kind of leather that fitted like a second skin and made bank officials see red. But then Karlsen was a bank official – unlike Jarvis, she could afford this kind of stuff.

The other package held a cardboard box. Jarvis was expecting more shoes so she was taken by surprise to find it contained a ribbed black dildo. The plastic phallus must have been over a foot long and thick like a stout stick. It was bigger even than Lovelace's cock – much bigger, Jarvis realised as she took it in her hands. Tucked inside the package was a jar of Electric Love Gel – 'Get Connected to a Climax Every Time'.

Jarvis stared at the shadows on the pink pastel ceiling. She felt soiled, guilty, *bad*. She also felt stressed to a pitch where she might break. She knew the feeling of old. It came when it was way too late in the small hours and her nerves were jumping and her thoughts were on freefall. At times like this she couldn't relax, even though she knew she must. Before she could yield to the exhaustion that waited to claim her in sleep, she knew she had to achieve release.

From the base of the dummy penis extended a black cord. Jarvis leaned out of bed and plugged it in, next to the lamp socket. She pressed the On switch at the base. The thing purred and throbbed in her hand. She ran the tip slowly up one arm. Let it rest on the back of her neck for a whole minute. Mmm, yes.

She got out of bed and threw off the schoolgirl's nightdress. She picked up the boots and pulled them on. She did it slowly, sensuously, imagining how Kate would have felt. They fitted her exactly, cleaving snugly to the curve of her calves and encasing her thighs high above the knee like fishermen's waders.

She looked at herself in the mirror. The boots made her seem taller. The leather clung to her legs, turning them a glistening black like wet paint. Above, the tops of her thighs were sleek and creamy. Between her legs the dark thatch of her pussy hair fluffed out brazenly. Her breasts were round, heavy and swollen. Her face was shadowed by the thick fall of her hair but her lips pouted and her jaw was set firm. She forced herself to acknowledge that she looked like the kind of woman men would pay money to enjoy.

She stopped at that thought and reached for the jar of cream. At first her labia smarted as she smeared the gunk on, then a spark lit in her nerves and her whole sex began to tingle.

'Electric love gel,' she muttered to herself. 'Sure.'

Her fingertip brushed the top of her crack and the spark flickered into flame. 'Oh,' Jarvis heard herself exclaim as her clit began to pulse.

She made herself wait before reaching for the vibrator. She lay on her back on the bed, her shiny black-leather legs spread wide and her mound thrusting, the oiled lips parted like a hungry mouth. She turned on the big machine and gently touched it to her thigh above the boot. Then higher up, on the inside. She tried to erase her thoughts. She needed what was to come. Needed to de-stress her body. It was purely physical.

'Oh Christ,' she moaned as the tip of the thing nudged her pussy lips apart. She held it still and moved against its bulk. My God, it was just so . . .

'Aah,' she gasped then 'Ohhh' and 'Ohhh' once more until the sounds were tumbling from her lips, merging and blending into a high note somewhere above the insistent buzz of the enormous black beast now lodged between her legs, deep inside her cunt.

No! she mustn't think that word. It was so crude – so *bad*. Instead she must imagine someone holding her tenderly, giving her pleasure. Someone secure, steadfast, faithful. Someone she could trust. Someone with *values*. Someone with . . .

. . . a big pulsing throbbing storming cock pounding hard and deep to the very depths of her *cunt* . . .

'Oh fuck me!'

She was coming, her pelvis squirming on the huge black dummy prick, her ass cheeks rubbing against the sheet, the liquid of her desire oiling her fingers as with both hands she jammed it into her again and again and again. Trying not to think of men and women, of bodies and flesh, of someone holding her fast, pressing hot kisses on her neck, gripping her ass cheeks in a hold so tight as he/she/they fuck-fuck-fucked her into the irresistible whirl of orgasm.

As dawn crept over the East River, Jarvis's last thought was of the missing woman in whose bed she lay.

I'm on your side, Kate. I just need a break.

In the morning she got it.

TEN

OAK VALE, IOWA. OCTOBER 1ST. 5.30 AM.

Felice watched the small blond hairs on the boy's forearm as he pumped gas into her rental car. There was something thrilling about the notion of a strong and handsome youth thrusting a big pipe into her vehicle and injecting it with fuel. She refrained from saying so. She didn't want him to think she was crazy. However she did want him to think of her as more than just another customer.

'Been working all night?'

'Yes, ma'am.'

'Busy?'

'Hell, no.' The boy flashed her a big white-toothed smile as he shook the last drops off the pump. 'We ain't got more than six cars right through. I don't know why he keeps it open.'

'Sounds pretty boring for you.'

'You bet.'

'Haven't you got any friends to keep you company?'

'Sometimes one of the guys drops by.'

'How about girls? I bet there's a few who'd come and hold your hand.'

He scowled. 'Well, I sure ain't met 'em.'

He stomped off towards the small office and Felice followed.

As she took money from her purse she said, 'Want *me* to hold your hand?'

'Ma'am?'

'Of course, there's a few other things I wouldn't mind holding as well.'

'Huh?'

He wasn't the world's brightest, she thought as she saw the incomprehension in his toffee-brown eyes. He sure was pretty though. The name tag on his shirt said 'Ben'.

She took a twenty from her purse.

'Do you want to earn a tip, Ben?'

'Sure.' His eyes had lit up.

She folded the bill small and tucked it into the open neck of her shirt, deep down into the crease between her breasts.

'Take it then.'

He hesitated.

'Hurry up, Ben. I'll give you ten seconds.'

His eyes flicked over her shoulder out into the empty forecourt where the grey light of dawn died in the garage lights. Nothing stirred.

He stepped towards her, the grin back on his face. She grabbed his hand as it hovered over her bulging shirt.

'With your mouth,' she said and pulled his blond head onto her bosom.

He did as he was told.

Five minutes later a yawning motorist pulled up outside. It was just as well he was half asleep and didn't notice how the pump jockey's hands shook as he unscrewed the gas cap.

When Ben returned to the office he found Felice sitting on the chair behind the counter. She was grinning.

'I've got another tip for you, Ben,' she said and pulled her skirt up her gleaming thighs.

The hair was lustrous on the base of her belly. The breath caught in the boy's throat as he gazed on the pink glistening lips of her labia and the fold of paper in-between. To his eyes, George Washington's face had never been so thrillingly framed.

This time he didn't hesitate.

ELEVEN

KARLSEN'S APARTMENT. 11.00 AM.

Jarvis felt better after some sleep. There wasn't much in Karlsen's kitchen but she rustled up dry crackers, canned juice and instant coffee – it was enough. The people who had bugged her yesterday didn't seem so terrible now. Hannah, Lovelace, Greg the fuckwit – they still annoyed her but she could handle it. What the hell? They were just guys doing what guys do. She mustn't let men get to her.

Then there was the job in hand – the disappearing women. Having spent the night in Karlsen's apartment – in her bed, no less – she felt much more attuned to the missing banker. What would Kate do in her shoes? Jarvis wondered. The thought occurred that she would probably do just what Jarvis did every morning: check her e-mail.

There were a dozen incoming messages. Jarvis ignored all but the last three – the others, she knew from Bureau reports, had already been read.

Two were from Karlsen's boss at the bank directing her to be in touch the moment she returned. The second of them was more recent and even more frantic. It appeared that Karlsen knew a whole lot about Rikard-Huysmann's key activities – probably more than her superior, Jarvis guessed.

The other message was dated September 30th, the day before.

Hiya Foxy

How's liberated life? Bet you're having a great time with

all those Manhattan Men. Oh, I forgot – these days they prefer their own company. Poor you. Not that I'm against same-sex preference as you know . . .

Anyhow, I've been thinking. We all had a life-changing experience chez Rolf. I can't just walk away from you and the others – why don't we get together? Does New England in the fall appeal at all? My house is huge and the garden right now is magnificent. You're welcome anytime.

Platonic kisses – Dale

Jarvis printed off the message and considered it for some while. It raised several questions and, whoever Dale was, the sooner she talked to her the better. She wondered how best to couch her approach. In the end she e-mailed back:

Your mail to Kate hasn't reached her because she's disappeared. I'm a friend who is most concerned for her whereabouts. Can we talk?

She added Kate's phone number, her own office and home numbers and her e-mail address. She signed off as 'Bonny Jarvis' with no mention of the Bureau. It worked. Within half an hour the woman was on the phone.

'What do you mean, she's disappeared?'

'What it sounds like, Ms—'

'Kennedy, but call me Dale, for God's sake. And who are you exactly?'

'Special Agent Bonny Jarvis of the Bureau. I'm looking into a number of missing person cases and Kate Karlsen is one of them.'

'You're serious?'

'Indeed I am, Ms Kennedy. Do you have any idea where she might be?'

'No, I don't.'

'Are any of these names familiar to you? Stacey Pine, Felice Cody and Madeleine Simons.'

There was silence for a moment. When the woman spoke

again she sounded far less self-assured.

'Sure, I know them. Don't tell me they're missing too?'
'Yes, they are.'
'Oh my God.' She sounded shaken.
'We need to talk, Dale.'
'Yes.'
'I'll come down today.'

Dealing with Hannah was not quite so easy.

'What are you doing in Karlsen's apartment?' was the first thing he said. 'You never told me you were flouncing off to Manhattan.'

'Something came up after you'd gone. I'm sorry.' She thought it wise to sound a placatory note. 'Anyhow, Hannah, it paid off. I think I've found a connection with the other vanishers.'

'What is it?'

'There's a woman called Dale Kennedy from New Bolton in Connecticut. She knows Karlsen and the others but I don't have the details yet. I'm going to see her as soon as I get off the phone to you.'

'Hey, hold your horses. If you've found the missing link, I'm coming too.'

'No, Hannah, I can't wait for you. I'll get a car and drive up there now.'

'You're not trying to ditch me, are you, Jarvis? Stone put me and you together. Just because you've got a problem with men you mustn't let it screw up this case.'

Jarvis took a deep breath. After a moment she said, 'That was not a helpful observation, Agent Hannah. I do not have a problem with men.'

'So it's just with me, is it? No, don't answer, Jarvis. I don't much care provided we can work as a team. As in you and me interviewing this Dale Kennedy together.'

Jarvis sipped her cold coffee. This was difficult.

'Look, Hannah, I'll level with you. I think Dale and Kate shared some kind of traumatic experience and it's most important we know what it was. But I've got a feeling if you and I go in flashing badges we'll just spook her. I'll do better one-on-one, I know it. It's a kind of woman thing.'

Hannah chuckled. Jarvis was relieved to hear it.

'I didn't think you were big on gut feel, Jarvis. I thought you only operated on bio-feedback.'

'Trust me on this. I'll share everything with you, I promise.'

'OK. But what am I supposed to do while you take in the scenery in New England?'

Jarvis breathed a sigh of relief. She'd won her point without too much bloodshed. It was time to throw him a bone.

'I found this woman through Karlsen's e-mail. We should check out messages on the other women's PCs – if they've got them. Cody has her own Web page, I know. We could get someone local to go to Simons' place and you could do Cody and Pine.'

'Oh shit, you mean I've got to mess around with computers? You don't know how awful I am with that kind of stuff, Jarvis.'

'Come on. You can look at someone's e-mail, can't you?'

'I can try but if these women turn up and I've crashed their precious systems you'll have to put them back together – deal?'

'Deal.'

'And one other thing. When you get back tomorrow you debrief me over supper at my apartment. I may know zip about computers but I can cook. Agreed?'

Inside her head Jarvis cursed as she pictured the dinnertime seduction that Hannah would be planning. Hannah guessed the reason for her hesitation.

'It's OK, Jarvis, it's strictly business but in a more friendly atmosphere. You can be gone by ten o'clock and I will respect your personal space at all times. If we're going to be partners we ought to try to be pals, don't you think?'

Jarvis didn't but she agreed to go all the same. She didn't have much choice.

TWELVE

BALDRY, PENNSYLVANIA. 12.45 PM.

Chris Shaw was rigid with guilt as he waited in the parking lot of the shopping mall. He was rigid with something else too. The thought of seeing Stacey Pine again had him stiff with desire.

It was as well her call had come through when Rita had gone for the day, though he'd guessed that Stacey had planned it that way. Rita would have recognised that low voice at once and been on to him about it. Been on to the police, too, without a doubt. The disappearance of Judge Pine was still the biggest mystery around.

'Do you remember me, Chris?' she'd said.

What a stupid question – not that Shaw would have dreamt of calling Stacey Pine stupid. But the five minutes he'd spent on the bed with her in the O'Rourke place had been the most exciting of his life.

'Judge Pine – where are you? Are you all right? The whole town's looking for you.'

'Calm down, Chris. I'm just fine. Now, listen, I need your help . . .'

Which was how come Shaw was sitting where he was, scanning the shoppers for the most mysterious woman he'd ever met. If Maxine – or Rita, come to that – found out about it, his life would be hell.

He didn't see her arrive until she was sitting in the passenger seat of his Volvo. She looked different. The ash-blonde hair was freshly groomed and she wore make-up. She had on a loose cream jacket over an emerald-green sweater and a short black skirt which showed off her legs. Thin silver bracelets tinkled on her wrists and her familiar perfume filled the car. She did not look like a harassed officer of the court or a fugitive or a stressed-out woman in early middle age.

'Stacey, you look fabulous,' he said.

'I feel fabulous,' she said.

'God, it's good to see you,' he said. 'I was so worried.'

She smiled indulgently. 'Once you're over the shock, Chris, I hope you won't express yourself entirely in clichés.'

His jaw dropped and she laughed.

'Do I frighten you?'

'A little, I guess.'

'Excellent. Some fear in a relationship can be most beneficial. If you report this conversation, for example, I shall tell your wife about your behaviour at our last meeting.'

'Oh my God – please, Stacey, don't do that.'

Her grey eyes bored into him. 'Just so we understand one another. Another thing – I've changed my mind about you calling me Stacey. Call me Judge.'

'OK.' He swallowed. Her skirt had ridden up to bare those lean thighs he remembered gripping his hips with such passion. 'OK, Judge.'

'Good. I'll call you Chris but sometimes I'll call you Prisoner.'

'Prisoner?'

'Wouldn't you like to be my prisoner? Tied naked to a bed so I could do what I liked to you.'

'Oh yes.' He didn't mean to say it like that, like he really wanted her to walk all over him. But then it had only just occurred to him that that's exactly what he did want.

'Excellent, Chris. I promise you can be my first prisoner when you've found me the kind of place I'm looking for.'

'What do you mean?'

She shot him a thunderous look. 'Did I give you permission to ask me a direct question?'

'No. I'm sorry.'

'I'm sorry, *Judge*.'

'Yes. I'm sorry, Judge.'

'That's better. I can see I'm going to have to train you a little. Undo your pants and show me your cock.'

'What!'

'Just do it, Chris.'

'But there's people out there. Don't make me, please.'

She hit him without warning, the bracelets jangling as the back of her hand landed on his cheek. He clutched his burning flesh, speechless with shock.

The sound of her voice sent a shiver through him as she spoke.

'Mind what I say, Prisoner. If you don't then I shall get out of this car and you'll never hear from me again. I'll find someone else to do what I want – I don't need you. Do you understand?'

'Yes, Judge. Please don't go. I'll do whatever you say.'

'Very well. Turn on the ignition.'

'The ignition?'

'Just turn it on. Then show me your prick.'

He did as he was told, turning towards her in his seat to try and block the view through his window.

His cock stuck up awkwardly beneath the steering wheel. She considered it with amusement.

'Open your pants more. Pull your balls out so I can look. Mm, you're very excited, aren't you?'

'God, yes. Stacey – Judge, I've never felt so . . .'

'Quite.'

She reached forward and plucked the cigarette lighter from the dashboard. The end glowed orange.

'Now listen carefully. I need a place to rent. Somewhere out of the way with no nosy neighbours. It should be soundproofed or so far off that no disturbances will be noticed. It would be ideal if it had a cellar. Do you follow?'

'Yes, Judge.'

'Good. You can stroke yourself, if you like, but you're not allowed to come. I'm in charge of your orgasms now, do you understand?'

Shaw shivered with fear and excitement. His eyes darted nervously over Pine's shoulder as a crowd of people got off a bus and headed for the entrance to the mall.

'A short lease will do. Put it in your name. I'll give you the money, don't worry. Besides, it will soon repay the investment. Speed up, Prisoner, I want to see you beat your meat.'

'But, Judge—'

A girl in a leather jacket walked by the car, for a second her eyes fell on the squirming realtor, his erect cock gripped tightly in his fist.

'Don't you dare stop!'

Pine's arm shot forward and the glowing cigarette lighter pressed into the back of Shaw's hand.

'Aah!' he cried.

'Don't take your hand away. It doesn't hurt.'

'But it does—'

'And you like it, don't you?'

He nodded. The hurt cut through the fog of confusion in his head. It gave this weird scene an edge.

'You're getting close, aren't you?' she said, watching his hand jack his stiff, solid shaft.

Shaw didn't reply but he was, indeed, getting near. He slid his fingers down to the base of his cock, away from the super-sensitive nerves of his glans. The end of his penis stuck up red and obscene. Two teenage girls had stopped ten yards away and were peering at the car.

'This afternoon I want you to go to my apartment and fetch a few things. Some of my toys. You'll love them.'

'Please, Judge – oh—'

'You'll adore my whips, Prisoner. I can't wait to show them to you. There's just one more matter to discuss then you are permitted to come.'

Shaw stared at her, his brain in a fever.

'What?' he said.

'Your wife is a problem. She might notice things about you. Do you have intercourse much?'

'No, she's not – well, we hardly ever—'

'Good. From now on you're completely off limits. Do you know why?'

'Why?'

'Because you're *mine*.'

As she pressed the ring of the lighter onto the shaft of his cock, a white fountain of spunk showered the steering column, spattering his trousers and his trembling hands.

The laughter of the teenage girls rang in his ears, blending with the agony in his loins and the taste of humiliation in his mouth. He had never felt so good.

Judge Stacey Pine may be evil but he worshipped her already.

THIRTEEN

CODY'S APARTMENT. 3.15 PM.

'I appreciate you letting me in but if you need to be somewhere else I can lock up on my own.'

Hannah was in Cody's study, gazing uncertainly at the outsize monitor of her PC.

'Oh sure,' said Brigitte. 'Just like you know your way around here, huh?' And she reached past him to tap in the log-in code. As she did so her bare raspberry-tipped breasts brushed his arm. He stepped aside and placed a companionable hand on her naked ass. They'd been at Cody's place since midday and had somehow only just got round to booting up the PC.

'Here we go then,' said Brigitte as she accessed her sister's e-mail. 'Twenty-five messages in the past week.'

'Great,' said Hannah. Maybe Jarvis's suggestion would pay off.

There were two messages from Dale Kennedy. The first requested Cody visit her, a similar invitation to the one Jarvis had found on Karlsen's machine. The second was very recent:

Felice

I just heard the weirdest thing – that you've gone missing. If you haven't, mail me quick. I hope you're OK.

Thinking of you – Dale

Other messages were from Cody's publishers – some sales figures she had requested and a smarmy note from her editor that was really a nag about the delivery on her new book.

'*Starlight of the Gods* sold one point two million,' said Hannah. 'Felice must be pretty rich these days.'

Brigitte shrugged, the creamy skin of her back rippling delightfully. 'It's wasted on her. She'll leave it all to UFO research.'

That was a possibility, Hannah could tell from her other mail. It came from correspondents all round the world, most of it based on *Starlight*. Cody obviously had an on-going dialogue with many of these people.

The last message hit the screen.

Dear Ms Cody

I don't know how you got my mother's name but I'm sending this message to ask you never to approach her again. I suppose there's not much I can do to persuade you not to write about the Lake Musgrave Incident but I can assure you that she will not talk about events in the distant past that brought shame and embarrassment on our family.

There's no need for you to reply to this as I shall not enter into any kind of dialogue. You may think you are undertaking a serious research project but I regard it as nothing more than muck-raking in order to turn a fast buck. Shame on you.

Celia Roberts

'What's the Lake Musgrave Incident?' said Brigitte. She was sitting at the keyboard and Hannah was standing by her side. His half-stiff cock was on a level with her chin.

'I don't know. Do you know your way around her files?'

Brigitte took hold of his prick and licked it like a lollipop. 'Yeah, a bit.'

'Brigitte, I don't think I've got the energy.'

'Me neither.' She slicked his foreskin back over the scarlet end of his cock and tickled the very end with the point of her tongue.

He slipped a hand under her arm and cupped her pear-shaped left breast. It was soft and warm in his palm.

'Can you look for other references to Lake Musgrave?' he asked as she took the head of his cock between her lips.

She sucked him for a moment then let him go. He was fully erect now.

'I'll try.'

She turned to the screen and began to tap on the keyboard.

'Your dick's whacking me in the face,' she complained.

'It's your fault. You made it get like that.'

'Put it away, Hannah. I can't concentrate.'

Neither could he. He pulled her to her feet and sat at the desk. He motioned to his lap where the spike of his penis reared up. She didn't hesitate.

'Is this on Bureau time?' she asked as the slick lips of her vagina parted for his cock and she sank down onto his pulsing member.

'Sure.' He slid a hand over the warm dome of her belly and pushed his fingers into the silky hairs at the crest of her cleft. He lifted his eyes to the screen. 'Get searching.'

She settled her ass into his loins and began to click the mouse.

'It just seems wrong somehow that you're getting paid and I'm doing all the work,' she said.

He ran his fingertip in a lazy circle around the hood of her clit. Deep inside her, the magic mouth of her sex began to flutter along the length of his cock.

'I'll make it up to you, Brigitte,' he said He placed his lips on the white stem of her neck and bit down softly. She arched her back and moaned.

If only Jarvis could see me now, thought Hannah. *At last I'm getting to grips with computers.*

FOURTEEN

NEW BOLTON, CONNECTICUT. 6.30 PM

Jarvis stood on the wooden deck at the rear of Dale Kennedy's house and peered through the window. Her hand froze in the act of rapping on the glass to call attention to her presence and her heart thudded against her ribs. What she saw explained a lot.

It had taken her longer to get out of Manhattan than she'd expected. She'd given up on the NY Bureau and hired her own car. It had been a hassle. She hated the damn city anyway. Then she'd got lost on the country roads.

She'd found the Kennedy place at last. It was big – a sprawling modern two-storey building miles from nowhere. The trees were beautiful but Jarvis was too pissed off to pay them much attention – especially when no one answered the door. She spent fifteen minutes leaning on the bell and knocking before she explored round the back.

Inside, the room was green with plants and she had to angle her head to look beyond the tumbling foliage and take in the scene.

Kennedy – she assumed it was her – sprawled on her back along a worn but cosy-looking couch. She had wavy brown hair, with red highlights, that fell to her jaw. She wore a scarlet-and-yellow knit sweater on top of which lay an open book – *The Shipping News*, Jarvis noted – in which, it seemed, she had lost interest. Her nose was long and her face oval, the pale skin clear. Her mouth was wide and curled up at the edges. Her eyes were closed. She looked like an attractive late-thirtysomething who had fallen asleep over a book – from the waist up.

From the waist down she was naked, her thighs alabaster white and spread wide to accommodate the second figure in this riveting tableau. Somehow Jarvis had expected the woman to be on her own. She had certainly not anticipated the presence of a bare-breasted blonde nymphet licking the older woman's cunt.

The girl had a long pink tongue and she used it with delicacy, going about her business with languorous strokes. She lifted her head and spoke to her supine lover. Jarvis couldn't hear what was said but she noted the girl's full wet lips, her cropped bleached hair and the tiny stud sparkling in her nostril. She was kneeling up on the long couch and her pert little rear pouted in skintight leather shorts. Everything about this designer punk screamed sex.

Jarvis watched with clinical fascination as the girl opened the woman's vagina with her hand. The pubic delta had been shaved and the long brown labia were fully displayed. The girl's little fingers toyed with the glistening lips, pulling and squeezing and tugging the fleshy folds until, at last, the woman began to squirm her butt and push her pelvis up for further attention.

The girl spread the woman wide and lowered her head. Jarvis clearly saw a flash of her pink tongue as it flicked inside Kennedy. Then the woman grabbed the cropped blonde head and held it fast against her pubis as she ground into the face.

After a moment the blonde pulled away and folded Kennedy's left leg upwards, into her body, spreading her even wider. She looked down at the woman's exposed flesh – the gaping mouth of her vagina, the brown star of her anus, the white globe of her buttock. She licked the index finger of her right hand and pushed it into Kennedy's ass as far as the second joint. Then she lowered her head once more and began to lap her eagerly, like a cat at the milk. The woman wriggled and bucked, faster and faster.

Jarvis pulled back from the window abruptly. As she walked away she could hear the sobs of Kennedy's orgasm through the glass.

She drove five miles down the road to a gas station and sat in the coffee shop for twenty minutes before she used the phone. She sure as hell wished they sold something stronger than coffee.

When the girl opened the door Jarvis was relieved to see she had changed. The leather shorts had been replaced by a tartan miniskirt worn over a skintight black body. The buds of her nipples were clearly outlined beneath the thin material and Jarvis tried to keep her eyes on the girl's face. She had a chipped front tooth and big brown Bambi eyes. She looked about seventeen.

'Hi, I'm Quinn.' Her voice had a Brooklyn squeak. 'We'd just about given up on you.'

'I was delayed. I should have called earlier – I'm sorry.' Jarvis had no intention of elaborating on her late arrival.

Quinn showed her into the den at the back of the house, the room which she had peered into earlier. There was no sign of the torrid lovemaking which she had witnessed. Everything was neat and there was the smell of tarragon in the air. Through a half-open door Jarvis saw the stripped counter and tiled floor of a large kitchen.

Kennedy still wore the scarlet-and-yellow sweater but her bottom half was encased in a floor-length cotton skirt in an oriental pattern. The woman took Jarvis's arm as if they were old friends and the musky scent of patchouli enveloped her.

'Thank God you made it,' she said. 'Let's have a drink and a bite to eat. Quinn will fix us up. What'll you have?'

'Water, Coke, anything soft,' Jarvis said quickly. She'd kill for a real drink but she'd better be on her guard.

'Only,' said Quinn, handing her a glass of fizzing mineral water, 'if you'll have wine with dinner.'

How could she say no?

Dinner was great, Jarvis knew it would be. She was hungry and found it hard to refuse a second plate of herb-poached chicken. She helped herself to more salad and home-baked bread. Quinn refilled her glass.

'I met Kate this summer,' said Kennedy in answer to Jarvis's unspoken question. 'I signed on for a self-help course in New Mexico. That's where we all met up – Stacey and Madeleine and Felice and Kate and me.'

'What course is this?'

'It's called "Voices From Within – Freeing Your Sensual Self".'

'Your sensual self?'

'Right.'

'She sure didn't ask for her money back,' Quinn said and giggled.

Kennedy stared at her. 'This is serious, honey. Don't interrupt me when I'm talking to Agent Jarvis.'

A mutinous look crossed the girl's face.

'That was the most enjoyable meal I've had in months,' said Jarvis and Quinn flashed her a grateful smile. Then she stood and began to clear away the plates.

'How did you hear about this course?' asked Jarvis when Quinn had disappeared into the kitchen.

'I was reading some psychology journal in my shrink's office and I saw an ad. At the time I was single, repressed, frustrated as hell and just petrified of sex. Freeing any part of myself sounded like a good idea. Plus it was a women-only course.'

'So you went to New Mexico?'

'I did. Scared out of my wits, I can tell you. I ran into Kate on the plane, actually.'

'That must have helped.'

'Hardly. She was one of the most aggressive women I've ever met. I put her down as a professional career bitch. That's what she thought about me too, of course.'

'I see. Were you all antagonistic to each other at first?'

'You bet. We hated each other on sight. Then within two days we were buddies for life. Rolf says it's always like that.'

'Rolf?'

'Dr Leonard. He runs the course. He's got a ranch in the Antelope Mountains. Not a ranch as such, more like a health farm. There's a sauna, swimming pool, tennis courts.'

'Sounds pretty ritzy.'

'It should be for twelve thousand bucks a week.'

Jarvis reached for her notebook. 'How many women were on your course?'

'Twenty or so. You're thinking that's a ton of money, aren't you?'

'It's a quarter-of-a-million-dollar turnover for one week.'

'All of us could afford it. What else did we spend our money on, anyway? Besides,' she added, leaning forward and laying her hand on Jarvis's sleeve, 'if it had cost ten times as much it was worth it.'

It was dark outside now and Jarvis looked at the image of the pair of them reflected back into the room from the window. With her thick reddish hair, pale skin and full figure, she realised Kennedy looked like an older version of herself. And not that much older. In ten years she could be her.

She looked into Kennedy's milky blue eyes. 'Why's that?'

'Because I spent all my life not knowing what a real orgasm was. I found out twelve hours into Leonard's course. Since then, you could say I've been making up for lost time.'

Jarvis sat back in her chair, moving her arm and breaking contact.

Kennedy laughed. 'It's OK, my dear. I'm not some horny dyke putting the make on you. But I *am* a convert of Rolf Leonard's. He's changed my life – for the better.'

Jarvis scribbled a note. She resented the fact that she was uncomfortable with this.

'Tell me, Ms Kennedy,' she said, 'what do you do?'

'How do I pay the bills, you mean?'

'Right.'

Kennedy stood up. 'Follow me.'

She took Jarvis up a flight of spiral wooden stairs into the room above the den. She pointed to the long window that ran the length of the wall facing the garden.

'Out there is forest and light and animals. I bring them in here,' she said, turning to the opposite wall. It was hung with canvasses and others leant up against it in piles. As Kennedy snapped on the lights at the far end, Jarvis saw shelves of paint, easels, a large angled drawing table, twin sinks and jars of brushes.

'You're an artist,' she said.

'For years I called myself an illustrator. I just did books, stuff for kids and struggled along. Then I got lucky with a bestseller and people started buying the originals. Now I do commissions and have a fancy agent. It's turned out well.'

'This is lovely!' cried Jarvis as she bent to examine a painting of a blue jay in a beech tree.

'Cute, huh?' said Quinn's Brooklyn twang from the doorway. 'Yours for five thousand bucks.'

'Oh, Quinn!' protested Kennedy.

'Or maybe she does a special price for sexy Bureau agents. Spend the night with the artist and take the picture when you go.'

Jarvis froze with embarrassment but Kennedy just laughed. She pulled the girl into the room and hugged her. 'Don't be jealous, darling. Agent Jarvis is not interested in bedding me, she's here to do a job.'

She turned to Jarvis. 'Quinn's only been here since I got back from New Mexico. Sometimes she gets a little insecure.' And she kissed the girl on the lips. Quinn reciprocated passionately. Jarvis didn't know where to look.

The pair finally broke apart and Quinn dashed to the far end of the room. 'All this wildlife stuff is old,' she said, pulling open a desk drawer. 'Dale's working on some great new things.'

'Put that back, Quinn,' said Kennedy as the girl returned, clutching a large portfolio. 'I don't think Agent Jarvis is interested.'

'I wouldn't bet on that, Dale. They say everything about the new you – isn't that why she's here?'

Jarvis was intrigued as Quinn laid the folder on the table and opened it up. The breath caught in her throat as the girl slowly turned the pages to reveal drawings in pencil, charcoal and pastels. They were exquisite, Jarvis could see. They were also obscene.

Not that the subject of the drawings seemed to care. Quinn was beaming broadly as she watched Jarvis drink in every detail of her own nude body. A few of them were modestly posed but in the majority the model's genitals were the focus of the artist's attention. With legs spread wide, the purse of her sex revealed by inquisitive fingers and other invasive objects, Quinn displayed herself shamelessly for the artist.

'Wonderful, aren't they?' said the girl. 'Sometimes they're hell to do. She wants me to keep still all the time and that's impossible. Try it sometime with a ten-inch vibrator up your cunt!'

Jarvis blushed as a memory of last night in Karlsen's bed sprang to mind.

'That's enough,' said Kennedy. 'Put them away, Quinn, and show Agent Jarvis to the spare room. You'll spend the night here, won't you?'

Jarvis wanted to say no but it was late and she'd drunk too much to drive. She just hoped there was a lock on the door.

There wasn't. Neither had she brought her earplugs. The moment she turned out the light the women in the next room started. From the sighs and moans she could picture what they were doing to each other. Not that she had to imagine much. What she'd seen earlier was explicit enough. But she was tired. She found eventually that even the sound of lovemaking could make an effective lullaby.

She was woken at one in the morning by the sound of her door opening. She snapped on the light.

'Ta-daa!' said Quinn.

She was naked but for a red ribbon round her neck.

'What the hell are you doing?' said Jarvis.

The girl held her arms out, the circles of her small breasts jiggling with the movement.

'A gift from the management,' said Quinn.

'Get out.'

'You don't mean that.'

She advanced on the bed, her thighs gleaming and the flat of her belly white in the dim light. Her slit was almost on a level with Jarvis's head. Like Kennedy, she too was smooth between the legs.

'You know you want me,' she said.

'No, I don't, you cheap slut.'

Quinn sat on the bed. 'Slut, maybe, but not cheap. You can buy me lots of nice things.'

'You have ten seconds to get out of this room or I'll throw you out.'

'Mmm, that sounds fun. You policewomen are so butch.'

Jarvis swung her hand but Quinn caught it before it could land on her cheek. She pulled it down onto the curve of her hip.

'Go away!' hissed Jarvis but the girl took no notice, launching herself at the agent, her nipples pressing into the swell of the woman's breasts through her thin T-shirt.

For a minute they wrestled. Quinn was slippery and experienced in close-quarter combat, Jarvis could tell. She tried to throw her off her without using maximum force. She didn't want the commotion to wake Kennedy next door. Then Quinn's hand found its way between Jarvis's legs and a finger thrust up into her vagina.

'Ooh, you hot bitch, you're wet for me,' whispered Quinn's voice in her ear and the girl's lips closed on hers, forcing an entry with her tongue. She tasted musky and salty. She tasted, no doubt, of Dale Kennedy. For a moment Jarvis was rigid with shock as Quinn plundered her fore and aft.

Then she threw the girl onto the floor.

'Hey!' she protested as Jarvis dragged her to the door and slammed her against the wall. 'And I thought we were getting somewhere.'

Jarvis jabbed a fist into the girl's ribs.

'Get out of here, Quinn, before I hurt you.'

'But you want me, you know you do.'

'Out!' and she thrust the naked teenager into the corridor.

It took Jarvis a long time to fall asleep after that. The adrenaline was rushing and the feel of the girl's smooth nude body seemed to envelop her like a blanket. In the end she put her hand between her legs and gave herself a quick functional release that allowed her to drift into an unsatisfying sleep.

Despite the protests of her two hostesses, Jarvis made an early start the next morning. On the car seat beside her as she drove off was a package containing the painting she had admired.

She dropped the car at the rental office in Hartford and flew out of Bradley International. Only on the plane did she discover the note that had been slipped into the wrapping of the painting.

'I'm at this number in DC once a month. You can always leave a message. Quinn Duncan.'

Jarvis wanted to throw the paper away but told herself it might be needed for the investigation. She put it in her pocket and tried to catch up on her sleep.

FIFTEEN

UNIVERSITY OF CARDINAL SPRINGS, W. VIRGINIA.
OCTOBER 2ND. 5.05 PM.

Wayne Moreau and Art Rosen were shooting the shit in the locker room when the woman walked in. The rest of the team had all mooched off but Moreau and Rosen had a few things to straighten out about the snap count. Then they'd got into more interesting stuff, like the miracle that was Sue Wahlstrom's ass, when the brunette just strolled in. That shut them up pretty quick. It was lucky they were decent.

'Hi,' she said and pulled a towel from her rucksack. 'The women's showers are on the fritz – you don't mind, do you?'

Mind what? thought the guys though they didn't say so. Then the woman pulled her sweatshirt over her head and their eyeballs damn near exploded at the sight of her bare tits.

'What's up, fellers – never seen a woman take a shower before? Let me tell you, we do it just the same as you guys. Only, of course, we've got more interesting bits to wash.'

All the time she was talking she was pulling off her clothes – kicking off her trainers, tugging electric-blue lycra shorts over her rounded hips, pulling panties down her long creamy thighs.

'Hey,' said Moreau, 'you ain't allowed in here.'

'Yes, I know, but I've got to clean up. You can watch if you like.'

Her breasts sure were big. They pointed out to the side of her body and they moved a beat later than the rest of her. Rosen was mesmerised. Moreau was yakking on some more, even though he had a boner in his shorts. They both did.

'But, miss, this is the *men's* changing room. You gonna get yourself thrown out.'

'Why, are you going to do it? Just try.'

And she turned her gleaming white ass to them and stepped to the shower stall. Moreau went after her.

'Lady, this is against the rules.'

'Absolutely. Now, show me how this water adjusts.'

Moreau's muscular black arm reached round her to the dial.

'OK but this sure ain't my idea. If there's any trouble . . .'

The water hissed down on the woman's naked flesh. She lathered soap into a flannel and began to wash.

'Hey, Wayne.' Rosen spoke for the first time. 'Get out of the way, man, you're blocking my view.'

Moreau stepped aside and the pair of them stood there watching the woman. She had turned her back but she looked at them over her shoulder as she luxuriated in the hot spray. She raised her arm to wash beneath and the swollen sphere of her breast swung into profile.

'What you doing?' cried Moreau as Art stepped out of his shorts.

'What do you think?' His dick slapped his belly as he stepped into the shower beside her.

'But—' Moreau was perplexed. He watched his friend embrace the woman, his hands on her white buttocks. She squirmed her chest into him and rubbed her loins against his thigh.

'Lock the door, Wayne,' said Rosen, breaking the kiss. 'Stick a chair under the handle or something.'

Moreau did as he was told – he usually did. When he returned, the woman was on her knees, kissing Rosen's thick circumcised cock.

She lifted her head, a crazy glint in her eye, her hand pumping the boy's shaft.

'Take your dick out, Wayne,' she said. 'I want it.'

'I don't understand,' said Moreau as he offered her his swollen prick. 'Why are you doing this, lady?'

'Because I love athletic young men. I like their arms round

my waist and their hands on my tits and their cocks in my cunt. Have you got a problem with that?'

On reflection, with her lips wrapped around his dick, Wayne found that he didn't.

SIXTEEN

HANNAH'S APARTMENT. 9.30 PM.

Hannah speared a shrimp and bit it in two.

'So you think it's this New Mexico trip that's sent these women off the rails?'

Jarvis considered his question. So far things had gone pretty well. She hadn't even been tempted to throw wine in his face.

'Has to be,' she said. 'Kennedy says that's how they all met.'

'But *she* hasn't run away.'

'That's true. However she's shacked up with a lesbian punk half her age and they're romancing round the clock. She says she's making up for lost time and that this Rolf Leonard changed her life.'

Hannah pushed the salad bowl across the table. Jarvis shook her head.

'I'm full. You weren't kidding when you said you could cook.'

He grinned and produced a bottle of Armagnac.

'Coffee's coming,' he said and poured two glasses. 'Does she have any idea where Cody might be?'

'No, nor any of the others.'

'It's hardly a crime for a woman to take off. Especially these women. They're mature adults and they can do what they want. It's not our business. But Cody's a top-flight research scientist and we've got to find her. The rest of them are on their own.'

Jarvis thought about that.

'This thing is bigger than just one person,' she said. 'There were twenty women on Kennedy's week. For all we know there's been courses all year. That's a hell of a lot of people to be missing.'

'If they are.' Hannah stood up. 'We only know about our four. The rest of them could be tucked up in bed at home, getting acquainted with their sensual selves like Dale Kennedy. I'll get that coffee.'

Jarvis sipped her brandy. She'd made a decision on the flight back to Washington and she didn't know how to break it to Hannah. He wouldn't be happy. She steeled herself to speak but he didn't give her the opening.

'Have you heard of the Lake Musgrave Incident?' he said as he set down a pot of coffee.

'Why?'

'I checked out Cody's e-mail, as you suggested. The only thing of interest was this.' He passed her a print-out of the message from Celia Roberts.

Jarvis read it twice. 'Sounds like some long-dead scandal, doesn't it? I'll see if there's anything on file. What about Pine's place?'

'Nothing. She doesn't even own a PC. But someone has been there recently. The old woman next door stopped me as I went in. She made quite a fuss till I convinced her I was on the level. Then she told me about a man she'd seen leaving with a suitcase.'

'What kind of man?'

'Tall, blond, snappy dresser, she said. He told her he was from the rental agency, keeping an eye on the property while the Judge was absent. Later on she started to get suspicious. She remembered that the key ring the guy had was like the one Pine herself used – shaped like a pair of handcuffs. She spent ten minutes telling me she was convinced this man had slaughtered Stacey.'

'She might be right.'

Hannah chuckled. 'I bet the Judge sent a boyfriend round to pick up some things.'

'We'd better look for him.'

'Yes, boss. Have another drink.'

He poured without waiting for a reply. Jarvis sensed this was her moment.

'Look, Hannah, there's something we need to talk about—'

The door buzzer sounded. Hannah looked puzzled. It sounded again, insistent this time. Hannah went into the hall and spoke into the entry-phone. When he returned Jarvis could smell his embarrassment.

'That's Brigitte, Cody's sister. She's on her way up.' Before he could say more there was a rap at the door.

Jarvis followed him into the hallway.

A blonde in a fuschia-pink minidress tumbled through the door and hooked a slim brown arm round Hannah's waist.

'Hi, lover. Pleased to see me?'

It was neither here nor there to Jarvis but she thought that, beneath his discomfort, he looked *damned* pleased to see her. She noted the familiar way his hands took the woman by the shoulders and turned her away from him to make the introductions.

'Brigitte, this is my partner, Special Agent Jarvis. She's helping me trace your sister.'

Brigitte was taken aback but shook hands with Jarvis firmly.

'I just dropped in on impulse. I'll go.'

'No,' said Jarvis, claiming her coat. 'We're done here.' And she marched out without looking at Hannah. Which was petulant of her, she knew, but she couldn't help it.

As the door shut, Brigitte backed Hannah against the wall and thrust her tongue into his mouth. Her eyes laughed into his as they kissed.

'I'm sorry,' she said when they broke off. 'I can't get enough of you.'

She pulled the dress to her hips and he saw she wore nothing underneath it. She turned and bent over the hall table, offering her ass.

'I haven't got long,' she said over her shoulder. 'Glen's out till midnight.'

Hannah admired her rounded rear and the pouting cleft at

the base of her divide. He pushed two fingers into her wetness.

'Ooh,' she whispered. 'I'm ready.'

'I can tell.'

He unbuckled his pants and took his cock in his free hand. They'd been fucking for most of the preceding day and night but he was as stiff as a post. He went into her like a homecoming sailor and she thrust back into him till he hit bottom.

'God, that's better,' she muttered as he began a steady beat. He pulled out to the tip and pushed back in again. The air was thick with the scent of sex and the rude sticky sound of cock in cunt.

Her buttocks clenched and pulsed as he poked her steadily and he reached underneath her to find her clit. They were making a lot of noise now, their bodies crashing against the small table, bumping it against the wall, their breathing short and their endearments hoarse.

He came first, he couldn't hold on longer. The kiss of her velvet ass cheeks on his belly and the sweet squeeze of her cunt on his cock had him ramming into her out of control. And as his passion erupted inside her, the orgasm she so desired overtook her like a breaking wave.

In the corridor outside, Jarvis heard every crash and cry of their coupling. She stood perfectly still, listening to it out of a curious sense of duty. It confirmed all her worst suspicions about her new partner. The man was a degenerate who preyed on female desire. A weakness he would never, *never* discover in her.

When all was quiet she walked slowly to the elevator.

SEVENTEEN

BUREAU HEADQUARTERS. OCTOBER 3RD. 7.45 AM.

Jarvis was at her desk in the basement. The fluorescents glowed and the machines hummed. It could have been any time, day or night. Jarvis liked it like that. She'd already been at work for twenty minutes.

Before her was a faded green folder, filled with yellowing paper, marked in bleached-out copperplate: SF/8/14/34. She'd retrieved it from a bank of ageing grey file cabinets hidden on the rear wall of her long office after a few minutes searching the database of her computer.

God knows what time Hannah would turn up. Which was fine by her. It meant she could trawl the archives and make plans just the way she liked it. By herself.

She settled down to read the SF folder at her leisure.

SF as in Sex File.

EIGHTEEN

TRANSCRIPT OF INTERVIEW WITH SHERIFF JIM McKEE, 14TH AUGUST 1934, FORT MUSGRAVE, WYOMING. AGENT DAN QUANTRILL INVESTIGATING.

QUANTRILL: OK, Jim, we can't put this off any longer. You've got to give me your story about what happened yesterday.

McKEE: Does *she* have to hear it? I don't know that I can talk about this in front of a woman.

Q: You know the rules, Jim. We have to have a stenographer to do it official. Mary's the best, she knows how to keep her lip buttoned. Pretend she's not here.

M: But what's going to happen? I can't testify to this in court. I'd be a laughing stock the length of the Rockies. I couldn't do my job no more.

Q: Stop fretting. This thing's stopping here. We're going to wrap it up tighter than a brown bear's asshole and bury it. The Bureau's more worried than you are. But first we got to record the truth. So, shoot.

M: OK. Well, first off, yesterday was hotter than hell, up in the nineties and climbing. So when we got a call that there was a problem out on the lake there was no holding the boys back. I had to insist that Walter stayed behind and the other two deputies, Frank Willis and Ralph Cooper, rode on out there with me. The report we'd had was that a bunch of young females on a church picnic were making a nuisance of themselves on Cottonwood Island. It sounded like some damn fool joke but we weren't complaining. At the time.

Q: What precisely was this report?

M: That a group of young women were dancing naked on the beach.

Q: And you three thought you'd better take a look?

M: We couldn't ignore it, Dan. Apart from the contravention of public decency, they was trespassing.

Q: What happened when you got there?

M: Well, Cottonwood Island's about a quarter mile off the south shore. There was a whole heap of people by the lake enjoying the sun and all. And watching these young girls over on the island with no clothes on.

Q: What were they doing?

M: Most of them were running in and out of the water, playing a game with a ball. We counted about a dozen of them. I was all for leaving them there and having a word with them when they came back. If it wasn't for the preacher I'd of done that. To be honest, they weren't doing no harm and they weren't spoiling the view either.

Q: What about the preacher?

M: Reverend Andrews had brought these gals out there but they'd stolen a boat and taken off for the island leaving him on shore. He was damn near close to having a coronary. It was him had called in and complained. He said if I didn't get'em back in quick time he'd bring down the wrath of the Almighty on my campaign to get re-elected.

Q: I didn't know you were such a God-fearing man, Sheriff.

M: At election time I scare easy. But it wasn't that entirely. While I was trying to calm the preacher down, Frank pointed out that two of these women were kissing. Now, that changed everything. They stood there in full view of us all on the other side and embraced like . . . you know.

Q: You'd better say, Jim.

M: Well, like a drunken cowpoke and a ten-cent whore. Only these two were bare-ass naked. And female of course. So we borrowed a rowboat from one of the houses along the shore and headed on out. I tell you, Dan, I was glad I had two strong boys to do the rowing because my hands was sweating so much we'd of gone round in circles.

Q: Why's that?

M: Because I had a premonition what a goddam calamity this was going to be. There were all these people watching from the south shore, hooting and laughing, and I could see we were going to look pretty lame-brained chasing a dozen females with no clothes on. I mean, it wasn't dignified and I knew it could only get worse. Which it did. Though I ain't making excuses.

Q: Calm down, Jim. Just tell me what happened, then we can forget all about it.

M: We fair flew across the water – I guess the boys were feeling pretty chipper at the thought of all that girl flesh. I got out first and said howdy and asked if there was any one in particular who wanted to speak for the group. This blonde gal came over, one of those who'd been smooching with a girlfriend and said she'd answer for all of them. So I asked what in tarnation they thought they were doing, stealing a boat and trespassing on the island and all. And she said she was glad we'd come to join them because what they really wanted – do I have to say what she said?

Q: Yes.

M: What they wanted, she said, was to get laid and would I care to screw her pussy into next Tuesday? I couldn't believe my ears. I mean, she wasn't no low-life hooker. She'd got flaxen braids and eyes bluer than the lake and freckles dusted all over this cute little turned-up nose. Can't be older than my youngest daughter. I was just thankful those wise-asses back on the shore couldn't hear what she was talking about.

Q: What did you do?

M: I tell you, what I wanted to do was put her over my knee and tan that pretty little fanny of hers. I started to say that that kind of disgraceful language wasn't going to do her any good when, out of the blue, she charged at me. It was like there was some kind of signal because three or four of them jumped me at the same time. It was stupid, there didn't seem anything to hang on to – nothing you could fight anyway – just this hot slippery skin. Anyhow I got pushed over and they were on top of me and then suddenly they were gone. And when I got up, they'd all disappeared up the beach and they'd got my gun. Ralph and Frank were just staring bug-eyed. I couldn't believe it. Me and those two boys took in the Eldridge Gang last year and here we were outplayed by a bunch of naked women.

Q: Did you go after them?

M: Of course we did. It was our worst mistake. All three of us went tearing into the trees after them and the blonde with the braids put a bullet through Frank's hat. That stopped us. Frank held his Stetson out and we could see he'd been less than an inch from the cemetery. The blonde stuck the gun in my face and told the other two to hand over their weapons. They didn't argue and I was damn glad. Pretty or not, that gal would have plugged me, I know. Then they tied us up.

Q: What with?

M: Belts mostly, from our clothes and they had some stuff from their clothes too. Frank had this pair of handcuffs and they used those on him. Strung him up from a tree with one hand cuffed above his head.

Q: And then?

M: Well, you know.

Q: You've got to say it, Jim. For the record.

M: The *secret* record, right?

Q: I swear.

M: Then they raped us. Sounds pretty funny, doesn't it? I'd always thought it couldn't be done. I mean, a man's got to want to play before the woman can make the connection. But I forgot a woman can make a man do near whatever she wants. At least if she's got a face like an angel and skin like silk and a dirty mouth. The blonde one—

Q: Martha Shannon.

M: That's her. She got down beside me where I was trussed up on this bank, put her head right close to me and looked into my eyes. Then she started talking, about how much she'd always looked up to me, how handsome I was and how she needed me inside her. While she was talking she stroked my cheeks, then my chest inside my shirt, then she opened up my pants. Behind her I saw Frank, one hand cuffed to the tree, the other tied behind his back and he was stark naked. This thin dark girl was kneeling in front of him, pulling on his, er, penis and when she leaned back I could see it sticking up. I looked into his face and he had his eyes closed and his head back and I couldn't tell whether he was in pain or having the time of his life. Then she stuck his pecker in her mouth and he went, 'Ooh, baby.' To think that after being shot at and then strung up he could want to make out with those bitches. I was shook.

Q: I can imagine. So, Jim, did you . . . ?

M: Yes, goddamit, I did. That Shannon girl sat on my thighs and I fucked her – or she fucked me. She rode me like a bare-ass rodeo rider, her tits bobbing and her braids flying. I'm sorry, Mary, but that's the way it was. For the rest of the afternoon the three of us did just what they wanted. At least half a dozen of them sat on my dick until they popped. They made me lick them too. Young girl's cunt juice – sweeter than strawberry wine. I thought I'd never get to taste it again in my life. Now I'm going to be dreaming about it for the rest of my days.

Q: Lordy.

M: I just pray to God Sarah never finds out about any of this.

Q: She won't.

M: She'll know something's happened to me, Dan. After all that young pussy, I don't think I'll ever be able to fuck my wife again.

NINETEEN

BUREAU HEADQUARTERS. 9.25 AM.

It burned Jarvis the way Hannah was behaving. Sure, there were comic elements to the events at Lake Musgrave but Hannah had finished the McKee transcript ten minutes ago and he was still chuckling to himself.

'Knock it off, Hannah. It's not that funny.'

'You don't think so? Three hunky lawmen raped by a bunch of girls? No wonder they hushed it up.'

'Actually, it's a politically sensitive issue.'

'You're right, Jarvis. Especially in nineteen thirty-four. It could have advanced the feminist cause by half a century. Imagine if it had caught on. There'd have been a pre-war tourist boom in Wyoming.'

'Since you find it merely amusing I presume you're not interested in the rest of it.'

Hannah leaned back in his chair. 'Of course I am. I just can't help thinking of that poor sap McKee – dreaming of nude teenagers for the rest of his life.'

'As it happened, it turned out OK for McKee. He ended up married to Martha Shannon.'

'What!'

'They put her in a mental hospital out of state and her family raised a stink because she was so far off. They appealed to McKee so he went to see her and she begged him to forgive her. He managed to get her transferred back to a place around Larkspur and they let her out after five years. His marriage had gone sour because of the whole business so he was free to marry her. They settled down and had three kids, two sons and a daughter.'

'Celia.'

'Right.'

'What about Martha's friends? Did they lock them up too?'

'Of course they did. They split the group up and put them in mental facilities throughout Wyoming and Nebraska. Basically, though, the doctors couldn't find much wrong with them. They were pretty nice girls, it seems, who just had a wild afternoon.'

'That's it?'

'Not exactly. There was a core group of five, including Martha, of course. These were the ringleaders. They'd stepped out of line before – not in the same way but staying out all night and putting out for the local boys. One of them was caught in a hotel with a married man.'

'Sounds pretty average adolescent behaviour to me.'

'These were good kids from reasonable homes. They all belonged to the same church, remember. This Reverend Andrews was shattered by events up at the lake. He had an interesting take on the whole thing though.'

'Don't tell me – the girls were possessed by the devil.'

'Wrong. You're not cynical about religion, are you, Hannah? Stone tells me you've got an open mind.'

'I have.'

'Open to hypnotherapy?'

'Sure.'

'Well, that's what Andrews thought had caused these girls to go bad. It seems they'd all been seeing a new doctor in town. A charismatic type with a load of certificates on his wall and a belief in the therapeutic power of hypnotism.'

'Weird.'

'I'll tell you something weirder, Hannah. This man's name was Rolf Leonard.'

'Now, wait a minute, you two.' Stone's chocolate-brown voice was as measured as ever but he was looking worried. There was a deep furrow running east-west on his high, domed forehead and two smaller ones north-south above the bridge of his nose. 'I send you off to find a missing research biologist and you come up with outbreaks of sexual hysteria sixty years apart. Just what are you suggesting?'

Jarvis glanced at Hannah but he was staring out of the window at the yellow brick wall opposite. He was going to leave the tough stuff to her, she could see. Well, that wasn't necessarily a bad thing.

'We don't know the answers, sir, but there sure are a lot of questions. Let me summarise.'

'Please do.' Stone relaxed a little on the other side of his big empty desk. He waited.

'One – we've got four missing women, including Cody, our primary target. All of them vanished after an uncharacteristic burst of promiscuous behaviour. There's no evidence of foul play. Two – we've established a link between the women. They attended the same therapy course on sensual self-discovery run by a character called Rolf Leonard in New Mexico. Three – we believe Cody, who is also an expert on inexplicable phenomena, is researching events that took place in Wyoming in nineteen thirty-four. We know from our own reading of the Sex File on the Lake Musgrave Incident that it concerns a group of hitherto modest girls who suddenly became aggressively promiscuous. Four – the file also reveals that these girls were treated shortly before the incident by a doctor called Rolf Leonard.'

'Hah!' Stone's laughter was a burst of contempt. 'Are you suggesting, Agent Hannah, that the Leonard in New Mexico is same one as at Musgrave?'

'No, sir, that's not possible. Dale Kennedy described her Dr Leonard as a man of about forty. If he were still alive, the Musgrave Leonard would be in his eighties at least.'

'Quite. I'm relieved to hear that working with Agent Hannah hasn't addled your wits after all. So it's a coincidence?'

'Could be. Or—'

'What?'

'Maybe they're related. Suppose New Mexico Leonard is the son of Musgrave Leonard. Maybe there's a family tendency to exploit vulnerable women by whatever techniques happen to be fashionable at the time. This New Mexico course sounds like a lucrative business and I'm sure the Musgrave Leonard didn't practise for free.'

Stone nodded. 'OK, I'll buy that but what about Cody? Got any idea where she is?'

Hannah spoke up at last. 'She mailed a card to her sister from Chicago almost a week ago. Said she was heading out West.'

'Has the sister heard anything since.'

'No but I'm keeping in contact with her.'

Jarvis admired the deadpan way Hannah said it. For his sake, she hoped Stone would not discover exactly how close that contact was.

'Any other signs? Credit cards? Car rental?'

'There's no paper trail at all.'

'Damn.' Stone stood up and began to prowl. 'So what do you propose to do now?'

Jarvis knew this was her moment. 'I've enrolled on Leonard's next course in New Mexico. I fly down on Saturday.'

'You never told me!' Hannah sounded predictably aggrieved. He appealed to Stone. 'This is not the first time she's gone running off on her own – we should both go down there.'

'I've been trying to tell you about it since last night,' said Jarvis, 'but you're so touchy there's never a right moment.'

'That's enough.' Stone's rich baritone cut in. 'It seems to me that someone's got to run a check on Leonard because he may be perpetrating a damaging fraud on female victims. And since Agent Jarvis is the female member of the team it seems logical that she should go. Do you have a problem with that, Agent Hannah?'

'Put like that, I suppose not.'

'Good. Meanwhile you can concentrate on finding these missing people. Maybe Cody's sister knows more than she's letting on. Breathe all over her, OK?'

'Well, that shouldn't tax you too much,' said Jarvis as they left Stone's office. She couldn't resist.

Neither could he.

'Aren't you worried about this New Mexico jaunt?' he said.

'Why should I be?'

'Because you fit the profile, Jarvis – female and frigid. When you come back a nymphomaniac, I'll be waiting.'

TWENTY

BALDRY, PENNSYLVANIA. OCTOBER 4TH. 5.10 PM.

Pine watched the two men hanging the cage with a critical eye. They had assured her they knew what they were doing – that the load was on the ceiling joists and that the motor would raise it easily – but she wasn't convinced. She wanted a demonstration.

The elder of the men was small and dapper, he wouldn't do. Besides, Mr Walters was far too knowing for Pine's purposes. His assistant, a strapping sandy-haired young man called Chuck was much more suitable.

'You,' said Pine, her steely gaze on the boy, 'get in.'

'I'm sorry, Mrs Joseph?'

She had placed her order under a false name. It was usual in matters of this sort.

'Get in the cage,' she repeated.

The metal structure was two-and-a-half feet square and four feet high, with a hinged door on one side and steel mesh on the floor and walls. For a big boy like Chuck it would be a snug fit.

'Uh,' he said, taking a step towards it.

'And take your clothes off first,' said Pine.

His face turned white. He appealed to Walters. 'Do I got to do this?'

The older man patted him on the arm. 'Mrs Joseph just wants to make sure it works the way she wants.'

This seemed to mollify him and he turned to the cage.

'The clothes,' commanded Pine.

For a moment Chuck's face turned mulish then he began to unbutton his shirt.

Pine walked to the door and called down the stairs. 'Kate!'

A dark-haired woman in a paint-spattered overall appeared.

Pine gestured to the centre of the room where Chuck was dragging his jockey shorts down the white ovals of his ass cheeks.

'I didn't think you'd want to miss this.'

'You bet I don't,' said the dark woman.

Chuck slipped his feet back into his trainers.

'No!' barked Pine. 'No shoes.'

'But it will hurt my feet,' the boy protested.

'Get on with it,' muttered Walters, opening the cage door.

Chuck had to bend down to climb inside. Walters shut the door after him. The boy looked most uncomfortable, crouching and holding on to the sides for support.

'OK?' he said.

Pine turned the key in the lock and pocketed it. 'Send him up,' she said to Walters.

The boy opened his mouth to complain but the old guy cut him off. 'Relax, Chuck. We got to test it for Mrs Joseph.'

Walters pressed a button, the motor hummed and the cable running from the roof of the cage to the ceiling became taut.

'Oh shit,' said the boy as the metal box lifted up in the air.

'Let me do it,' said Pine, taking control.

The cage rose higher, turning now. Chuck peered down at them, his face flushed and miserable, his big body cramped against the metal frame.

'Well, it seems to work,' said Pine.

'Should do,' said Walters. 'You got a breaking strain of over a thousand pounds there. You could squeeze a couple more boys inside.'

'That sounds like fun,' said the other woman. 'I can see right up his ass. He's a hairy ape, isn't he?'

Chuck was now twirling sedately beneath the high ceiling. 'Let me down,' he called.

'Do you want to have some fun, Kate?' said Pine.

'Sure do. Bring him down to my level.'

The motor whirred and the cage descended. Pine stopped it about three foot above the floor.

'Let me out now, *please!*' the boy pleaded.

The women ignored him. Pine opened a leather case that lay on the table and removed a black lacquered cane. She stepped up to the cage.

'Wait a minute,' said Chuck.

She moved behind him and prodded his left buttock through the mesh.

'Hey,' he said.

She prodded him again and he tried to grab the stick in his hand.

She rammed the metal tip into his flesh.

'Aah,' he cried and let go.

She dug it into him again and he squealed.

'This boy of yours has a real soft centre,' said Pine to Walters.

'I'm sorry. He's new,' the man replied.

'Don't apologise,' said the dark woman. 'I like someone who's sensitive.' She pushed a long finger through the mesh and stroked the boy's cheek.

'Kneel down,' she said and he scrabbled onto all fours.

'Get up on your knees. Put your stomach against the side.'

The boy hesitated then saw Pine lift her stick and did as he was told. His thighs and belly now pressed tight against the mesh, the sandy bush of his pubic thatch escaping the prison.

The dark woman slipped two fingers through the grille and took hold of his cock.

The boy whimpered.

'I shan't hurt you. Not if you do as you're told. Don't you find this just a little bit exciting?'

'No, ma'am.'

'Then I guess you need help.'

She removed her hand and unbuttoned her overall. She threw it to the floor. Beneath, she wore black panties cut up on the hip and a push-up bra that squeezed her flesh together to form a line of cleavage. She unclipped the bra and her high round breasts bobbled free. The ruby-red points of her nipples were hard. In the vee of her crotch her dark pussy hair bulged beneath the see-through material.

Chuck swallowed, his eyes bugging in disbelief.

'Now, look at that,' said the woman as the boy's cockhead began to lift of its own accord. 'How gratifying for a girl.'

She put her fingers back in the cage and pulled Chuck's semi-erect dick through the bars. Her lips pursed in concentration, she began to massage it to full erection.

'Ooh-wee,' she said as the thick rod became fully extended. As she masturbated him, the cage swayed slowly, the boy's loins suspended right in front of her face.

The dark woman opened her mouth and engulfed Chuck's glans. She didn't even have to bend her neck.

Pine pushed the cane through the bars again and ran the tip down the divide between his buttocks. The boy jerked and the brunette folded her fingers round the pale shaft of his cock protruding from her lips.

Pine's cane slid between his legs, probing his testicles from the rear. The other woman lifted her head from his gleaming red knob and began to jack him with long slow strokes.

'Don't,' said Chuck without conviction.

Pine inserted the cane between the boy's twitching buttocks.

'Oh!' he cried as she pushed the tip into the bud of his anus, his ass jerking forward and back, impaling itself further.

The dark woman stepped aside as Chuck boiled over. A bolt of semen shot from his cock, followed by another and another, falling like rain on the polished wooden floor.

The boy slumped, his face pressed against the bars, the shiny black stick protruding from his rear. Pine left it there and walked to the door.

'Congratulations, Mr Walters,' she said. 'You have constructed this apparatus precisely to my specifications.'

TWENTY-ONE

ANTELOPE MOUNTAINS, NEW MEXICO. OCTOBER 5TH.
6.35 PM.

The man had the greenest eyes Jarvis had ever looked into, the irises a dazzling spring-leaf shade she found mesmerising. The sun was slipping over the hills across the valley, shining directly into his face, but his pupils were large as he stared at her. Such intimate scrutiny was unnerving.

'Welcome,' he said. 'I'm Rolf Leonard.' He clasped her hand in both of his, the grip warm and dry.

'Joanne Martin,' she said.

'I know.' The pupils grew even larger, as if he were downloading personal data directly from her brain. She regretted signing on under an alias. The way he was looking at her, he'd seen through her disguise already.

He moved on to the woman next to her, a twitchy-looking anorexic who'd been on the flight to Albuquerque. Lena Altman had introduced herself as they boarded the helicopter which flew them north to the Leonard spread. Apart from a few obligatory remarks about the scenery the pair of them had not conversed during the forty-five-minute flight.

Jarvis tried to take in her surroundings. They were on the tarmac drive of a large, two-storey wooden building, flanked by pines and spruce. She could see cabins amongst the trees. In her ears was the *thwock* of tennis balls from the courts to her left and the hiss of sprinklers working to keep the lawns a vibrant green. Above her towered the pitted crags of the Antelopes and the air in her lungs was without the familiar taint of the city. It was as if some ritzy country club had been plucked from the east coast and dumped five thousand feet up in the air.

'Our first session is tonight,' said Leonard. 'You have a couple of hours to unwind and eat dinner. Then I'd like to start as soon as possible. Is that OK with you?'

He was looking at Jarvis again, expecting a response.

'Sure,' she said, willing herself to conquer her nerves. It was unreal to feel like this in front of a man, no matter how beautiful he may be.

'Don't worry, Joanne,' he said as he separated her hand from her case and handed it to a female attendant. 'Uncertainty is good. Preserve that energy and channel it.'

Jarvis cursed as she was led away to her cabin. How come the most attractive man she had met in years spoke in clichés from the *West Coast Book of Psycho-Babble*?

She was feeling more relaxed when she entered the conference room for the first session and she stifled a chuckle at the sight before her. The floor was strewn with cushions and mattresses. About a dozen women sprawled around, most of them looking uncomfortable – particularly those in tight skirts and freshly pressed slacks, some clutching notebooks and clipboards. Surely they didn't expect some high-powered management-style meeting?

She slumped onto a bean bag next to the youngest person in the room – a slim brunette with a fringe who introduced herself as Alex. Jarvis was spared making conversation by the arrival of Leonard, dressed in a blue sweatshirt and sand-coloured chinos. His leaf-green eyes sparkled even at a distance and Jarvis was struck again by how impossibly handsome he was – if you liked chiselled features, an upright powerful body and loose-limbed grace. His audience were not averse to those things, Jarvis could tell. She reminded herself that the guy was doubtless a charlatan, adept at separating frustrated women from their money.

He didn't waste any time.

'Will you stand and form a circle please, ladies,' he began. 'Take the hand of the person on either side of you. I want you to realise you're in this together.'

Jarvis laced fingers with Alex and, on the other side, with a thin blonde. For a moment they all stood in silence. Then Leonard began to sing.

Jesus Christ! thought Jarvis, *this is more corny than Kansas.* Then the man's voice took root in her, a big baritone sound reverberating up from her toes, swirling through her veins like smoke. She'd once stood next to a music student in a street in San Francisco as he'd sung through the great tenor arias of Puccini. The boy's voice had been raw but to stand close to a sound so vast and passionate had been awe-inspiring. She thought of that now as she listened to the strange, wordless singing of Leonard, holding the hands of two strangers who, she knew, were as thunderstruck as she was.

The singing changed everything. After it was over they sat obediently and listened to the seductive murmur of Leonard's speaking voice. *This is crap*, Jarvis told herself but she stood up when bidden and told the group who she was – Joanne Martin, a physician from Washington DC. As her companions did the same she noticed that already they seemed just a fraction less uptight and on the defensive. These women really wanted to believe, that was plain.

Leonard gave good therapy-speak, as far as Jarvis could judge. New Age psychology and alternative medical treatments were not her style. Sure, she'd read some background material but all this touchy-feely group-bonding stuff was anathema to her. Nevertheless, as eager-to-please Joanne Martin, she did as she was told, turning to one-on-one with her blonde neighbour and intoning with her, 'We are not alone.' She even felt quite comfortable with it.

Her comfort zone evaporated at the end of the session.

Leonard placed a straight-backed chair in the centre of the room.

'Let's get practical,' he said. 'I need a volunteer.'

Alex rose to her feet and made her way to the chair. As she crossed the room Jarvis observed how tall she was, like one of those beanpole super-models. Her short skirt bared her thighs as she sat in front of them.

'Thank you.' Leonard was off to the side, out of the

group's sight. The lights grew dimmer.

'Now, I'm going to ask Alex a few questions and I want you all to watch her reactions. OK, Alex?'

'Yes.'

She didn't seem to be in the least apprehensive. She closed her eyes exuding, Jarvis thought, an air of serenity.

'Tell me, do you masturbate?'

There was a collective intake of breath. From Lena Altman came a muttered, 'Oh my *God!*'

Alex said, 'Yes.'

'How often?'

'Lots. At least once every day.'

'So you enjoy it?'

'I *love* it.'

'How does it make you feel?'

'Good about myself.'

'Anything else?'

'It makes me feel free.'

'Do you want to explain?'

'Yeah. Shall I tell you a story?'

'Go ahead.'

'I was in love with this boy at high school. James Dolin. Black wavy hair and killer eyes. Tall and wiry, very laid-back with an acid tongue. He had no time for me because I had acne. It wasn't that bad but it got much worse when I was about sixteen. Every day there'd be some new spot and he always noticed. He'd call me Pizza Face and shout, "Here comes Zit City," when I came into the room. "Imagine kissing *that*," I heard him say to another guy once, "you'd need medication after a hot date with her." '

'What a pig,' murmured a voice from the floor.

'Right,' said Alex. 'But I guess I'm a masochist. I used to hang around him. My eyes would follow him around the room. At night in bed I'd play with myself and imagine him driving me to the woods and making love to me on a blanket under the stars. Telling me he only said that stuff to hide the fact that he was passionately in love with me. I was still a virgin. I knew nothing about sex – apart from what I saw my brother get up to sometimes. But the orgasms I got when I fantasised about Jim were the real thing, I knew that. And the more he trashed me, the more I'd diddle myself at night, sometimes till I could hardly walk the next morning. It was like we really were having a hot and secret affair.

'Then a funny thing happened. When summer came my acne cleared up and I'd grown three inches. My stepfather treated me to a whole new wardrobe and my brother's friends started hanging around even when he wasn't there. Suddenly I was a desirable person – even though I was exactly the same as I'd always been underneath. Then, guess what? My dream came true – Jim asked me on a date. I told him to come to my house when I knew everyone would be out. He turned up with a bouquet of roses and a box of chocolates. I took him into the living room and pulled the curtains tight even though it was as light as day outside. He had on a smirk a mile wide when he saw that. I made him sit opposite me across the room and then I stripped off my dress.

'The smirk disappeared real quick when I pulled my panties down my legs and stood there in just a black-and-white lace garter belt and stockings held up by suspenders. I sat down on the couch and I spread my legs so he was staring right at my pussy. "What do you think?" I said. "Does the sight of me still make you sick?" "You're beautiful," he said and got up to come over to me. I took my stepfather's pistol from where I'd put it underneath the cushion and aimed it right in his face. That stopped him. "Get back," I said. "You can watch. Or you can leave." Of course, he didn't leave. I could see a boner busting a hole in his pants as he sat back down. Just thinking about it makes me hot.'

Suddenly Alex jerked her tiny skirt to her waist and spread her legs. She was nude underneath. A triangle of dark hair pointed down like an arrowhead to the shaved split of her gaping vagina. The sight hit Jarvis like a slap in the face. She watched in disbelief as Alex ran a hand over the gentle curve of her belly and began to caress her long, glistening labia.

'What happened next?' said a woman's voice and Alex

resumed her tale, her fingers strumming the strings of her sex as she spoke.

'I kept the gun on him. I showed him the safety was off so he wouldn't do anything stupid. Then I gave myself some of the best orgasms I've ever had. It was wild, a pistol in one hand and my clit in the other. My finger was on the trigger that night, all right. And as I did myself I talked to him. I said, "If you hadn't been so shitty you could be doing this to me. I worshipped you. If you'd been kind I'd let you do just what you want to me. You could fuck my cunt and my ass and I'd suck the come out of your dick every night of the week. But you couldn't see past my pizza face, could you? Now you'll never get to touch a hair on my head – or my bush. But you can look just this once and see what you're missing!" And all the time I'm telling him stuff like that I'm humping my hand and getting off. Just like this . . .'

Her thumb pressed down on the hood of her clit, pushing the bright red nub into view as she thrust her bunched fingers inside herself, her hips squirming and her pale cheeks blazing. The orgasm rippled through her like a wave through water and the breath hissed from her lips as she took herself over the top.

After a moment she spoke again.

'Finally I got tired. But I was curious about one thing. I told him to stand up and take his dick out. It looked red raw though he hadn't touched it. It was weeping juice from the eye in the head and the shaft was shiny and wet. I made him stand like that while I took photographs with a Polaroid. He was so terrified and turned on, I suppose, that he didn't try anything even when I put the gun down. I told him if he ever spoke to anyone about this I'd show the photos round. Then I ordered him out of the house with his cock sticking out of his pants. The moment I shut the door he put his hand on his dick and the come just squirted up into the air. I was watching from the porch window and I swear his spunk landed on the roof of his father's car about six feet away. If ever I'm having trouble getting off, I always think of that.'

She flipped her skirt down and smiled at her stunned audience.

'That's my story. Self-stimulation is power. It liberated me.'

'Bedtime,' said Leonard's voice from the back of the room and the lights came up. 'We'll leave discussion till tomorrow.'

Jarvis looked around her as the group got to its feet and made for the door. There were a couple of angry faces and a few pale with shock. Others, however, held a thoughtful and distracted look. She had no doubt that some were turned on. She had to admit she herself was not unaffected. Though she wasn't entirely satisfied.

She took hold of Alex's arm and said quietly, 'You were planted, weren't you? You're not like the rest of us.'

The girl's dark eyes met hers. 'Every word I said was true.'

'Maybe but you've said it before. Do you do your party piece on every course?'

The dark eyes flashed for a second then she covered Jarvis's hand with her own. 'Every party needs an ice-breaker, Joanne.'

Jarvis jerked her hand away and moved towards the door.

Alex called softly after her. 'Your turn tomorrow, I believe. I'm looking forward to it.'

TWENTY-TWO

U.OF CARDINAL SPRINGS. OCTOBER 5TH. 10.00 PM.

Tork was sidelined for the game – a stomach upset he'd told Coach – so he'd taken up his buddy, Art's, invitation to visit for the weekend. Truth was, he didn't feel up to hard-assing around a football field right now, not since the business with Miss Simons. After her disappearance and the shit he'd had to take from the school and the cops, he hadn't felt up to much. So when Art invited him to Cardinal Springs, he'd agreed. His mom had been pleased about it, that was something – he needed to get back in her good graces. He promised to check out the university facilities real good. That put a smile on her face.

But she wouldn't be smiling now if she could see into the back parlour of Big Biff's Bar, a rowdy hang-out for college jocks. The last thing she wanted was that nymphomaniac schoolteacher, Madeleine Simons, back in her son's life.

Tork watched Miss Simons serve a table on the other side of the room. She wore white tasselled cowboy boots, red velvet hotpants and a skintight scoop-necked pink vest with 'Big Biff Says Hands Off' written across her chest. Her chestnut hair was tied back in a matching pink ribbon and she slid frothing steins of beer across the wooden table with a flick of the wrist. She seemed like any other good-looking good-time waitress, a little mature for this clientele maybe but far from over the hill. She did not look like a runaway high-school teacher.

'Why didn't you tell me?' said Tork, following her every move.

'Figured you'd like a surprise,' said Art.

'Have you talked to her?'

'I've done better than that. Hey, Angela! Over here!'

The waitress waved – a gimme-a-minute sign – as she made change for a table of rowdy jocks.

'Angela?'

'That's what she calls herself. For God's sake, don't come out with any Miss Simons shit. Anyhow, it might not be her.'

'Of course, it is. You took her classes, too.'

'Yeah, but this ain't no Miss Simons I can relate to. She might look like her but I tell you she sure don't behave like her.'

The waitress came over to the table. 'Hi there, Art. Let me guess – two draughts, right?'

'I want you to meet my friend Tork. He's a buddy from high school. Gonna join us next year.'

'Is that so?' The woman's smile held no sign of recognition. 'I'll bring your order right up.'

'See,' said Art as they watched her retreating rear, the solid hemispheres of her ass like two beckoning pillows. 'That's no Miss Simons, no way.'

'Oh yes it is. I'm gonna ask her.'

'OK but first I'm gonna prove to you she couldn't possibly be Miss Simons. So wait till later.'

'What's that about later?' The waitress was back with their beer. 'You want to have a coffee at my place, Art? Your friend is welcome too.'

Tork blinked at her in disbelief. It had to be her – and yet . . .

'You bet,' he said.

The waitress winked at the pair of them. 'Give me half an hour.'

The woman's apartment was ten minutes walk from the bar. Forty-five minutes after their conversation she stood in the centre of a cheaply furnished living room and pulled her vest over her head. She reached behind her with both hands and unclasped her bra. Her swollen breasts swung into view and she rubbed the undersides, hefting the big white loaves of flesh in her hands as she did so.

'God that's better, I always let my tits out when I get off shift. I hate having them constricted.'

Tork gaped at the puckered saucers of her areolae.

'Your friend doesn't mind, does he, Art? I can cover up if he likes.'

'C'mere,' said Art in a hoarse voice, catching her hand.

She made to pull away from him but not so he'd take any notice.

'Not in front of a stranger, please,' she said as Art's hand closed on her left tit and squeezed. The flesh spilled over his cupped palm and he put his tongue in her mouth.

Stranger! thought Tork as he watched the two of them trade tonsils. *Screw that!*

He stepped forward and palmed the velvet cushion of her buttock.

She broke the kiss with Art and turned her head to Tork. She kissed him as if she were dying of thirst and ground her ass back into his crotch. Art cupped and fondled her breasts, his tongue flicking over the upstanding knobs of her nipples.

The three of them stood like that for what seemed like an age, savouring the moment before they got down to some real action.

Then the boys got impatient.

Art tugged at the waist of her panties and Tork helped him ease them over the satin-soft curve of her hips and down her legs. They left her boots on and laid her on the moth-eaten couch. Her legs were spread wide for them to feast their eyes and Tork gazed once more on that neatly trimmed black bush with the pink groove down the centre. He dropped to his knees and pressed his lips to her sex. She tasted melon-sweet – just like before.

Then, with the sound of Art's moans in his ears as Miss Simons gobbled his prick, Tork got down to work. He felt better than he had for weeks.

He felt like he was coming home.

TWENTY-THREE

ANTELOPE MTS. OCTOBER 6TH. 6.30 AM.

Jarvis woke sweaty and irritable – though there was nothing new in that. The sheet was plaited into a single strand between her legs, as if she'd been riding it all night. She probably had been, abrading the cotton rope across her mons while images of Alex's lewd tale of masturbation haunted her sleep.

She showered quickly with the water as blistering hot as she could stand, then turned it to full cold. The trick worked, as it usually did, clearing the fog of a bad night's sleep from her head. But, while dressing, she noticed her fingers were shaking as she buttoned her blouse. She knew the reason at once. She wasn't cold or ill. She was downright terrified.

It was plain this course was to be a full-frontal show-and-tell. Alex's performance had been a set-up, no doubt, but the others would let it all hang out in their turn. That's what they'd paid for, after all. Though some would kick and scream, they'd come here to have their sexual reservations blown away. Well, that was OK for them but how the hell was she going to get through the next week?

More precisely, what was she going to say when it was her turn to sit on the chair in front of the group?

Jarvis took a yellow legal pad from her case and sat at the desk in the corner.

After some thought, she began to make notes.

At breakfast she sat next to Lena Altman, who looked as

flaky as Jarvis had felt an hour earlier.

'I'd get out of here right now if I could,' said Altman as she sipped black coffee. 'But we're miles from fucking nowhere. I feel like I'm in prison.'

'You can't keep on running,' Jarvis heard herself say.

'I'm sorry?' Altman's black eyes were piercing.

'All of us have been running away from ourselves. We can't handle sex and relationships, so we compensate in other areas of our lives. Now we've had the guts to face up to it. We're here to make a stand, Lena.'

'I suppose so.'

'It's just as well there's no easy way out. You wouldn't be the only one heading for the airport.'

Altman gripped Jarvis's hand. 'Thanks, Joanne. Maybe you're not the prissy bitch I took you for.'

Jarvis laughed, surprising herself. Usually a remark like that would have had her spitting. Joanne Martin was obviously more relaxed about life. Maybe there was a way to survive this ordeal-by-confession after all.

When Altman left, someone quickly took her place. Jarvis found herself staring into the unnerving eyes of Rolf Leonard.

'There's always a surprise package on my courses,' he said. 'I think this week it might be you, Joanne.'

'You heard what I said to Lena?'

The tanned skin on his face was impossibly smooth, as unlined as a fresh sheet of paper. When he stopped smiling – as he did now – the creases disappeared as if they'd never existed.

'I saw you offer support to a woman in need. That's particularly admirable when you are in need yourself.'

For a second Jarvis glowed – God, it was good to get a stroke once in a while, even though the stroker was probably a crook. But she wanted to take the initiative.

'Tell me, Dr Leonard, would one of your previous surprise packages be called Felice Cody?'

'You know Felice?' His beam was as broad as the Grand Canyon – but was there a glint of suspicion in those unreal green eyes?

'Actually, I know Dale Kennedy. She was here with Felice back in the summer. She stayed in touch with quite a few of her group.'

'Really? How gratifying. And it's her recommendation that has brought you here? '

That and the need to find out how the hell you turn respectable women into runaway sluts.

Jarvis didn't share that thought, however, but simply nodded.

Leonard rose from the table. He placed a hand on her shoulder and said, 'I'm really looking forward to your input.'

CONFERENCE ROOM. 9.15 PM.

In my freshman year I roomed with a girl called Robyn. She was very athletic, the tall willowy type who did more aerobics classes than economics, it seemed to me. Her father was the chairman of some mail-order business in Minneapolis but she wasn't a stuck-up rich kid. Her dad had built the business from scratch and it had taken years to make money. Anyhow, Robyn was really enjoying her time in college. She said the work ethic in her home had damn near worked her to death in high school and now she was going to play.

There were guys running after her round the clock. She had this long raven-black hair and a big smiling mouth. Most of the time she wore sloppy sweaters and sweatpants but when she bothered to dress up for a date she looked like a front-page sensation. At the beginning of the summer semester she cut her hair off, said her father would kill her but a bob was easier to manage. Actually the cut was great, made her look like a drop-dead gorgeous guy.

About then I was going through a bad time. I'd fallen for a law instructor who, so I thought, was all brains and no balls. Just when he'd convinced me that intellectual compatibility was the foundation of true romance I'd caught him dry-humping a waitress with a couple of footballs in her sweater. There were other things too. My dad had left home again and I knew my mom was taking it hard. I felt I should be with her but she'd insisted I returned to college. Anyhow, I thought Robyn wasn't too aware of any of this. We were friendly enough, we had to room with each other after all, but we didn't confide in each other. Next year, no question, we'd make other arrangements – that's if I came back at all.

This particular day, Robyn asked if I'd like to play tennis – her regular partner had begged off. She talked me into it, even though my game wasn't that strong and I knew she was hot stuff. Actually, she was better than that and one of the things that made her so good was her killer instinct. She just creamed me on court. She didn't even try to ease up. She insisted we play a match and went about it like it was an ATP event. She even disputed my line calls. Then I got pissed and walked off. She came after me. "We haven't finished the game," she said. "What's the point?" I said. She laughed. "You got something better to do with your life than get your ass whipped by me?" So I went back and let her stomp on me some more. I don't know why.

That evening I was lying on my bed, feeling sorry for myself. It was hot so I was almost naked, just a T-shirt and a pair of briefs. I knew Robyn had a date with a third-year guy who was taking her to a ritzy French restaurant with a celebrity chef. She'd been excited about it. So I was amazed when she came in at around eight.

'What happened to the dinner date?' I said.

'I blew him out.'

'Why? You were looking forward to it.'

She gave me this mysterious look and put some packages on the table. I could see they came from a deli, the only good one near campus. 'I told Ed I had some unfinished business,' she said. 'That means you.'

'What are you going to do? Wipe the floor with me at Trivial Pursuit?'

'No. We're going to eat and talk. And see how things develop from there.'

I didn't have a clue what she meant but she was a darn sight more fun than my own company. I'd forgiven her already for humiliating me at tennis. It wasn't her fault that I was hopeless. And the food she'd brought was amazing: smoked salmon, *foie gras,* crusty white bread, peaches and lots of gooey French cheese. And wine, a Chablis and a Burgundy. She opened both because she said we should drink the white with the salmon and the red with the pate and the cheese and, as this was a picnic, we ought to eat everything together.

So we shoved my books off the table and sat down with two glasses of wine each and wolfed the lot. As we ate she got me talking about my troubles. She turned out to be a damn sight more perceptive than I'd thought. Basically she just helped me get everything off my chest. Then she got up and took her clothes off.

I'd seen her without clothes before, of course, and it was perfectly reasonable for her to strip. It wasn't as if I was wearing much. However, it changed things. As she undressed she looked at me, like she was challenging me to say something about it. Then, when she'd got down to her panties, she came over to my chair and said, 'You take them off.'

'Why?'

'Do it and you can have one of these.' And I saw she was unwrapping a box of chocolates, the kind with cherry liqueur in them and real cherries with stalks. I'd had some like that on my birthday – she knew I liked them.

My fingers were shaking as I took hold of the waistband of her briefs. They were a very sexy pair, almost a G-string, which left her hips bare and clung to her pussy mound in a vee of cream satin. I tugged them downwards, unveiling her belly and a vertical strip of hair that ran down between her legs. The hair was long and wavy, rather than curly. It kind of fanned over her sex, hiding her lips and everything. I wanted to part it with my fingers but I didn't dare.

'I bet your boyfriends go ape when they do this,' I said.

She laughed. 'They should be so damn lucky,' she said. 'Come and get your reward.'

I looked up to see she had the stalk of one of these cherry chocolates between her lips and the cherry was hanging down. I could have taken it with my fingers, I suppose, but I knew that wasn't the idea. I stood up and closed my lips round it. She held on to the stalk with her teeth so we were staring right into each other's faces. Though her lips were smiling her eyes weren't laughing.

I bit into the chocolate and the alcohol burst over my tongue. I felt her arm go round my waist and she kissed me. It was like an explosion of sensation in my mouth – the taste of her and the chocolate and the cherry liqueur all at once. She put her hand into my briefs at the back and ran her finger right down the crack of my ass and up my cunt. It sank right in, I was so wet.

She kept me there like that, pressed up against her, feeding me chocolates with one hand and fondling me with the other. It was the most extraordinary sex thing that had ever happened to me. No boyfriend had ever been able to give me an orgasm but she made me come halfway through the third piece of candy.

Then she said, 'I want one now,' and got me to lie on the bed. She pulled my panties off and reached for the chocolates. She held one up in front of me, said, 'Now for the *real* gourmet experience,' and pushed it deep into my sex. Then she ate me out. Literally.

I'd been with men before but you could say that was the night I really lost my cherry.

Alex caught up with Jarvis as she unlocked the door to her cabin.

'Slick pay-off, Joanne,' she said. 'Was any of it true?'

Jarvis shrugged. 'I was so nervous I can't remember half of what I said. We're not all professional members of this group.'

Alex tilted her pretty head to one side as she gave Jarvis a searching look. 'I could be offended by that but I'm not gonna be. Do you want to come in and chat? I'm just next door.'

'I'll take a raincheck. I'm tired.'

Jarvis ducked inside her door and locked it behind her. Her mind was in a whirl – and so was her body.

She went into the bathroom and turned on the shower. She threw her clothes on the floor and climbed into the warm water.

My God, talking about it had brought everything back. She'd not made up a word, not even changed Robyn's name. But she'd not spoken about the agony of the following weeks when she'd discovered the girl was in love with her. Poor Robyn. She hoped she was happy now. She'd not thought about her for years but right now the feel of that tall lissom body in her arms was almost tangible.

With one hand Jarvis opened herself up, with the other she brought herself off, hard and fast, screaming her release into the sound of falling water.

She could almost taste those damn cherry chocolates.

TWENTY-FOUR

SUNFISH CITY, NEBRASKA. OCTOBER 7TH. 1.30 PM.

Maynard Jeffrey sat in the city library, his eyes fixed on the doors behind the reception desk. He'd been in that spot since opening time, toiling at an essay, but looking up every time someone came through the door. Now he'd given up the pretence of working and the knot of excitement inside him was turning to disappointment. She hadn't exactly promised she'd meet him at noon but she'd said she'd try. Obviously not hard enough.

A teenager shouldered her way into the room, her arm full of books. She had tumbling golden locks and an uncommonly pretty face. Maynard groaned. He yearned for a middle-aged female with mousy hair and spectacles whose picture he had seen on the jacket of a book. In his estimation no nymphet sex goddess could compete with the author of *Starlight of the Gods*.

The door banged again and an elegant woman in a designer suede jacket with a leather shoulder-bag came in. Beneath the jacket the hills of her breasts were encased in an embroidered cream sweater which tucked into the waist of her tight black skirt. She bore not the least resemblance to Felice Cody. Maynard swore under his breath.

The woman looked around and spotted him Her face broke into a smile as she flowed across the floor and thrust out a slim hand.

'I'm sorry I'm a bit late,' she said, not sounding it. 'You're Maynard Jeffrey, aren't you?'

'Ms Cody?' he said, his irritation wiped from his mind in an

124

instant. 'Ma'am, I'm honoured to make your acquaintance.'

She laughed, a husky sexy peal. 'Did you get my stuff?'

He nodded and pointed to a yellow file tied with string on the desk.

To his amazement she gave him a hug, the kiss of her sweatered breasts lingering through the cotton of his shirt.

'Great!' She thrust the bundle into her bag and took his arm. 'This calls for the best damn lunch this town can provide.'

Bewildered but elated Maynard followed her switching hips out of the door.

Three hours later his eyes followed those same hips, unclothed now, as she walked to the window of her hotel bedroom and peered between the curtains, down at the traffic below.

'It's weird to think what this place must have been like ninety years ago,' she said.

'Yes.' He was interested, sure he was, but the sight of her nude ass drove most other considerations out of his mind. He'd fucked her twice already but the jut of her creamy buttocks and the rearward pout of her pussy lips had his cock stiff again.

He got up off the bed and pressed his flaming member against the lush flesh of her rear. She wiggled back companionably, so the barrel fitted into the groove between her cheeks, and continued to talk.

'I wonder,' she was saying, 'what the hell it was like back at the beginning of the century. Especially for some stranger from out of town, trying to get a little business going.'

'You're talking about the guy in the newspaper clippings I got you, right? The animal doctor.'

He reached around her to cup her tits and buried his face in the dark cloud of her hair. Could he be in love after just a few hours? He'd never met a woman like Felice before.

'Indeed. The handsome blond stranger who had a magic way with sick cows and horses.'

'And farmers' wives.'

Maynard let his hand roam over the sumptuous body in his arms, down over the gentle swell of her belly to the thicket of hair nestling in fork of her thighs.

'Till he seduces one too many and they get up a lynch mob and string him up outside the courthouse right here in Sunfish City. Do you want to bugger me, Maynard?'

'Christ, Felice, I—'

'You do, don't you? You're practically screwing my butt as it is. If you fetch some cream from the bathroom you can.'

When Maynard returned she was still at the window, leaning down with her elbows on the sill. Her ass was thrust back into the room like a round white target with a dark bull's-eye at its centre. With shaking hands he began to slather cream into her crack. He'd never thought he'd meet a woman who'd let him do this to her. She was incredible.

He put his finger in first and she moaned. Then he pressed against her with the head of his cock.

'Uh,' he said as the glans stuck there, like a cork plugged in the neck of a bottle.

She shimmied her ass with a flick of her hips and suddenly he was buried to the root.

'Oh yes!' she muttered. 'Take it slow.'

He held it deep inside her, the pair of them quivering like fever patients.

'They probably still string you up around here for doing this,' she said.

'Like the animal doctor, you mean?'

'That's right. Like poor old Dr Leonard.'

He found her clit with his fingers and, by way of an answer, she clenched her internal muscles around his cock, rushing him to orgasm all too soon. If a lynch mob had burst in at that moment he'd have paid them not a blind bit of notice.

TWENTY-FIVE

BALDRY, PENNSYLVANIA. 4.05 PM.

The fall afternoon was fading but the overgrown garden of Stacey Pine's rented house was warm enough for Chris Shaw to sit out in shirtsleeves. No human noise interrupted the peace. Which was a tribute to the sound-proofing installed by Mr Walters and his team. The Judge was in session within.

Before the court was a guy called Brown who had made contact with Shaw through the Elks. He liked the kind of justice Pine meted out and Shaw had the money to prove it – five hundred dollars in an envelope in his briefcase. There were other envelopes in there too. The number of men prepared to pay for punishment was amazing.

Chris Shaw let the last of his beer slip down his throat and congratulated himself on finding Walters and customising the property to Pine's specifications. Had he failed her, he knew she would have got herself another Mr Fix-It and he couldn't have borne that. He worshipped her too much.

Notwithstanding the sunshine and shirtsleeves and beer, Shaw was far from relaxed. He was waiting for the moment when he, too, would be summoned to the room within to pay for his recent misdemeanours. Not that they were serious but the object of his veneration was so strict. He had been late that morning but it was essential he kept up appearances at the office. The delay had been unavoidable. Well, almost. And now he was to pay for it. The suspense was agonising – and delicious.

'Hey, Chris.'

He jumped at the sound of the voice. Kate Karlsen stood in the doorway. She was wearing thigh boots. His heart began to pound.

'You're on, baby,' she said. 'I wouldn't dawdle if I were you, she'll flay you alive.'

A high-pitched ring interrupted him before he could respond.

'I'd better get it,' he said and picked the cellphone off the chair. It was Rita.

'Mr Shaw, are you coming back to the office this afternoon?' She was pissed off, he could tell. She was pretty much always pissed off these days. 'I've been fielding calls all day and the Pattersons say you were due to appraise their apartment at eleven this morning and failed to show. They've called in another realtor.'

'Don't worry about it, Rita. Those folks are just pulling my chain. I already told them their place won't fetch within twenty of what they're looking for.'

Karlsen smirked as she listened in to the conversation. Her expression said that Shaw was going to pay for this delay.

'You wife's been on a couple of times, says don't forget dinner with her mother at seven sharp. And there's a man who must have phoned at least four times since midday. He won't leave his name but says he's desperate to come and see the old courthouse – is that a new property we're handling?'

'Did he leave a number?'

Karlsen pointed to her watch as Shaw rang off.

'Another client,' he said. 'I'll get him later.'

Karlsen looked pensive. 'Aren't there any ordinary guys around? I mean, ones who're just looking for some regular fun.'

'With you?'

'You catch on quick, Chris.'

'I'll see what I can do.'

'You'd better, or I'll tell the Judge you've let me down.'

'No – please.'

She shrugged and walked away from him, back inside the house. He followed her along the hall to the big oak door.

'I'll rustle up some business for you, I promise,' he said as she placed her hand on the doorknob.

'Great. You take care of the money, Chris. Just make sure I get some action.'

The door swung open.

'You're late!'

Pine's voice rang out like a whiplash.

'Judge,' Shaw croaked as Karlsen shoved him from behind. He stumbled into the room, his eyes not yet accustomed to the gloom. A hand cracked across his cheek, caught him again on the back sweep. He fell to his knees.

'How dare you keep me waiting? *Twice* in one day!'

He could see better now. She was standing over him, the black leather basque cinched at her waist, her breasts drawn tight together in a severe line of cleavage.

Above her, the man called Brown was suspended in the metal cage. His body was naked and his hairy flesh pressed against the wire mesh. His head was encased in a leather mask, zipped at the mouth, with holes for the eyes and nose.

'Have you anything to say, you pathetic creature, before your punishment begins?'

'Judge – I – I'm sorry.'

Pine picked up a cane. She brought it down on the table beside Shaw with a crack like a pistol shot.

'You will be, my little Prisoner, I promise you that. Now, strip.'

As Shaw pulled the shirt from his back, a bud of terror bloomed in his chest. He'd never felt more . . . alive.

In the cage beneath the ceiling, the masked man's eyes were ablaze.

TWENTY-SIX

CARDINAL SPRINGS. OCTOBER 8TH. 3.10 PM.

Hannah took a stroll round campus to kill time – he wanted to arrive at Big Biff's after the lunchtime crowd had gone. It turned out to be a mistake. As he stood in the central quadrangle the bright sunshine shut off like a closing door. Then the heavens opened. The sky was black as he reached the bar and rain was trickling down his collar.

He took a seat in back and draped his wet jacket over the chair next to him. A buxom brunette in hotpants laid a menu on the table and said, 'Pretty rough out there, huh?'

'Yeah. "So foul and fair a day I have not seen".'

The woman gave him a piercing look.

'*Hamlet*, right?' said Hannah. 'Got any soup?'

'*Macbeth*, actually. Ham and pea.'

'Surely not. Just bring me a coffee.'

'His first line in the play. Anything else?'

'Yeah. You could tell me why a high-school English teacher is waiting table in a student bar dressed like a refugee from the *Playboy* mansion.'

The woman gaped at him like a landed fish. Hannah took his ID from his pocket and held it up.

She looked around. The place was empty apart from two jocks lolling on the bar, watching a game show on TV. She took the seat across the table from Hannah.

'Tork Jackson, I suppose,' she said.

'The boy's obsessed with you. When you packed him off home Sunday night he rang a New Jersey cop who'd interviewed him when you took off. He was heartbroken you claimed not to recognise him.'

'He's a nice young man. I didn't want him mixed up with me.'

'Didn't stop you fucking his brains out on Saturday night.'

Madeleine Simons looked past Hannah at the rain beating on the window. 'What's this got to do with the Bureau? Tork's old enough to enjoy himself like an adult.'

Hannah shrugged. Water dripped from his hair onto the table.

'I need to talk to you about Felice Cody.'

'Felice?'

'Yes. Do you know her current whereabouts?'

'So I'm not under investigation?'

'Not by me.'

'Or under any obligation to cooperate with you at all.'

'No.' Hannah sneezed. 'The only obligation you're under, I'd say, is to help me locate a friend of yours who's missing. In other words, a moral one. That must mean something to a former guardian of youthful minds.'

'Don't lecture me, Agent Who-ever—'

'Hannah. Ashoo!' He sneezed again.

She got up. 'Come on, before you freeze to death. The bartender's got an apartment upstairs. We'll find you some dry things.'

Two minutes later he was standing in a scruffy living room lined with Kurt Cobain posters, clutching a bundle of clothes Simons had unearthed.

She stood in the doorway and watched with open curiosity as he unbuckled his belt.

'Aren't I a bit old for you?' he said, dropping his pants.

'Actually, Agent Hannah, I've got catholic taste in most matters. But I'll spare your blushes and fix you that coffee.'

Five minutes later he was sitting in dry clothes, sipping a hot drink. His wet things were hanging in front of a heater and the room was warm. He felt a hundred percent better. Outside the rain still lashed against the window.

Simons stood a bottle of bourbon on the scarred old coffee table and took a seat next to Hannah on the couch.

'What makes you think I know where Felice is?' she asked.

'You were on that course with her, weren't you? Down in New Mexico.'

'Sure. That's where I met her.'

'How did you get along?'

'How much do you know about the course, Agent Hannah?'

'Very little.'

'It's about getting in touch with yourself – the real self that's buried under years of fear and doubt. That's why we were there, a bunch of old-maids-in-waiting. When I first saw Felice I thought, that's one uptight lady.'

She took a drink and continued.

'All of us changed over the next week. Dr Leonard showed us our fear and showed us what it amounted to – nothing. He made me listen to my body and he put me in touch with my senses. All my senses, you understand. I came back a different person – we all did.'

'And Felice?'

'Rolf made spectacular progress with her. When she started out she was this crotchety intellectual in clothes like sacks. If she could have, she'd have put her head in a sack too. When she left she was like a butterfly emerged from a chrysalis. Rolf's people had made her over – he's got a hairdresser and a beautician resident on the ranch. She looked gorgeous. She told me she was going home to change her wardrobe, buy some contact lenses and get some guys. It was the exact same thing for me. I hope she's had as much fun as I have.'

'So that's why you just walked out on your life? To have fun?'

'Uh-huh.' She put down her glass and leaned towards him. He was conscious of the shifting mounds of flesh beneath her scoop-necked vest. Her eyes were large and luminous and her lower lip was swollen and wet.

'After what happened with Tork I had no choice. I needed to be surrounded by virile young men, where it didn't matter if I behaved like a slut. Here's perfect.'

'Is this what Felice is doing, would you say?'

'That's my guess.'

'But you don't know where.'

'Haven't got a clue.'

'Well, you've been most helpful, Miss Simons—'

'Here I'm known as Angela.'

'Oh, OK. I guess that's it, Angela. I won't take up your time.'

'How disappointing. Don't you want to know what we actually did in New Mexico? You know, how we conquered our fears?'

She was up to something. If he were Stone, he knew he would be pulling on his wet clothes right now and heading back into the rain. Thank God he wasn't Stone.

'Sure,' he said. 'I'd be interested to hear about it.'

'I can do better than that,' she said. 'I can give you a demonstration.'

She reached for something on the shelf above his head. For a moment his face was in her full bosom, the protruding button of a nipple almost in his eye. She sat back down holding a glass jar. Inside it, Hannah could see some folded twists of paper.

'Rolf used to make us play games to get rid of our inhibitions. I play one with the boys here.' She held out the jar. 'Take a piece of paper.'

Hannah did as he was told.

'What does it say?'

He unfolded the slip. Two words were written there: Tit Fuck.

She beamed at him. 'Couldn't be better, huh? You've not been able to take your eyes off my chest since you walked in.'

'I don't understand,' he said.

'Of course you do.' She pulled her vest over her head and turned her back to him. 'Undo me,' she said. 'Get my tits out, you know you want to.'

'Look, Angela, you were going to tell me about Leonard—'

'Sure, I'll tell you.'

Somehow Hannah's fingers had found the clasp and released her straining bra. She pulled the straps from her arms and turned to face him.

Her tits were fabulous.

'You like them this size, don't you?' she said. She cupped them in her hands and the soft white flesh billowed over her fingers. The saucers of her areolae were pinky brown and ridged, the nipples long and swollen.

She took his hands and placed them there instead.

He kissed her – it seemed the right thing to do. Just as it seemed right to stroke and fondle and pull on her enormous breasts. Her mouth was hot and wet and the globes in his hand were heavy. She ripped open his shirt and squirmed their satiny smoothness against his bare skin.

After a moment she stood up. He watched with a hammering heart as she shucked her shorts over her hips and kicked off her panties to reveal a neat black bush of hair on her mons, pink lips pouting below. He remembered the Tork transcript – 'sweet as a cantaloupe' the boy had said – and reached out to taste for himself.

'No,' she said, pushing him away. 'That's for later. Right now . . .' She held up a bottle of moisturiser and pooled some into her palm.

He watched, mesmerised, as she slicked it onto the slopes of her breasts, above and below, oiling the glistening hills for his aching penis.

He stood and kicked off his clothes.

She pulled the back cushions off the couch to make it wider and lay down face up.

'Straddle me,' she commanded, 'put your lovely cock in here.'

He was in no mood to disobey. He placed his knees on either side of her ribcage and laid the barrel of his tool in her cleavage. As it touched her glistening flesh it leapt and twitched of its own accord.

'Why, Agent Hannah,' she murmured as she took a breast in each hand and folded her creamy flesh over his trembling prick, 'you're quite a tit man, aren't you?'

Hannah made no reply. He couldn't. His mind was drunk on the sensation of his cock encased in silk, the nerves singing and leaping as he began to plough the slippery channel she had made for him. She laced her fingers together, pressing her tits tight around him and completing the stimulation along the topside of his shaft.

Resting his hands on the arm of the sofa above her head, he watched himself fuck her cleavage, the scarlet head of his glans emerging on the up-stroke and then sliding back out of sight on the down. As the tip of his prick showed, her tongue shot out to flick across the glistening cap, her face aglow with the joy of giving.

The experience was new to Hannah. It was possibly the rudest sex act he had ever committed. It was also, he realised now, exactly what he had wanted to do to Simons the moment he had set eyes on her. Was that something to do with Leonard and his mystic methods?

It couldn't last long.

It didn't.

'OH!' he cried, just once, and fountained over Simons' lovely upturned face.

Her smile broadened as he shivered through a long and shattering orgasm, inundating her with his seed.

When he was finished, she licked the spunk from her lips.

'My turn next,' she said.

The room was hot from the fire and the rain still beat down. Right now Special Agent Hannah was going nowhere.

TWENTY-SEVEN

ANTELOPE MTS. OCTOBER 9TH. 8.05 PM.

More than half the course was over and Jarvis couldn't claim to have made any great progress.

'I still think Leonard's a charlatan,' she'd told Hannah on the phone that evening. 'Probably gets his rocks off watching women making fools of themselves. So far I can't pin anything on him apart from that.'

Hannah had called to say he'd located the runaway schoolteacher, Madeleine Simons.

'She says Leonard is a miracle worker who made her into a sexually liberated woman. How does he manage it? How can he turn nuns into nymphomaniacs inside a week?'

'I don't think he does.'

But, though she didn't want to get into it with Hannah on the phone, she wasn't so sure about that. Maybe it was the whole charade of being Joanne but Jarvis was feeling different about herself, more in tune with her physical needs. For one thing, the nightly masturbation session was turning into more than just a functional means of getting to sleep. But she wasn't going to discuss that either.

'Goodnight, Hannah. Good work in tracing Simons.'

'Take care, Jarvis. Don't play any funny games of lucky dip.'

Now what the hell did he mean by that?

But Jarvis knew. They'd played it that afternoon. Leonard had asked the group to write down something personal about another woman in the room. The slips of paper had been placed in a small Indian basket then picked out at random and read aloud by the subject. Most were suitably positive and anodyne – 'Kirsty has a great laugh – when she lets herself go', 'I admire Anya because she says what I feel.' It was harmless, if puke-making, stuff.

So Jarvis's turn came as a shock and she turned crimson as she looked at the slip with her name on it. She would have refused to read but she felt Leonard's gaze resting on her. This was a test. *I'm not me, I'm Joanne,* she said to herself.

'Joanne is stone-dead gorgeous,' she read hesitantly. 'I'd like to lick her pussy.'

She glared defiantly at the group around her. When she found the joker responsible she'd smack her in the mouth. Or him – it could be Leonard. He wouldn't look so damn smug when she hit him with charges of fraud and corruption. If she could make them stick.

After she'd spoken to Hannah she was still seething. She couldn't face the evening session – some kind of film show on relaxation techniques – but she was damned if she was going to sit in her room. There was, thank God, a bar. A small drink might help her calm down.

She ordered a large one – a Bloody Mary with plenty of spice. She sucked it down like mother's milk and asked for a refill. The buzz was immediate and she felt the tension in her body ease just a fraction. The red mist drained from her mind and she willed herself to contemplate her discontent. It was more than the public humiliation of the afternoon session. And more than professional frustration at not making progress with the Cody case. What was it?

'That looks good,' said a voice by her side. 'Gimme one of those too,' Lena Altman said to the waitress, 'and another for my friend.'

'Thanks but . . .' Jarvis started to object but then thought, what the hell? She'd get to bed early and sleep it off.

'Here's mud in your eye,' said Altman, drinking deep and snagging a handful of peanuts at the same time. She wore a bright red slip of a dress and a casual black jacket with an art-deco pin in the buttonhole. The past few days seemed to have fleshed her out somehow, made her seem more whole. And it struck Jarvis that this kind of change in her fellows was what was bugging her. Everyone else was blooming like a rose and she still withered on the vine. *For Christ's sake,* she said to herself, *you're not here for the ride!*

'I owe you an apology, Joanne.'

'You do?' Jarvis was miles away. She'd started her third cocktail.

'I wrote the message you read.'

'*You* did?'

'Sure. I thought you'd be relaxed about it. That you'd be more, shall I say, receptive.'

'But why did you do it?'

Altman's black eyes were piercing. 'Why the heck do you think?'

'Oh my God.' Jarvis gulped the rest of her drink.

Altman laughed. It was a warm rippling sound. 'Don't look so shocked, Joanne. You're a fabulous-looking creature and you did tell us that horny story about your room-mate. I'd never thought about making it with a woman before but you lit a little spark in me, you know? However, I can tell you're not interested in fanning it into flame.'

'No!' said Jarvis more firmly than she intended.

Altman simply grinned. 'That's OK. I guess it's being cooped up here without any guys, apart from the dreamy doctor, of course. I tell you, I'm going to have a heck of a party when I get home.'

Jarvis killed her drink and stood up. Altman didn't seem phased by her sudden departure. As she left, she heard the dark woman ask the waitress her name. What the hell had got into her?

She bumped into Alex in the hall and asked her the same question. The girl laughed.

'Lena had her one-on-one with Dr Leonard this morning.'

'What's that?'

'You don't know? It's your personal session alone with Rolf in which he unblocks the river of your sexuality.'

'No one's said anything to me about it.'

'He's probably saving you for last, sweet pea. Believe me, it will be worth the wait.'

Alex opened the door of the meeting room and, without

thinking, Jarvis stepped inside. The room was dark, a large screen on the wall reflecting light and shade across the watching women who sprawled on couches and cushions.

'Here, next to me,' said Alex and pulled Jarvis down onto the seat beside her.

It took Jarvis a moment to work out the image on screen. There was milk-white skin and a hand, a woman's hand with a wedding band and short unpainted nails, and what looked like a black cloud. The hand pushed aside the cloud to reveal petals of pink and, within, the opening of a tunnel walled with scarlet. The fingers probed and re-emerged filmy with wet and, of course, by now Jarvis was well aware she was watching a vast close-up of a vagina.

The camera pulled back. A thirtyish woman with dark hair falling across her face was lying on a rug, pleasuring herself. The camera pulled back further. There were other women there, some nude, some semi-clothed, but all with bared loins and probing fingers. A female voice was heard above a sitar soundtrack '. . . and now comes the most significant step in the ritual of self-stimulation – the re-imaging of the clitoris. For each woman, her love-bud is visualised differently. For some it is a flower, for others a burning torch or a precious stone. Whatever the form, it should act like a personal lightning conductor of her sensuality as she brings herself to the pinnacle of . . .'

'Uh, uh, uh . . .' the voice came from a few feet in front of Jarvis and, simultaneously, she became aware of other voices around her, of the rustling of clothes and shifting of bodies, and of the thick must of female arousal that hung in the air like a fog. Christ – she had walked into a group *wank* session!

'Joanne.' Alex's voice was husky in her ear, her hand resting on the bare skin of her forearm. 'Just lie back and relax. Why don't you let me . . . ?'

Jarvis yanked her arm from Alex's grip and got to her feet. Her head swirled with alcohol and outrage. Before the door banged shut behind her she heard the breathless squeal of a woman in orgasm, whether on or off screen she had no idea.

She almost ran back to her cabin and her fingers shook as

she chained the door behind her.

She didn't like herself for it but she knew what she must do. She dragged out her suitcase and unzipped the side compartment. Inside, wrapped in several layers of paper, was the big black dildo she had removed from Karlsen's apartment. When she'd taken it she'd rationalised her action. She'd told herself she felt a special sympathy with the missing banker and that she needed a symbol of the erotic chaos in Kate's life. Besides, she hadn't wanted the police or other Bureau colleagues to discover it.

She'd lied to herself, of course. She'd taken it because she wanted to fuck herself with it and now she was going to.

Jarvis had not used it since that night in Karlsen's bed but her need was urgent now. She pulled off her underwear and plugged the thing in. And she tried very hard not to think of black-eyed Lena and husky-voiced Alex and a roomful of self-pleasuring females as she brought herself gasping to orgasm.

A girl had to get herself to sleep somehow.

TWENTY-EIGHT

HANNAH'S APARTMENT. 10.30 PM.

Hannah's hands and mouth were occupied when the phone rang. He would have left it but Brigitte picked it up with a giggle. Evidently she liked the idea of being eaten out while playing receptionist.

'Thomas Hannah's residence. How can I help you?'

There was a longer pause while Brigitte listened. Hannah stopped what he was doing with his tongue but she pushed his head downwards in an unmistakable signal. He sucked her sugar-pink pussy lips into his mouth in response. He knew his duty.

'How the hell did you know that?' said Brigitte to the unknown caller, rocking her pelvis to the rhythm of Hannah's caress. 'OK, I'm listening.'

There was a longer pause this time. Hannah licked upwards to the head of her crack, slipping a finger into her as he found her tiny pleasure button with his tongue.

'Right. Got it. I'll tell him when he gets back.' She dropped the phone back into its rest and grabbed his head with both hands, pressing his face hard into her crotch as she squirmed against him out of control.

'Oh my God,' she panted a moment later, after the storm had subsided. 'That was a blast. I thought I was going to come down the phone.'

'Who was it? What did they want?'

'Not going to tell you.'

'What!' Hannah sat up in indignation. His face was raw and wet with pussy juice. She was grinning fit to burst.

'Give me some of *that*' – she pointed to his cock which was rearing upwards, the head red and slick – 'and I might.'

'You little bitch.' He was grinning too.

'It was a *very* important message. He said to tell you immediately.'

'He?'

'Uh uh. Not till you've made me happy.'

'I'll make you happy all right.'

He was quick but she was quicker. She was off the bed in a flash, her ass cheeks bouncing, white and inviting, as she reached the bedroom door.

He caught her in the living room.

Smack!

'Ooh!'

Smack! Smack!

The white was swiftly turning pink.

Smack! Smack! Smack!

And crimson.

'Hey, that hurts!'

'Tell me.'

'No!'

She squirmed round in his lap and bit his ear. His hand was still on her hot ass, not smacking now but squeezing and probing and plunging into the divide between her flaming buttocks.

She put her tongue in his mouth. He lifted her onto his cock.

She got what she wanted all along.

Much later so did he. The message was a puzzle – who the hell was this character Lovelace? And what did he care about Karlsen and Pine?

The information, however, was very interesting.

TWENTY-NINE

ANTELOPE MTS. OCTOBER 10TH. 7.00 AM.

Jarvis had finally got her break. She was awake early and took a jog up the mountain to clear her head. Her real purpose was to take photographs. The long lens was bulky and awkward to carry but she was glad she made the effort. From a ridge a hundred feet above the ranch she was able to get some great shots of the entire spread. Then came her real stroke of luck. Leonard was on the putting green.

Jarvis dropped down lower, fortunately the pines provided plenty of cover. She framed Leonard as he doodled around, knocking in balls from all angles on the small green rectangle. She'd never seen anyone out there before. She guessed it was an expensive indulgence maintained entirely for him. She looped back on the trail so he wouldn't see her and headed for a shower, then breakfast.

As she nibbled wholewheat toast and drank black coffee, one of the Leonard harem – which was how she termed the small army of female staff who worked the centre – dropped by her table.

'I've got great news for you, Ms Martin. Dr Leonard has scheduled your personal assessment for two o'clock this afternoon.'

'What exactly is this assessment?'

'Oh, it's fabulous. It will make all that's gone before seem worthwhile, I guarantee.'

'And you are?'

'Dolores.'

'Do you have any qualifications, Dolores? Did you go to

med school? Are you trained in psychotherapy? Or any alternative medical techniques?'

'Sure I'm trained, I'm a beautician. Come by later on and I'll give you a fabulous makeover. If you don't mind me saying so, you could use one. You look a little stressed out.'

'Joanne, I've really been looking forward to this.'

They were sitting in Leonard's study, a small room on the first floor of the main lodge. It was sparsely furnished – a desk, two chairs, a cactus in an earthenware pot. Navajo and Apache masks hung on the wall and, behind the desk, some books on a free-standing shelf. One among them caught Jarvis's eye.

'You've got Felice Cody's book – *Starlight of the Gods*.'

'She was kind enough to inscribe a copy for me.'

Leonard picked it off the shelf and handed it to Jarvis. The inscription read: 'To RL, one of the Gods. With respect and love, FSC.'

'That's very gracious,' said Jarvis.

'A smart woman – a true scientist. More than just an enquiring mind but also a fierce intelligence. I feel some of that intelligence in you, Joanne.'

'Really? I'm flattered.'

'There's no need to be.'

His smile was warm, his face seemingly lit up from within. In the small room his presence was awesome. Jarvis couldn't look away from him. *That pale gold hair*, she thought, *and smooth unlined skin is unreal. And those eyes* . . .

'Listen to me, Joanne. We're going on a journey. Just you and me, in this room. All you have to do is look at me. Look into my eyes. I will remain seated here and you there and we will travel together on a voyage to meet your real self.'

He's trying to hypnotise me, she thought. *So this is his trick – brain-washing* . . .

'Don't fight me, Joanne. Have no fear. This is what you've come here for.'

That's what you think, you slick medicine-man. You'll not get me with your hypno-jumbo and your angel curls and . . .

. . . floating, drifting, sailing on a sea of turquoise. A friendly swell bearing me along as I swirl on my back with the sun on my face and the breakers roll me high up onto the beach. The white sand is warm on my bare feet, the grains crunching between my toes as I walk along the strand, the waves breaking in a line of white surf along the curve of the shore which stretches to the horizon.

The wind is balm on my skin, perfumed with thyme and a hint of far-off lemon groves. It wraps the thin cotton of my wet sarong around my bare legs, pushing me along like a boat under sail as I walk beside the surf. I'm naked beneath this clinging shift and I relish the swing of my hips, the kiss of my thighs, the sway of my breasts. A happiness bubble bursts in my head.

There's a dot in the distance, getting bigger. Someone or something travelling towards me along the beach.

I can see now – it's a weird beast shape. A man. An animal. Both. A man on a horse. Coming closer. Fast.

The horse is white. Dainty but powerful with a high step and a tawny mane.

The man is broad and bronzed, naked to the waist. His hair is long and golden, blowing in the spicy breeze.

Then they're upon me and I see it's Leonard – a not-quite, almost-Leonard. Bigger, muscled, more savage. But with those new-minted green eyes laughing as he bends and sweeps me up in his arms.

I am captured by this bare-back bandit, bound to him in a grip of silky strength as he pins me to his body on top of his still-bounding steed.

I hear myself laugh. I feel no fear. I'm safe.

His eyes are smiling into mine as he says, 'Hello, Birdie.'

My heart flips. No one has called me that since . . .

Marty Brennan. First boyfriend, first lover. The high-school dropout Mom made me promise to never ever see. But a forced promise can be honourably broken.

Lean, mean and bad, she said – but she didn't know Marty like I knew him. His worst sin was a stubborn streak. He wouldn't be told. Wouldn't be told to study, bow his head, keep the peace. Wouldn't be told to stay away from me. Wouldn't listen to a girl who loved him either. Got squished on the road like a squirrel under a truck when running from a cop. Gentle, sweet, stupid Marty. Broke my heart at sixteen. Hot summer nights in his arms beneath the stars spoilt me for other men.

A bit of me thinks of Marty every day and the rest of me blocks it off. Till now. The little icicle in my chest melts in an instant. Long-frozen nostalgia and pain washes over me, floods my senses.

I'm weeping as Leonard turns my body on the horse, placing me astride a broad strong back, facing ahead, my hands in the silk of its mane. His arms are round me like a girdle of muscle and he kicks on.

We ride fast, hooves drumming on the wet sand in the spray of the surf. The salt of the sea whips into my face to join the tears which flow for my long-lost adolescent self. And as we thunder on my skirt rides higher and my thighs are bared and I'm aware of the strong male body pressing into my back. The skin of his chest is hot through the single layer of cloth and the arm circling my waist binds me tight. Between my spread legs my sex is glued to the pelt of the animal beneath us. I'm not crying any more.

Slowing now, I feel the air on my skin. He's unwinding my sarong. I help him. As my hands pass behind my back they skid on his naked skin, then stroke and seek, slipping down to the thong around his waist.

Suddenly I must have his cock in my hands. He chuckles as my trembling fingers scrabble at his pouch. I laugh too as my fingers close on his wand of flesh. I want it like I've never wanted any man's part in my adult life. And I don't feel fearful or guilty or needy. I just feel horny as hell.

He doesn't stop the horse but pushes me forward, so my face is round the beast's neck and my ass is in the air. Then he sheathes himself deep within me.

As we connect I shout for joy. I am pure animal desire, naked and breached on the back of a prancing beast. This sensation cannot be denied. The drumming hooves. The wind-blown spray. His pulsing pillar of a cock buried inside me. God, I need this in my life . . .

My climax goes on forever until I am delirious. Ecstatic. Spent.

The horse slows to a halt, blowing hard and quivering. Like me.
I turn in the arms of this god who has liberated me. The fabulous Dr Leonard.
But it's not Leonard. Nor Marty.
I'm looking into the face of a different man altogether.

THIRTY

BALDRY, PENNSYLVANIA. 10.35 AM.

'There's another of those men on the line, Mr Shaw.'
'What men, Rita?'
'One who's asking about the courthouse. When are you going to give me proper details about this place? What's so all-fired special about it anyway?'
'Soon, Rita, I promise. Right now, can you just put him through?'

'Hi. Chris Shaw. Can I help you?'
'Jack Lovelace suggested I ring.'
'I see.'
'I'm interested in viewing the old courthouse.'
'Gotcha. What's your crime, Mr . . . ?'
'Hannah. And it's curiosity.'
'That's an original offence. Who would you like to see? Judge Stacey has a full list today. Do you like brunettes?'
'Love 'em.'
'I could arrange a hearing with Mistress Kate for this afternoon. She's not as strict as the Judge, of course, but she's more . . . flexible.'
'Flexible sounds fun.'
'Cash up front, Mr Hannah.'
'Surprise, surprise.'

Hannah had little experience of whores – as a consumer, that is. Nevertheless he'd bet big bucks that the dark-haired babe with the red nipples and big brown eyes currently sitting on his chest was no true professional. For one thing she was too enthusiastic. No sooner had the door closed behind him than she was in his arms with her tongue down his throat and her hand in his pants.

She'd sensed his alarm because she'd backed off a fraction, taking her mouth from his and whispering, 'I'm sorry, I just get carried away when I meet a sexy new guy.' She'd kept her fingers on his dick though, giving it the kind of thoughtful massage that suggested she had other uses in mind.

Which she had. Right now she was poised over his erection, about to feed the shiny red glans into the honey-sweet gate of her black-furred sex. At this point he could still – just – come clean. Push her smooth limbs from his body and produce his ID. At any rate, he could state his official business and proceed to interrogate her on the many matters related to the case.

'Oh God,' she muttered as she settled her slim hips on his loins, the length of him burrowing deep inside her. 'God, I love it when it first goes in, don't you?'

Hannah did not reply. At least, not in so many words but his eyes were on those cute jiggling tits and one hand had somehow settled on the satin of her thighs, the tips of his fingers grazing the coal-black strip of hair that framed the pretty pink lips of her cunt. Official business or not, it would be churlish not to stroke those quivering sex petals.

'Oh, yeah, touch me!'

And tickle the peeping pearl of flesh hiding just *there* at the top of her crack.

'Ohmigod, I'm gonna come if you do that.'

Of course, should he ever be asked to account for his current behaviour, he could always explain that it was necessary to conceal his identity. Would Stone go for that? he wondered, retracting his finger from the woman's clit so he could keep her on the brink a little longer.

'You see,' he could say, 'I was working undercover. I had to get to both of them, Karlsen *and* Pine. It was necessary to establish that I was a bona fide john. For God's sake, Stone, you don't think I actually *enjoyed* having sexual intercourse with that woman?'

'Ohfuck, ohfuck, ohfuck,' she was going, one hand on his chest, fingers splayed, helping her balance as she swayed and bounced on his bursting dick.

Hannah let his other hand snake round her body and roam across the curves of her buttocks. They were pert and firm, boyish almost but for the pouting ripeness that filled his palm. He explored her rear divide. Would she go for that?

'Yeah, yeah, that's gooood!'

Affirmative.

He found the dimple of her anus and pressed. Her up-and-down motion did the rest.

'Christ, that's wonderful!'

Time to put her out of her misery maybe. The hand at the join of their bodies returned to her clit. The finger in her rear slipped in to the second joint.

'*Yes!*' she shouted, her body convulsing.

She went off like a Roman candle, in such a display of pyrotechnics that it took him a moment to realise that his own firework had exploded at the same time.

As she lay panting on top of him she muttered, 'You don't say much, do you?'

It was hardly the moment to reach for his ID.

THIRTY-ONE

ANTELOPE MTS. 3.25 PM.

The white fog cleared from her brain. The room looked just the same. Same bookshelf, same Indian masks, same plant. And there was Leonard on the other side of the desk looking at her just as he had done before . . . before what exactly?

Jarvis felt different. Something fundamental had changed within her. She could feel her sex throbbing and her whole body racing with a familiar sensation – if a distant one. Once it had happened to you, you never forgot the afterglow of being well fucked.

She was wet between the legs. Had that charlatan hypnotised and assaulted her? But she knew he hadn't. What he had done was even more invasive than that – he had ravished her mind. This was what he did to women. What had happened to Cody and Karlsen and the rest. *And now he's done it to me!* Half of her wanted to put a bullet between his sea-green eyes, the other half of her was ecstatic. *I wonder,* she thought, *if he's freed me too?*

'Can I have a glass of water?' she said.

He filled a tumbler at the water cooler and handed it to her.

'How do you feel?'

She sipped.

'You know how I feel. May I go? I must lie down.'

There was concern in his eyes as he opened the door for her.

'How did you know about Marty?' she said.

'I know nothing about him, only what I read in you. It is

you who have made whatever took place on your journey. That's why it is meaningful. Believe me.'

She didn't.

She left the room, still holding the glass. In her cabin she threw away the water and wrapped the container carefully in her luggage. Then she lay down on her bed and fell utterly asleep.

It was dark when she woke. Someone was knocking on the door. She splashed water on her face before answering. It was Alex.

'Are you OK? You missed dinner.'

'I just woke up.'

'You've been with Rolf, haven't you? How'd it go?'

Jarvis turned back into the room. She felt light-headed and light-limbed. The sensation wasn't unpleasant.

'I'm hungry,' she said.

'I'll go and fetch you something. Give me five minutes.'

Jarvis dressed in a dream state. She pulled on leggings and a thin vee-necked sweater. She couldn't be bothered with underwear. She dragged a brush through her hair and let it fall loose to her shoulders. She looked pretty damn good considering, she thought.

There was more knocking on the door. Jarvis opened it to find Alex had returned, accompanied by Lena Altman. They wheeled in a food trolley set for one.

'Room service,' said Altman. She was carrying a bottle of vodka.

'Lena liberated this from the kitchen,' said Alex.

Jarvis laughed. 'How did you manage that?'

'Lena's pretty tight with some of the staff, aren't you, darling?'

'Up yours,' said Altman cheerfully, in the middle of laying out dishes on the table. There was quiche, chicken and salad.

'Go for it, Joanne,' said Alex, pouring drinks.

Jarvis obeyed. The meal vanished down her throat in about ten seconds flat. She'd not felt so hungry in years.

'Thanks, guys,' she said. 'What's for dessert?'

'Glad you asked that,' said Alex and reached inside the trolley.

Altman took the box from her and broke the cellophane seal. 'Fancy a chocolate, Joanne. Cherries are your favourite, I believe.'

'You bitches,' said Jarvis. 'You've set me up, haven't you?'

But her voice lacked its usual venom and her eyes were wide with interest as Alex began to unbutton her blouse.

THIRTY-TWO

BALDRY, PENNSYLVANIA. 9.20 PM.

Hannah was working overtime, though he doubted if Stone would see it that way. Fucking a missing person in the ass was not an official part of his job description.

On the other hand, though the sodomy itself was technically coincidental, it was during this act that he had located yet another missing person – Judge Stacey Pine.

Hannah was standing in what had once, he assumed, been a broom closet. It was a pretty tight space, though big enough for two people to cosy up together and look through the spyhole that offered a view of the room next door – the 'court' in which Judge Pine was still holding session.

'I oughta go through,' muttered Karlsen. 'She likes another pair of hands for a whipping.'

Next door, a naked pasty-fleshed man was kneeling on all fours before Stacey Pine. She wore a black leather basque, stockings and spike heels. So far Hannah had only viewed her from the rear, the black straps of her suspenders drawn tight over the full creamy moons of her buttocks. She was a hell of a horny sight. His cock twitched and bounded within the slick sheath of Karlsen's rear.

'You can't go yet,' he said, his voice thick, his hands busy with the sharp-pointed flesh of her hanging breasts. 'I'm not done.'

She turned her head, her teeth gleaming in the dark.

'So, take yourself in hand, buster.'

Her soft ass pressed back against his belly. He knew she wasn't going anywhere for the moment – she was enjoying herself too much. He slipped a hand into her crotch and began to gently diddle her clit.

Another man came into the room next door. Though he wore a mask Hannah had no trouble recognising him.

'That's Shaw, isn't it? The real-estate man. I paid him enough to rent your ass for a month.'

She giggled. 'If he's there I don't have to go in. It's just that this guy likes an audience.'

And so he did, Shaw could tell, for now he could see the kneeling man's cock jutting down, the shaft thick and the head a flaming scarlet.

'He's hung like a horse,' he said and then fell silent as Pine hit the man with a crop.

He'd never watched a sex beating before. There didn't seem much real whipping in it though the blows were delivered with all of the woman's might.

Pine raised her arm high and laid an angry stripe the full length of the man's back. He jerked in pain, his head thrusting upwards, his teeth bared in a rictus.

The woman waited for him to compose himself then barked an order at Shaw. The realtor moved closer.

She hit the man again, a cross-wise stripe this time.

'She likes a pretty pattern,' said Karlsen, her breath getting shorter.

Hannah pulled his cock out to the tip and then sank it in again slowly. He felt like he could go on all night.

Others were getting more impatient.

The man on his knees was crying out loud as the woman struck. Shaw had his cock out, his hand stroking the shaft to full erection.

Pine landed a thunderous blow and the man's entire body shook, then twitched and danced some more. From the end of his distended cock spunk pooled onto the floor.

'God, look at all that juice,' muttered Karlsen.

The man shook his head as if to clear it of all sensation. He sat back on his haunches carefully and reached for a towel that lay within reach. Then he said something to Pine that Hannah couldn't catch.

The Judge bent over the table and called to Shaw. He

came up behind and entered her from the rear. Hannah could clearly see his thick prick nosing into her vagina before Shaw's body blocked his view. The pair of them coupled like dogs in heat while the kneeling man looked on.

Beneath him, Karlsen thrashed in climax. Hannah could tell it was not done for his benefit but to answer her own need. She was no whore – though she was like no financier he'd ever met before.

The tight ring of her anus pulsed around his shaft, slipping back and forth like a hand in a velvet glove. In the room next door Stacey Pine's ash-blonde hair whipped across her bare shoulders as she shook in ecstasy, her bare white buttocks punching back to meet Shaw's impatient thrusts.

It was too much for Hannah. He shot off inside the liquid ass of the woman beneath him and buried his face in her black mop of hair.

He'd remember for a long time the day he shafted a Wall Street banker.

THIRTY-THREE

ANTELOPE MTS. 11.15 PM.

It was many years since Jarvis had been in bed with a woman – with Robyn that summer at college – and she'd never been with *two* women at the same time. But somehow that made it better. It was new, it was fun – it was incredibly exciting.

The three of them lay tangled on her sheets, the covers strewn on the floor. Jarvis was in the middle, as she had been ever since they'd stripped her and laid her down. She'd gone along with it with a smile on her face – at first. But when Lena had slipped between her thighs to slide her mischievous tongue deep into her sex, the smile had fled from her lips. This was too damn good to be taken simply as a laugh.

They'd done plenty more to her since then and she had lain back and let them. Her story about the chocolates had fired them up, that was plain, and they'd made her pretty messy what with popping them in her mouth and up her pussy and crushing them into her breasts. Not that it mattered, because they'd licked her clean, like two hungry cats, scouring her skin with their busy tongues while she revelled in their attention.

Beside the two of them she felt big. Lena was skinny, lean as a whippet with no breasts and big pointy nipples; Alex was more fleshy but so tall and slender it hardly showed. Jarvis enjoyed the contrasts between them. She liked the fact that her breasts were full and womanly and her hips rounded. She wondered why she'd ever been embarrassed about her blooming female form. She could remember resenting every lustful glance from a man, standing with her shoulders slumped and her arms folded across her bosom in denial. My God, many women would kill for a figure like hers. Lena Altman for one.

'Joanne, you are so fucking delicious I could eat you,' she murmured.

'You already did, honey,' said Alex.

'You know, I've gotta do it again. Would you mind, Joanne, if I licked that sweet pussy of yours once more?'

Jarvis didn't mind. She spread her legs to accommodate her admirer and sighed with sensual delight. They could do what they liked with her – for the moment.

About an hour later, Alex yawned and said, 'I'm beat. I'm going back to my own bed.'

'Me too,' said Altman.

'No chance,' said Jarvis. 'You started this orgy, I'm going to finish it.'

They looked at her in surprise as she got off the bed and pulled open her suitcase. Their jaws dropped as she turned to them with Karlsen's dummy prick in her hand.

Alex giggled. 'What do you aim to do with that?'

'Not what,' said Jarvis. 'Who.'

She climbed back on the bed between Altman's legs and pushed her thighs apart. The woman's sex yawned wide, the lips puffy and loose from the pleasure she had already enjoyed.

'Joanne, please,' she murmured. 'I'm not sure I can take any more.'

But Jarvis's fingers were already in her fleece, opening the well-juiced passage between her pussy lips, the black monster buzzing in her other hand.

'What do you say, Alex? Shall I give her some of this?'

'That session with Rolf's certainly had an effect on you,' said Alex. 'Sure, go ahead, I'd like to see someone take that thing.'

Jarvis held it in front of Altman's face. Her black eyes were huge and gleaming. In them, Jarvis read apprehension – and desire.

'Are you game, Lena?'

The woman nodded once and Jarvis lowered the instrument between her legs.

She set about it slowly, running the buzzing tip through the tangled bush of Altman's pussy, then along the tops of her thighs. She let it rest for the moment on the pad of flesh just above her clit and Lena began to thrust her pelvis forward, the juice leaking from her sex lips. The woman might be uncertain but her cunt was aching to be satisfied.

Jarvis put it in, just the first few inches to let Altman adjust to the sensation. It was like plugging in a light bulb – she lit up.

'Yes, fuck me, Joanne,' she cried. 'I don't think I've ever – oh!'

Jarvis slid the big machine all the way home – it wasn't difficult. Then, with the humming beast buried to the hilt, she began to massage Altman's clit.

She came almost at once.

'Let me do it,' said Alex, moving closer.

Jarvis let her work the dildo and returned to the swollen folds of the woman's sex.

'Please,' moaned Altman between orgasms, 'I don't think I can take much more.'

'How do you know,' said Jarvis, 'until you've tried?'

They took her through one more climax, her reed-thin frame thrashing against them as they held the vibrating penis inside her. It took her the best part of a minute to calm her twitching limbs and her sex seemed to release the black monster with reluctance.

Jarvis was burning with curiosity to see what effect the big dildo would have on Alex. She turned to the tall slim girl.

'You're next,' she said.

'You're wicked,' said the girl, spreading her beautiful legs.

'I feel wicked,' said Jarvis, sliding a finger into the slippery groove of the girl's vulva. 'But you can leave if you like.'

'No. I want you to do me with that thing.'

'I might keep you all night.'

'OK. Just get on with it.'

Jarvis bent her head to kiss the girl's sex. She sucked the long lips of her pussy into her mouth and slipped her tongue between, savouring the salty taste of her. Her clit was a hard nub of flame-red. She sucked it gently and felt Alex shudder.

She lifted her head, sex juice glistening on her mouth.

'Put it in, Joanne, please!' The girl's voice was hoarse with longing.

Altman cuddled up on the other side of Alex, her face bright with curiosity as Jarvis nosed the humming tip of the big black prick between the girl's wet labia.

As she did so, Jarvis had to restrain herself from laughing out loud. What she was doing was rude, obscene, shocking – but she didn't care. For once, she wanted to let her hair down and indulge her sensual self. Tomorrow, she'd be good. Once she'd got these wild impulses out of her system.

'Oh!' cried Alex, the dildo deep inside her and Altman's hands on the white flesh of her breasts.

'Yes, darling,' murmured Jarvis, her fingers finding the girl's swollen pleasure-bud. 'Come for momma.'

THIRTY-FOUR

FORT MUSGRAVE. OCTOBER 12TH. 11.35 AM.

Until recently, at least, Felice Cody would have described her life as sheltered. It had certainly not included the experience of being held at gunpoint.

She was on the dirt driveway of a timber-framed house on the brow of a hill outside the small town of Fort Musgrave. The Roberts spread was not large but she could glimpse stables out back and jumps laid out in the paddock.

Not that she was of a mind to look around with the twin barrels of a shotgun aimed at her face from ten yards.

Cody held her hands up instinctively – *just like they do in the movies*, she thought to herself – and opened her mouth to say . . .

'Git!' The wild-haired woman with the gun beat her to it.

Cody tried again. 'I think there's a mistake here. My name's Felice Cody and—'

'I know who you are. And I already told you, you ain't welcome here.'

Cody tried to stay calm though the barrel pointing at her was unwavering. 'But we've never spoken before. I wrote to Mrs McKee at this address—'

'And I wrote back. I'm her daughter and I told you never to try and get in touch with her again.'

'Well, I'm sorry, I never got that letter.'

'Don't you check your e-mail? I e-mailed you off your letterhead.'

'Oh.' Cody felt pretty foolish. This was one weird woman but she appeared to know exactly who Cody was and what she wanted. And she didn't approve.

'Call yourself a writer,' said the woman, 'and you don't even check your mail. I know what you're after – to harass my poor mother and drag my family through the dirt. Well, I ain't havin' none of it. You just sling your fancy east-coast ass out of here and git!'

Dumbfounded, Cody walked back to her rented Taurus expecting, at any moment, a volley of shotgun pellets in her butt. She'd seen enough Westerns to know there was only one winner in this scene.

She was contemplating her next move in a motel three miles down the road, when there was a heavy knock on the door.

'Ms Felice Cody?'

He was a big man in uniform with a firearm on his hip that looked powerful enough to blow down a house.

'Sheriff Byron Clare,' he said. 'And this here's Officer Casey Roberts.' In the passage behind Clare, partially obscured by the sheriff's bulk, stood a tall downy-lipped youth similarly armed.

'Come in, gentlemen,' said Felice – unnecessarily, as the sheriff had already marched into the room with a heavy tread. Roberts followed, bobbing his head by way of a greeting. He really was a very tall boy.

The poky room seemed even smaller with the pair of them inside.

Clare looked around. 'Ain't you packin', m'am?'

'I'm sorry?'

'I don't see no luggage bein' got ready though it's comin' up to check-out time.'

'I'm not leaving, Sheriff.'

Clare cocked his head on one side and squinted at her through piggy eyes. 'My, you're a handsome woman. Time was, if we got an out-of-state troublemaker round here we'd just run 'em out of town on a rail. Especially if they looked like you.'

Cody was beginning to get anxious – and irritated.

'I don't know what you're talking about, Sheriff, but I strenuously object to being referred to as a troublemaker.'

'What are you then? I'd call pokin' your nose into other people's family secrets and trespassin' on private property makin' trouble.'

So that was it. The trigger-happy daughter of Martha McKee had called in the local law to make her point.

'Now look, Sheriff, I am an internationally published author carrying out research on a future project. I would like very much to talk to a lady called Martha McKee but her daughter appears to have decided that I have sinister intentions. That's not the truth. All I've done is make legitimate approaches to my intended subject which have been rudely rebuffed.'

'You mean Celia ran you off her place with a shotgun. All the fancy language under the sun don't disguise the fact that she don't want nothin' to do with you. Ain't that so, son?'

'Er, yeah.' The younger policeman spoke for the first time. 'My mother's dead set against you. I'm sorry.'

'Celia Roberts is your mother?'

The boy nodded. Cody rushed on, maybe this was her opportunity.

'Look, it's your grandmother I'd really love to meet. If she's well enough, that is. I suppose she must be in her eighties.'

'Oh, she's in great shape,' said Roberts with a grin. 'Goes ridin' most every day, out at choir rehearsal and the bridge club three, four nights a week.'

Clare shut the boy up with a sour look. 'That ain't the point. The point is that the Roberts family don't want muck-rakin' outsiders trashin' their lives. So I suggest, Ms Cody, that you pack your things and head back where you came from right now.'

'That's outrageous, Sheriff, and you know it. I am a respectable woman on legitimate business and my travel arrangements are my own affair. I resent being ordered around by a small-town bully who feels it necessary to invade a woman's privacy wearing a canon on his hip.'

Clare's face flushed beet red and his small mouth pursed as he fought to control his anger. He took a step closer to her and spoke with low deliberation.

'I'm only considerin' your personal safety, ma'am. There are some folks here who resent a rich woman from DC comin' round, makin' a nuisance of herself. Folks like that do things the old ways. They'd think nothin' of cuttin' a few hickory sticks and touchin' up your fine white ass till it turned purple. Then sittin' you buck naked on a rail fence for a couple hours. Think about that – a sharp wood fence wedged right up there while you contemplate the folly of your ways and all the people watch you wrigglin' your pretty butt.'

'Get out!' Cody was enraged – and scared.

Clare took a step back, a gleam of pleasure on his mean face now he had provoked the desired reaction.

'Of course, notwithstandin' how much I might personally enjoy that particular sight, as an officer of the law I'm only doin' my duty in warnin' you of the possible consequences of your visit to our locality extendin' beyond, say, ten o'clock tomorrow mornin'?'

'You have just put your career in jeopardy, Sheriff Clare. I know many influential people in Washington—'

'And unless you're out of here by ten, as I said, it may be that you won't be able to sit down when you go and see them.'

THIRTY-FIVE

CHICAGO MIDWAY AIRPORT. 7.10 PM.

Jarvis had switched her ticket on impulse. She told herself she didn't want to sit with Lena Altman on the plane back to the east coast – which was true enough. She preferred to sever her connections right now to avoid any complications. So she'd got on the Southwest flight to Chicago, telling herself she could spend what remained of the weekend with her sister. In her bag were two Apache dolls she'd picked up for her nieces from the souvenir shop in Albuquerque. She'd had a few minutes before the plane left but, somehow, she'd failed to call Carol and tell her of her change of plan.

The truth was, Jarvis was strung out like some despairing junkie. But the fix she craved was not chemical. She was dying for a man. Her eyes had crawled all over the males she had encountered at the airport, from the gangly boy at the concession stall to the fat fellow who'd changed her reservation. She knew this urge wasn't exactly normal but she couldn't ignore it. And she wasn't going to indulge it on her home turf back in DC. Especially since the first hound to sniff her scent – she'd put money on it – was bound to be Hannah.

The guy on the plane next to her had been a God-send, a late thirties businessman in a suit who couldn't keep his eyes off the way her skirt rode over her thighs. She'd made no attempt to pull it down the entire flight.

Franklin was going a little thin on top but his eyes twinkled in a mischievous fashion and he had a fund of dry one-liners that came fast on one another after the first scotch went down. Jarvis stuck to mineral water, it was her new resolution. It was hard to handle more than one vice at a time.

Her travelling companion was en route for a national convention of optometrists in a large and swanky hotel on the Loop. In her current mood that sounded just perfect.

Franklin was guarding her case by the exit on the airport concourse. She'd made a show of trying to call Carol.

'Gee, I don't know what to do,' she said, her face crestfallen. 'My sister's not in and, now I remember, she said she might have to spend the weekend with her in-laws. I don't have that number. I guess I'd better hang around and try her later.'

'But if she's away for the night you could be stuck here.'

'Hey, it's not your problem. You've been more than kind to me, Franklin. You hurry along – I don't want to make you late.'

'You wouldn't consider coming on to the hotel with me? We could have dinner and you could call your sister later.'

'Well . . .'

'I promise you'll be perfectly safe with me, Joanne.'

'Don't say that, Franklin, or I might say no.'

The hotel had some style about it. Wood-panelling and marble floors decorated a lobby the size of a railway station. On the tables by the velvet banquettes, where guests hovered, vast bouquets of flowers sweetened the air. A golden cage of canaries was suspended above the check-in counter, the trilling of the birds swelling the noise of hearty hellos. The conference attendees were meeting and greeting en masse and the press of besuited males had Jarvis in a lather. The optometrists had a keen eye for female flesh and she bathed in their lustful glances.

Franklin was playing it cool as the bellhop ushered them into his room but Jarvis noticed that his hand shook as he palmed the youth a twenty. He was obviously feeling expansive.

'Would you like to try your sister again?' he said.

'No,' she said and tested the bed with her hand. It was soft and inviting.

'Oh. Well, perhaps I'd better make a dinner reservation.'

Jarvis kicked off her shoes and lay back on the bed. Her skirt was riding high again.

'What kind of food do you like? French? Chinese? I can ring the desk for a recommendation—'

'Franklin, just relax. Let me ask you a question.'

'Sure.'

'Do you optometry guys do anything for women besides looking?'

'I'm sorry, Joanne, I don't follow.'

'I mean, Franklin, do you like to screw? Because if you don't I'm heading back to the lobby right now to find someone who does.'

It turned out, of course, that Franklin liked to screw just fine. In fact he probably screwed brilliantly but Jarvis had been celibate so long she had no means of comparing his performance. It wasn't a state of affairs she intended to maintain, for this weekend at least. Right now she was still Joanne Martin and on time out from her real life.

God, how she'd needed that first fuck! There'd been no finesse – which was how she'd wanted it. She'd pulled her skirt to her waist and spread her legs. Taking no prisoners, as it were. Still in his blazer and sport slacks, Franklin had covered her, his prick plunging into her well-juiced sex in one smooth glide. She'd held him fast, her legs hooked over his hips, her arms locked around his neck, her loins in a fever of want.

She came hard and fast, twice, before he did. But that hardly scratched the surface of her desire. She restrained herself, however.

'Do you want to phone your wife?' she asked as she peeled Franklin's shirt off.

'Huh?' He looked bemused. This kind of action was a little fast for him.

'You know, just to say you've arrived safe and sound and you're off to have dinner with some old conference buddy. To save her worrying and calling you when we're busy.'

He'd taken her advice and, out of guilt probably, had got

into a long lovey-dovey dialogue with his wife about what she was going to do while he was gone. Frankly it was damn boring and Jarvis had no qualms about popping his shrivelled dick into her mouth while he was gassing. At which point the dick rapidly unshrivelled and she'd played with it, weighing the heavy balls and slipping the foreskin up and down the purple head. It occurred to her that never in her life had she toyed so unselfconsciously with a man's sexual equipment. Even with Marty she'd been pretty shy that way. A surge of regret claimed her. She wished she'd let Marty do all the things he'd wanted to do to her.

So it was her fault really, the way she was going at Franklin, that the moment he replaced the receiver his cock spurted into her face, hosing her with thick gummy spunk which glistened on her lips and cheek. She laughed.

'You're one crazy lady,' he said. 'What exactly do you want from me?'

'Just this,' she said as she licked his juice off her fingers, savouring the salty taste.

As it turned out, the phone stunt was a mistake. After that, Franklin didn't have much more left to give. They ordered steak and fries from room service and he drank most of a bottle of California red – she couldn't stop him. So it was no surprise when, after she'd ridden him to an after-dinner climax that seemed torn from his guts, he'd subsided into a slumber close to coma.

Jarvis showered and dressed perfunctorily. She had an emerald green slip at the bottom of her case. She slipped it over her nude body and examined herself. She looked – she knew it – like a complete slut. Her lush satin-packed flesh seemed to radiate sexual heat. Bonny Jarvis would have died rather than be seen in this condition. Joanne Martin, on the other hand, couldn't give a fuck.

Rather, that's just what she intended to give.

She put Franklin's room key in her cocktail purse and, without a glance at her snoring lover, headed for the door.

THIRTY-SIX

FORT MUSGRAVE. 8.45 PM.

Felice Cody was in a quandary. She pondered her problem as she ate a piece of blueberry pie in the coffee shop, swallowing without tasting.

She had to admit she was scared. She could still feel Sheriff Clare's eyes all over her – he'd just love the chance to whip her ass, that was plain. And though her response had not been idle – she did know people of influence back in Washington – out here alone in cowboy country she felt damn vulnerable. Besides, there would be precious little satisfaction in taking revenge after the event.

On the other hand . . . she was on to something wonderful. Her next book was taking shape in her mind and the events at Lake Musgrave in 1934 were crucial to it. And Martha McKee nee Shannon was the central figure in that whole drama. The old gal, she now knew, was hale and hearty and right here. It was frustrating to be so near and yet so far. Especially since she had no idea whether Martha had any idea of her existence. It would be a damn sight easier to take a no from her than from her crazed daughter or that pervert of a sheriff.

'May I join you, ma'am?'

Felice looked up in surprise to see Casey Roberts hovering by her table.

She shrugged. 'Go ahead. Where's your Obergrüppenfuhrer?'

'I'm sorry?'

'That revolting man you work for. Sheriff Clare.'

'Oh – Cousin Byron.'

'Cousin? Jesus, are you all related? I'm not surprised – in-breeding encourages mental degeneracy.'

His boyish face crumpled. 'That's a little extreme, ma'am.'

'What else would you call it, Officer Roberts? Only a degenerate would talk of treating a woman in that manner.'

'That's just Cousin Byron, Ms Cody. He likes to mouth off. He just got called out to a car wreck. Big smash – six in hospital and a dead cow. So he sent me over.'

'Why?'

'Well, first off to see if you was still here. And to give you a hand packin' if you wasn't.' He had a most engaging grin.

'Officer, I don't like being pushed around. I may not be leaving.'

The grin disappeared.

'Please, ma'am, it would be best. You wouldn't want to get the sheriff all riled up.'

'You mean he really would do those things to me?'

'Maybe not, but he can be pretty mean. He might take you in and strip-search you, for instance.'

'Strip-search?'

'He does it to hitchhikers, specially the pretty girls. Searches 'em for drugs. Searches everywhere, if you know what I mean.'

Cody could imagine. 'The man's a menace and you're no better for helping him.'

The young policeman looked aghast. 'That's not true. I ain't like that sonofabitch, I swear.'

Cody laughed in derision. 'It's obvious you don't have the courage to stand up to him.'

'I do too!' His reedy voice was swollen with defiance. Cody recognised the look in his spaniel-brown eyes as well. He wanted her. And the thought of those rangy arms around her body was not without appeal. She decided to test his sincerity.

'OK, Officer, prove it. Put me face to face with your grandmother tonight and I promise I'll leave first thing in the morning.'

★ ★ ★

It was Martha McKee's bridge evening over in the nearby town of Renegade. Casey Roberts had called his mother and volunteered to pick the old lady up. Now, Cody sat in the back of his bruised old pick-up, watching the door of a house twenty yards down the street. Casey was inside, collecting his grandmother.

Suppose the old girl really did not want to see her? She could be on the phone right now to Celia. Or Sheriff Clare. The thought of either of those two maniacs showing up chilled Cody to the bone. She might not get home in one piece.

The light came on in the porch and Casey stepped out, a woman following close behind. He took her arm and the pair of them began to walk towards the truck. Casey had his head bent and Cody could see him talking.

She had been expecting a frail and grey old lady. Casey's grandmother was grey all right but otherwise the description was way off-beam. Her silver locks were cut in a stylish bob and she wore jeans and a suede-fringed jacket. She walked upright, holding Casey's arm in companionship, not for support. At this distance Martha McKee scarcely looked sixty.

They reached the pick-up and Casey opened the door.

'Felice,' he said, 'it's OK, she's not mad or anything. But she says she's gotta look at you first.'

Martha McKee peered into the truck. 'Let me see your face,' she said in a firm but pleasant voice.

Cody leaned forward into the beam of the streetlight. The woman peered at her, her own features obscured.

'Mrs McKee,' she said. 'I would very much like the chance to talk to you.'

'Give me your hand.'

Cody reached over the seat and the woman's fingers closed over hers.

'Ah yes,' she said, her grip warm and strong. 'I can feel it.'

'Feel what, Mrs McKee?'

'Call me Martha, child.'

She climbed in. Casey started the motor.

Martha turned to face Cody. 'You've been touched, haven't you? Like me.'

'That's why I wanted to meet you.'

'I've got my own quarters at the ranch. We can talk there. Casey will stand guard – won't you, son?'

'Yes, grandma.'

'Then you can take the pretty lady home.' She smiled at Cody, her eyes laughing. 'I imagine you might both enjoy that.'

It was three in the morning but Cody was ablaze with excitement. She pulled Casey into the room with her and pressed herself against the length of his tall frame.

'Uh, Felice—'

'Shut up and kiss me.'

She didn't want to talk, there was too much going through her mind. Her body, on the other hand, needed the satisfaction of a strong man's arms and hands and – cock.

'Oh God, ma'am.'

Even as their first kiss broke she had his pants open and his dick in her grasp. It was youthful and eager, just like its owner. He was pawing at her clothes, desperate to get his hands on her nude flesh. She heard a button fall to the floor as he ripped open her shirt. She didn't care if he shredded her entire wardrobe – provided the mini-cassette and tapes in her pocket were not damaged.

What she had learned from Martha was all that she could have hoped for and more. Right now she wanted to celebrate.

She pushed Casey backwards onto the bed, still holding his cock in her fist. From the way it was jumping she ought to put it somewhere safe.

'Tear my panties!' she hissed, hauling her skirt up.

Casey was no expert with female underwear but his hands were strong. The thin cotton snapped in his grip as she straddled his slim hips. She aimed the big dome of his glans into the notch between her thighs and sank down with relief.

He muttered something but she fastened her lips over his to shut him up. God, that felt good. He was on the brink, she knew, but he was young and eager. She'd let him come soon then they could take things at a more leisurely pace.

There was plenty of time. After all, she didn't have to leave till ten.

THIRTY-SEVEN

CHICAGO. 11.20 PM.

Conversation didn't exactly stop when Jarvis walked into the room – most people were too far gone to react that fast – but she could feel the men looking at her as she sashayed to the bar. She liked it. Just as she liked the feeling of near nudity under the thin slip. She relished the roll of her hips and the rise and fall of her unfettered breasts. She knew everything was on show, the hem riding up on her thighs and her nipples pressing into the satin like small thumbs.

The lustful stares of the men were just what she wanted. The bout with Franklin had done nothing to quench the fire that roared within her. On the contrary, it had simply fanned the flames. Tonight she wanted men. Plural. Wanted them in every shape and size, crushing and mauling and poring over her body. She was in the grip of a fever – sex fever. It was weird and scary but she couldn't think about that now. Now was no time to think. She was drunk with the need to fuck.

'Perrier,' she snapped at the barman, slamming Franklin's key down before he could ask her to leave. She knew she looked like a hooker but that was fine by her.

She scanned the bar, searching the men's faces and bodies. There were women in the room too but she scarcely looked at them. Her eyes lit on a gathering of seven or eight guys in the far corner. They were younger than the rest and one man in particular, dark and Latin-looking, was a hunk. After Franklin, she decided she deserved a treat. She made straight for the group.

'Hi,' she said. 'Are you fellows with the optometrists' convention?'

'That's right,' said one. The others all looked too stunned to reply.

'See anything you like the look of round here?'

'Sure,' said the first man. 'You.'

Jarvis grinned. 'Good answer. Any particular part of me?'

There was a whoop of laughter.

'Your red hair,' said one.

'Your swinging hips,' said another

'Your great jugs,' said a third, bolder and drunker. The whole group guffawed except for the Latin looker.

'So you want to see more?' Jarvis was enjoying this. She was really going to let her hair down tonight. 'Well, you guys are in luck. The management is running a competition during the convention for Slut of the Week.'

There was a collective whoop of excitement.

'Now, I'm aiming to win and I need your help. Here's the deal. One of you takes me up to his room—'

There was more whooping.

'—and we have some fun together. After he's finished, he goes and another of you comes in. One at a time, got it? And when I say enough, that means enough – OK?'

'Sure,' said a man on her right. 'I've got a suite. Let's use that.'

'Perfect,' said Jarvis, placing her hand on the arm of the Latin guy. 'And I want this one first.'

'What are you up to, lady?'

Jarvis had her back against the door of the bedroom. Her Latin hunk was by the bed. He looked suspicious.

'Isn't it obvious? I want to get laid.'

'I don't pay for pussy.'

'And I don't charge.'

'So what's the catch? Are you drunk?'

'Come over here and find out.'

His hair was thick and black, falling to his collar. His cheekbones were sharp, the mouth full and slightly girlish, so too the long-lashed midnight-black eyes. He was the kind of guy Jarvis always fell for. Correction – *used* to fall for. Before she'd got fed up with having her emotions torn into shreds. But back in her dating days she'd had other needs beyond the physical. Right now she just wanted the cheapest thrill she could get.

'Come on,' she said and leaned back against the door, her slip riding just that bit higher on her thighs. Men had always told her she was beautiful but she'd never believed them. Now she knew she was. She was a sex slut just begging for it. And this man was not going to say no.

He didn't. He seemed to come to a decision and the next moment his arms were round her. His lips were dry on hers, just resting on her skin. She parted her lips a fraction and waited for him. He traced the outline of her mouth, then gently kissed her lower lip. She giggled, the sound surprising her – Bonny Jarvis was not a giggler. But Joanne Martin had a whole repertoire of sexy laughter. *What the hell*, Jarvis thought, *this is fun!*

She flicked her tongue into his mouth and he thrust back hard. Then they were embracing at full throttle, their bodies grinding together, hearts thumping. His hands began to explore. She could feel his excitement kick up a gear as his touch confirmed that she was nude beneath the flimsy satin garment.

He held himself back for a moment.

'You're feverish.'

'I'm horny.'

'Look, I'm a trained physician. You may not be well.'

'I'm well enough to know what's good for me, doctor. I want a fuck.'

'Let's get on the bed then,' he whispered, his fingers in the bush of her pussy.

'No. Take me here. Standing up against the door.'

He chuckled. 'You dirty bitch. You want them all to hear, don't you?'

She hadn't thought of that but the idea excited her – to be screwed against a door while a queue of would-be lovers waited impatiently for their turn on the other side.

'Yes,' she said. 'I want them to hear what they're going to get.'

He didn't waste any time. Somehow her slip was round her waist and his cock was between her legs. She took it in her fingers and squeezed. It was satisfyingly hard, a rigid baton of flesh with a broad circumcised tip. He bent his knees and she guided it between her lips and into the tunnel of her sex.

It was as if they had rehearsed it, the way he straightened up, lifting her round the waist so that she was riding on his pole, her bare buttocks flat against the door. Then he began to pound her.

It was hot and fierce and short. He cupped the undercurve of her ass as he fucked her. She clung round his neck and thrilled to the sheer energy of his excitement. She hadn't been fucked like this in a long time.

When he was done he walked her to the bed on his cock and threw her onto the covers. She sprawled happily, legs spread, the green satin bunched below her breasts.

'Send the next one in,' she said. 'And tell him to hurry.'

time and so are the jocks. Everybody's happy, apart from the odd lovesick kid but she can handle that. You could say she's still in the teaching profession.'

'And the other two?'

'They're running a house of correction in Baldry. Pine has set herself up as a professional dominatrix and Karlsen is helping her out. We could close the place down and put them on vice charges but I can't see the point.'

'We don't want this story out in the open,' said Stone. 'At least until we know exactly what's at the bottom of it.'

'Leonard's at the bottom of it,' said Hannah. 'That's what they say. I've talked to all three of them and they think he's some kind of genius who liberated their sensuality.'

Stone turned to Jarvis. 'What do you say? You've met him and checked out his set-up – what's going on?'

Jarvis dismissed from her mind the image of Stone lying with her in bed, that great barrel chest crushed to her bare breasts . . .

'It's a psycho-babble scam,' she heard herself say. 'He's very smooth and charming. He organises touchy-feely sessions and discussions on personal growth for lonely women. His clients can't make relationships because they've lost touch with the pleasure principle. He closes the gap.'

'So, that's it? He's a sex therapist whose therapy is so successful that his clients become sex addicts?'

'Yes – and no.' This was the hard part, Jarvis had to struggle to marshal her thoughts. Stone had come round from his side of the desk and was leaning back against it facing them, his arms folded. If Jarvis slipped to her knees her face would be just inches from his crotch. She could take his zipper in her teeth and pull it slowly down . . .

'Are you OK, Agent Jarvis?' Stone's earnest face was creased with concern. 'You look like you're burning up.'

'I'm fine,' she said, dabbing her temple with a paper handkerchief. Christ, she was sweating! She was wet between the legs, too. She had to wrap this meeting up quick and escape.

'Look,' she said forcefully, 'there *is* something strange

THIRTY-EIGHT

BUREAU HEADQUARTERS. OCTOBER 14TH. 10.00 AM.

To her relief, Hannah was all business when they met up on Monday morning. Jarvis had prepared herself for an onslaught of snide remarks but all he said was, 'Hi, there. Nice trip?' and she'd nodded. 'Nice' was hardly the word to describe what had happened to her in New Mexico but she wasn't going to get into that if she could help it.

So here they were, sitting in Stone's office, trying to get a handle on where they stood. Jarvis wore her frumpiest clothes, a dark suit over a blouse buttoned to the throat. She'd left off her make-up – minimal though it was – and wore her heavy-rimmed reading glasses. She did not look like a woman who had chain-fucked a dozen strange guys throughout Saturday night.

She regretted it now. Not because it hadn't felt great to let it all hang out for once but because the orgy hadn't achieved its purpose. She'd thought she could blast the sex fever out of her system and, for most of Sunday, exhausted and tender, she'd thought it had worked. But now she knew it hadn't. Sitting here, trying hard not to look at the two men in the room with more than professional interest, the illness was back. She had banked the fire not smothered it – now it was ready to burn.

She tried to concentrate.

'So,' Stone was saying to Hannah, 'you've located three of these missing females?'

'Correct. Madeleine Simons is up in Cardinal Springs working as a waitress in a bar for jocks. She's having a great going on. I pulled a few favours yesterday with the technicians. They developed photos of Leonard – or tried to.'

She stood and placed a set of ten-by-eights on the desktop.

'As you can see, they show everything but what we really want.'

They poured over the photographs. There were the mountains, the tennis courts and cabins, the unreal lawns and the hissing sprinklers – but no Leonard. On the shots of the putting green where Jarvis had carefully framed him a dozen times over, there was nothing but a dark blur with no discernible features. The surroundings were clear as day but the figure at the centre was just a black smudge.

'There's more,' she said, opening another envelope. 'I took his fingerprints, hoping I could match them from the archives. This is what I got.'

The images generated off the computer were roughly fingerprint-shaped but there the resemblance to regular prints ended. There were no whorls and ridges but a kaleidoscopic scatter of dots and star shapes.

'These are meant to be fingerprints, right?' Stone was not amused. 'They look like some joke you knocked up on screen. It's not what I expect from you, Jarvis.'

'I'm entirely serious, sir. I took these off a water glass he handed me.'

'Maybe he's playing the joke on you,' said Hannah. 'He knew you were after his prints and came up with this.'

'*No!*' The sound came out more shrilly than she intended. If she didn't get out of here soon she would scream.

'You're not well,' said Stone. 'You're shaking.'

It was true, her whole body was trembling. The men were on either side of her and their proximity had her body throbbing with lust.

'Go straight home,' said Stone. 'Get yourself fixed up. Hannah and I can progress this.'

She didn't have the will to protest – other needs were more urgent.

'Call me,' she said to Hannah as she collected her papers. 'Keep me informed – please.'

★ ★ ★

In her office, she ran to the phone, scrabbling in her pocket for the piece of paper she had discovered that morning. Thank God she hadn't thrown it away.

When the phone was picked up at the other end she launched straight into the speech she had prepared in her mind. 'This is Special Agent Jarvis of the Bureau. I wonder if you can help me – I'm trying to make contact with a Ms Duncan. She gave me this number a little while ago and—'

'Hi, Special Agent. To what do I owe the pleasure?'

The Brooklyn twang was unmistakable.

'Quinn – I didn't think you'd be here.'

'Well, you're in luck. So you kept my number, huh? I was right about you.'

'Can I see you?'

'Maybe. Fancy slapping me around a bit more, do you?'

'I'm sorry about that, really. Let me make it up to you.'

There was a snigger on the other end of the line.

'Now look here, Agent Jarvis, I could make you crawl. Especially after how you treated me a couple of weeks back. But since I'm a sucker for punishment – sucker, geddit? – I'll give you one more chance.'

'OK.' Jarvis tried to sound cool but she felt like a teenager begging for a date.

'You know the Jefferson Mall? Meet me in the coffee shop in thirty minutes. They've got a great lingerie shop next door. You can buy me something sexy then go home and see how it looks. Whaddya say?'

There was only one thing *to* say and Jarvis said it on a gleeful rush of breath. 'Yes!'

THIRTY-NINE

HANNAH'S APARTMENT. 1.30 PM.

When the street buzzer sounded, Hannah simply pushed the release button. He knew who it would be.

She pushed past him into the apartment with a scowl on her face. It didn't make her look any less attractive. She threw her jacket onto a chair and faced him.

'This really can't go on,' she said.

'OK, Brigitte.'

'I'm a married woman. I can't keep sneaking off to fuck some other guy when Glen's back's turned even though he's a rat. Especially since the other guy can't keep his pants zipped either. We've got to pack it in.'

'If that's what you want.'

'Well, I do.'

She fell into his arms and nuzzled her blonde head into his chest.

'So why did you come here, Brigitte?'

She licked the hollow of his throat and dug her nails into his back through the cotton of his shirt. 'To tell you there's no word from Felice.'

'I see.'

'I'm very worried and Glen doesn't care. The least you could do is hold me.'

She pulled his shirt free of his waistband and slipped her hands beneath to circle his chest.

'I *am* holding you, Brigitte. It also strikes me that your behaviour is not entirely congruent.'

'*Congruent?* What the fuck does that mean?'

She ripped open his belt and plunged a hand into his pants.

'It means that your body language is inconsistent with your stated desires.'

'So, you don't believe me when I say we should break up.'

'Not when you're clinging on to my dick, no.'

'Don't you like it?'

'Brigitte, I like it so much I'm going to cream your skirt if you keep it up.'

She let go of his prick and yanked her sweater to her chin. Then she pulled his shirt up and rubbed her bare tits on his chest.

'Is that better? I don't want you to come just yet.'

'Brigitte, if you want to get laid just say so.'

'Well, I guess one more time wouldn't hurt, would it?'

Quinn Duncan had the upper hand and she was making the most of it. She looked delicious in the peach silk slip and matching briefs with little bows on the hip that Jarvis had sprung for at the lingerie shop. She'd sprung for quite a bit more too and the spoils lay strewn around Jarvis's bedroom, a few hundred bucks' worth but Jarvis wasn't counting. She was too damn turned on.

Quinn pulled her panties off and threw them in Jarvis's face. They were warm and musky already. The petite blonde posed in front of her. Her big brown eyes gleamed, so did the stud set in her nostril. But what drew Jarvis's eyes and set her heart thudding in her ribs was the girl's quim.

In comparison with her dainty frame, Quinn's pubic delta seemed out of proportion. Shaved bare, her sex seemed huge. The girl stepped closer, almost thrusting her vagina into Jarvis's face as she perched on the edge of the bed.

'You like it, don't you?' said Quinn. 'Go on, have a good look.'

It was the labia, Jarvis concluded. They jutted forward like a pouting mouth just begging to be kissed. Above, at the top of her sex groove, her clit thrust up, a wine-red knob of flesh that took Jarvis's breath away.

The girl put her foot upon the bed so her cunt mouth

yawned wider. The smell of her filled the room, rich and complex and exotic.

'Get to it then, Special Agent,' said Quinn. 'Lick me out.'

Jarvis pressed her lips to the skin of the girl's thigh. She had been in bed with two women just a couple of days ago but this was somehow different. With Alex and Lena, the three of them had been each other's man-substitutes. She hesitated.

Quinn laughed and grabbed her hair, jamming Jarvis's face into her crotch.

If she hadn't been so sex drunk would she have been turned off? Jarvis couldn't figure it out as her mouth closed on that other mouth between the girl's thighs and her hands gripped the taut ass that had been driving her crazy as Quinn had displayed herself in her new finery.

The girl tasted salty yet sweet, a honeyed sea of erotic sensation on her tongue. Jarvis licked her hungrily, knowing there was no need for delicacy. Quinn was as desperate for release as she was. She fastened her lips on the blonde's big clit and took her over the edge in seconds.

To her credit, Quinn didn't slow down the action – she knew the state her new lover was in. She pushed Jarvis back onto the bed and burrowed a hand up the agent's skirt even as she shivered in the aftershock of her own climax.

'Mmm, you've got a bushy little puss,' Quinn said as she pulled Jarvis's panties to her knees.

'Don't you like it?'

'Oh it's adorable but—'

Quinn had a finger inside her and Jarvis was half out of her mind already.

'When I used to date guys—' the blonde continued.

There were two fingers inside her now and Quinn's thumb was tickling her clit.

'I always preferred kissing the ones without beards. Know what I mean?'

'Uh, I'm not sure . . .'

All four fingers were in her and the thumb was massaging in earnest.

'Don't worry, baby,' whispered Quinn, 'I'll take care of

you in a minute. I've got a razor in my bag. And when I've shaved you clean, I'll show you just how good I really am.'

There was no answer to that. Which was just as well for, in the throes of orgasm, Jarvis was incapable of speech.

Later, in the kitchen fixing a drink, the phone rang. It was Hannah. Thankfully the session with Quinn had cleared her head.

'How you doing, Jarvis? Feeling any better?'

'Much better.'

'Look, after you left, Stone decided I should talk to Leonard. I'm flying to New Mexico tomorrow.'

'What about me?'

'We didn't think you'd be up to it.'

'You just want me off the case.'

'Not true. You looked damn sick this morning, that's all.'

'Get me a plane ticket. I'm coming with you.'

'If you're sure you're up to it.'

'I'm sure.'

'Great. I'll look forward to your company.'

Jarvis replaced the phone, anxiety already gnawing at her. She was learning fast about the erotic obsession that gripped her. It could only be kept at bay by frequent sexual activity. The prospect of a couple of days in the close proximity of Hannah was appalling. The things she had done with strangers and casual pick-ups were one thing but she was damned if Hannah was going to get his hands on her.

'Quinn,' she barked as she marched into the bedroom.

The girl turned over lazily in bed.

'Something wrong, sugar?'

'Can you stay the night?'

She eyed Jarvis lasciviously. 'Can't get enough of me, huh?'

Jarvis nodded. 'Something like that.'

'C'mere.'

The girl pulled Jarvis down beside her onto the bed and folded her into her arms.

'Sure, I'll stay. Is there a problem? Do you want to talk about it?'

Jarvis swivelled round so that they lay head to toe.

'Thanks, Quinn, but I don't want to talk at all.'

'I understand.'

And to show that she did, she lowered her lips to Jarvis's newly shaved pussy and went to work.

FORTY

ANTELOPE MTS. OCTOBER 15TH. 5.05 PM.

'Damn!' said Jarvis for maybe the fiftieth time. 'I'm sorry, guys, I've screwed this up.'

The helicopter had been raking back and forth across the mountains for nearly an hour as Jarvis searched in vain for Leonard's ranch.

'Take it easy, honey. It's one thing knowing where you are on the ground but it looks a damn sight different from up in the air.'

Jarvis shot Pete, the Indian pilot, a poisonous look – though he was trying to be sympathetic the 'honey' rankled.

'But it should be simple to find,' she exclaimed. 'There's a dozen buildings and tennis courts and lawns. There's even a putting green.'

Pete's brown eyes twinkled and his big white teeth showed as he grinned. 'So you say, honey.'

'Well, I do say and I'd be grateful if you didn't call me honey.'

Pete's head dipped in acknowledgement but his smile did not fade as he said, 'I mean, it would be most unusual to find a rinky-dink leisure complex like you describe way up here in the mountains. I guarantee I'd know about it and if I didn't it would stick out like tits on a tree trunk, if you'll pardon the sexist allusion, ma'am.'

'How about down there?' Hannah pointed at a clearing beneath the pines on the other side of the valley. Half a dozen log cabins surrounded a two-storey ranch-house.

'No, it can't possibly—' Jarvis stopped as a rock formation

ahead caught her eye. It looked familiar – surely Leonard had pointed it out to her? 'Well, maybe. It must be somewhere near here.'

Pete was already taking the helicopter down. The land in front of the main building had once been levelled though now it was overgrown with weed. A cloud of dust rose as the chopper settled.

The place looked derelict and empty.

'I don't see no summer lawns and tourists in tennis whites,' said Pete.

Jarvis ignored the remark. 'Wait here,' she said, unclipping her safety harness and opening the door even as the rotor blades still turned. There was something damned funny going on but she knew, deep in her guts, that this was the place she had visited just a few days ago.

Hannah followed close behind as Jarvis strode across the neglected clearing towards the house.

The door wasn't locked. It opened on creaky hinges and dust rose from their feet as they walked into what had been the reception area. The place smelt musty and unused. There was no sign of the cane chairs and glass-topped tables and Indian rugs that had brightened the room before.

Hannah clicked the light switch – there was no power. Jarvis searched the drawers of the reception desk. She found only paperclips and staples. On the board next to the desk was a curling Antelope Reservation calendar for 1992.

She rushed from room to room. The dining room was full of stacked chairs and folding tables, the bar was a wreck – it looked like a family of raccoons had used it as a playroom – the meeting room housed what looked like farm implements wrapped in plastic sheeting.

Upstairs Leonard's study was bare but for a bad watercolour of an Indian pueblo hanging askew on the wall.

'Goddamnit!' Jarvis muttered. It was incredible.

She had once watched a TV series in which derelict properties were transformed in a couple of days – mostly to surprise families who had been lured away on weekend trips. When they returned their broken-down barns and fire-damaged basements had been turned into guest bedrooms and dens with wet bars. The show was called *Your Magic Makeover* and the returning families usually burst into tears of joy. Right now, Jarvis felt that she was on the receiving end of *Your Magic Makeover* – in reverse. And the tears she was on the point of shedding were born of confusion. What the hell was going on?

She looked out of the window of the study, up at the ridge across the valley. The sun was beginning to slide down to the west, catching that rock she had noticed from the helicopter . . .

'Hannah!' she called.

He appeared in the doorway, grime on his hands and a rueful smile on his face.

'Surely this isn't the place?' he said.

'It must be.'

'But, Jarvis—'

'Yes, I know. I can't explain it but look up there.'

She pointed out of the window.

'Do you see that big rock?' she said.

'Yeah.'

'What does it look like?'

'Jarvis, it's a rock.'

'What *shape* is it? Doesn't it remind you of something?'

'Now you point it out, it looks like a bear.'

'Exactly. Which means I am not crazy. Don't ask me what the hell has gone on here – I can't explain it. But I know I was in this room with Leonard five days ago. He showed me that rock formation. It's called Bear Peak.'

Hannah digested this information.

'Tell me, Jarvis, do you believe in time travel?'

'Only in science fiction. What are you getting at?'

Hannah shrugged. 'Just trying to figure it out. It seems our Mr Leonard can work miracles.' He glanced out of the window. 'Though it's comforting to know he can't move mountains.'

Jarvis walked up the hillside into the pine forest, following as best she could the path that she had taken the previous week. The track was overgrown but passable. She paused at the spot where, she reckoned, she had taken those photographs of Leonard.

A hand closed on her arm.

She whirled and kicked, it was a reflex action.

'Hey, now,' said a deep familiar voice. Pete had caught her foot in a big shovel-like hand. 'I know you don't like me all that much but—'

'Let me go!'

He relaxed his grip and stepped back.

'What the hell are you doing here?' she snapped.

'Answering a call of nature, ma'am. Or should I have asked permission?'

'Don't be stupid.'

He chuckled, his eyes dancing, his big brown face alive with merriment. Jarvis reined in her irritation – the frustrations of her situation were hardly his fault – and he was a striking figure of a man. She took in his broad shoulders and the lustrous sheen of his thick black hair and her stomach flipped. The puzzle of Rolf Leonard had wiped her other problems from her mind but now, alone in the woods with this burnished hunk of manhood, her sex dilemma came flooding back in all its intensity. Come to think of it, there *was* one of her frustrations he could help her with.

'I've not been very polite to you, have I?'

'That's OK, ma'am, I'm used to it from some of my lady customers. At least you got some compensations.'

'Like what?'

'You're a damn sight easier on the eye than most other tourist women, ma'am.'

'Knock off the ma'am stuff, Pete. I'd rather go back to honey.'

'You would?'

'Yes. Please.'

There. She could hardly be more obvious without being downright blatant – which, in her current mood, she was quite capable of. Fortunately, there was no need. Pete was right up close, an arm snaking round her waist.

'Well, honey, I got to tell you you're the cutest piece of tail that I've had in my bird all year long. I don't know why it is that I go for you snot-lipped types.'

A big hand was under her jacket enclosing her left breast. She pushed her chest into him, a throb of anticipation shaking her entire body.

'Maybe,' he continued, 'it's because I know that, deep down, you ball-breaking upscale women just want to climb between the sheets and spread your pretty legs for a red man like me.'

'Oh God,' muttered Jarvis as his fingers unbuttoned her shirt.

'Would you like that, honey? For me to strip your cute white body and lick it all over till you beg me to stuff you full of big brown cock?'

'Yes, please.'

He had her shirt open to the waist and her tits out in the air, squeezed together in a tarty push-up bra that Quinn had insisted she buy.

His fingers were at her waist, unbuckling the belt of her jeans. She helped him push them down over her hips. She was shaking like a leaf.

'Tell me more,' she whispered. 'Tell me what you're going to do to me!'

'Jarvis!' Hannah's voice floated up from the house below.

Pete's fingers, already in the slick folds of her pussy, ceased their exploration. She ground herself against his hand as Hannah shouted again.

'Jarvis, where are you?'

'Come on!' she hissed. 'Fuck me quick.'

'Wait a minute—'

'Come *on!*' She unzipped his pants. 'We've got time.'

'Uh—' Pete was hesitant but his penis, thank God, was not. She pulled it into view – a long dark truncheon, pulsing with desire. She turned and bent forward, clasping the trunk of a tree. Her gleaming white ass thrust back at him, the split lips of her bare pussy pouting in invitation. Few men could have resisted – and Pete the pilot was not one of them.

'Hey, come on, Jarvis, stop mucking around!' Hannah's voice was nearer this time.

Pete was fumbling between her legs, pressing the smooth

head of his cock into her fork. She reached between her legs and gripped his thick shaft.

'I can see him,' mumbled Pete as he sank into her. 'He's getting close.'

'So what? Don't you want me?'

'Sure, but not like this. You're such a horny witch, I want you for the night.'

He was in her and pumping. She kept her hand in her crotch, feeling the slippery thrust of his prick as he ploughed her, pressing the quivering pip of her clit. It was a race against time.

'OK,' she muttered, pressure building in her loins. 'You can have me all night. You can do what you want.'

'He's coming up the path—'

'Don't stop – I'm almost there.'

'But—'

'Oh God!'

'Hush now!'

But Jarvis couldn't give a damn as his pounding cock and her urgent fingers did the trick and she yelled her release across the mountain side.

Hannah crashed through the woods towards the cry that still reverberated in his ears. It was Jarvis, he knew. Something terrible had happened to her.

To his surprise, he found Pete bending over her as she leaned with her back against a tree, breathing hard. There was a smear of bark across one cheek and her clothes were dirty and dishevelled.

'Are you all right?' he asked.

'It's OK, Hannah. I tripped on a root and banged my head. It's nothing.'

'It sure sounded like something.' He looked suspiciously at Pete and Jarvis caught his expression.

'I asked Pete to come up here with me. It's the route I took when I photographed Leonard last week. I'm certain this is the place.'

'I agree with you.'

'You do?'

'I've found something in the house. You'd better come and see.'

The three of them descended slowly, Jarvis leaning on Pete's arm. Hannah tried to ignore how much that irritated him. He guessed she was more shaken by her fall than she cared to admit.

He took her into one of the cabins. It was piled high with furniture. He pointed to a battered desk.

'In here.'

'That's Leonard's desk,' said Jarvis.

'Open the top drawer.'

Inside were some medical textbooks and—

'*Starlight of the Gods,*' she cried and picked it up. She flicked quickly to the flyleaf and read once more the author's inscription: "To RL, one of the Gods. With respect and love, FSC.'

'I'm sorry I doubted you,' said Hannah. 'This is one damn weird business.'

'What do we do next?'

'Let's get back to Washington. Leonard's not here – he could be anywhere.'

'You can't reach DC tonight, folks.' Pete's voice sounded from the doorway. 'But if I may be permitted to recommend a quality motel in my neighbourhood I can guarantee to get you to the airport first thing tomorrow morning.'

Hannah hesitated but Jarvis was already heading for the door, the book tucked under her arm and no trace of a limp in her step. He admired the swing of her denimed ass. She ought to wear jeans more often.

'Sounds fine to me, Pete,' she said.

What the hell was she so cheerful about all of a sudden? Hannah couldn't figure it out. Unless it was the prospect of spending a night in the boonies in his company. Maybe now was the time to discover whether Jarvis's week with the wacky doctor had had the kind of effect on her that had transformed Cody and co.

Hannah began to feel a little upbeat himself.

FORTY-ONE

HOUND DOG, NEW MEXICO. OCTOBER 16TH. 5.15 AM.

Jarvis peered at her face in the mirror over the sink. She looked pretty good, all things considered, since she had swapped vices. Trading booze for sex was certainly better for the complexion.

Pete was snoring in the bedroom. He had earned his sleep. She would have no qualms about interrupting it, however. There was time for a little of what she fancied before she left his apartment and headed for her motel room across the street.

She clicked on the bedside lamp, angling it away from his face and down the length of his magnificent body. Apart from the raven-black hair on his head he was almost as hairless as she. His broad chest gleamed against the white sheet and she bent to lick his nipples, leaving a trail of moisture which sparkled in the light.

She admired him for a minute before resuming her handiwork, leaving a snail trail of kisses down his ribs to his flat, smooth belly. She stripped the sheet from his body and started again at his feet, tracing her lips upwards along his sinuous, muscle-packed thighs. He had performed this same ritual for her at some time during the night, lapping her skin in the dark while she moaned with pleasure at his touch. As he did now, summoned from his slumber by her caress.

'Hey now, honey,' he murmured as she reached his cock, lifting the slim cylinder of flesh to nuzzle into the crook of his thighs and tongue the soft sack of his balls. One by one she took his testes into her mouth, as gently as if she were holding an egg.

'What you doin' to me?' he sighed, the slim cylinder now swollen to a thick branch thrusting upwards from his groin. She gripped it in her fist and squeezed, relishing the silk-on-steel resilience in her grasp. God, she needed that big thing shuttling deep inside her.

She climbed over him, silencing his sleepy moans by pushing a taut-nippled breast into his face. His lips closed over her teat and she nursed him for a minute, relishing what was to come.

He'd been a good lover in the night though she wasn't unhappy that morning had broken. She scuttled her ass down his prone form and lodged his cock-head in the moist nook between her thighs. One more time to savour her Native American's fabulous pipe of peace . . .

Hannah, too, woke early. He pulled shorts and an undershirt from his bag and took off for a run. As he pounded the streets of what seemed to him a tedious suburb he tried to get a handle on the whole Leonard business. None of it made much sense. He believed Jarvis when she swore that the place they had looked over yesterday was Leonard's. At least, he believed the Jarvis he knew – cool, level-headed, analytical. However, he wasn't so sure about this new Jarvis – the woman gripped by hot flushes who needed a man's arm to lean on and who made eyes at helicopter pilots . . .

As Hannah rounded the block in front of the motel he saw her. He was so surprised he almost ran slap into a fire hydrant.

She was in the doorway of an apartment building across the street – the building where Pete lived. Hannah stood stock still in the half light and watched as Jarvis crossed the road. She vanished inside the motel without a backward glance.

He cursed himself for a fool – not for the first time where a woman's sexual appetite was concerned. If she had the hots for Pete it explained quite few things – her strange cry in the woods, her eagerness to stay the night, not to mention the way she had ducked dinner, pleading fatigue, the night before.

Hannah knew he had no right to be jealous. He was pleased Jarvis had at last proved herself to be made of flesh and blood. In the context of the Cody case that was mighty interesting – obviously Jarvis had not been impervious to Leonard's influence after all. Hannah's overwhelming feeling, however, was that he was damned pissed off. If Jarvis was going to free her sensual self then why not with him?

Later, on the flight back to Washington, he tried to talk to her about it.

She sat in the window seat with the sun setting off sparks in the beaten copper of her hair. The jeans were gone, replaced by a tight black skirt that revealed a spectacular expanse of creamy thigh. Her loose linen jacket hung open to reveal a thin vee-necked pastel blue sweater that seemed moulded to her breasts. Hannah's palms itched as he contemplated the sweet curves of her body. To think that Pete the pilot had had proprietary rights on that sumptuous flesh just a few hours earlier drove him crazy.

'Tell me, Jarvis, did Leonard's therapy have any effect on you?'

She shrugged. The way her superstructure rippled drew the knot of lust in his stomach even tighter.

'Come on, you can tell me, I'm your partner.'

She turned her pale blue eyes on him full beam.

'Exactly. I'm your professional associate, nothing more. I don't trust you. Whatever I say could go straight back to Stone.'

'Hey, Jarvis, I'm not in league with that desk jockey.'

'So you say. You can tell him one thing. In my opinion, Leonard's techniques are highly dangerous and capable of destabilising vulnerable women, whatever their intellectual capacity.'

Hannah placed his hand on hers. 'So – are you all right, Jarvis? Can I help?'

For a second her hand trembled then she ripped it from his grasp and thrust her angry face into his.

'You can help by keeping your hands off me, you arrogant asshole!'

Nothing further was said throughout the rest of the journey.

Hannah reached his apartment in a lather of pent-up fury. Which explained the stupidity of what he did next.

The only message on his machine was from Brigitte.

'Hi, Special Agent,' she said. 'Come on over tonight. Glen's out and I've got some hot news that won't keep.'

Hannah had promised himself to steer clear of Brigitte in the future. Delicious though she was, he could see her games would do him no good in the long run. But tonight he was in no mood for self-preservation and, boy, did he need to take his frustration out on someone.

He took it out on Brigitte as they screwed violently on the marital bed. She loved it. He smacked her pretty white ass till it turned puce and then plugged her till she popped, twice, before the dam of his rage burst deep inside her hot tight pussy. He didn't tell her that his passion had not been stored on her account.

They were lolling back, nude and indolent, gathering breath for round two, as it were, when the door burst open.

Glen, Brigitte's husband – at least, that was Hannah's assumption though they were never formerly introduced – was built like a Redskins' linebacker and just as pumped up. His eyes bulged as he took in the sight of his wife lounging in Hannah's arms, her sex steaming and her fingers playing doh-re-mi on his stiffening cock – then he charged.

Hannah ran for cover but he didn't get far. Glen caught him in the hall and smacked his jaw with a crunch that filled his face with pain. He followed up with a jab to the ribs that slammed Hannah against the wall and shook loose a framed print of a Georgia O'Keeffe flower the colour of blood.

'Don't, Glen, don't!' shrieked Brigitte, tugging at the man's ham of a forearm as he raised it again.

'I'm a Federal Agent,' spluttered Hannah. It was all he could think of to say.

The giant slammed Hannah in the ribs once more, with his foot this time.

'I don't care if you're fucking double-oh-seven,' he roared, 'get out of my house or die!'

Hannah scuttled down the stairs and into the kitchen. He spat blood into the sink.

There was more shouting from above and the crash of a door slamming. Hannah heard the wronged husband pacing the bedroom above. Then Brigitte appeared at the door with his clothes.

'I'm sorry,' she said as she dabbed at his face with a towel. 'Will you be OK?'

'Sure – he's all talk.'

'Really?' Hannah hugged his battered ribs, wondering if any were broken.

'Don't worry, I can handle him.' There was a gleam in her eye and Hannah didn't doubt her words. What a fool he'd been to get tied up with her.

She pushed him along the hall towards the door. He went willingly.

'Hey,' she said, 'I nearly forgot. Felice.'

'You've heard from her?'

'More than that. She's back.'

And she closed the door behind him with a bang.

FORTY-TWO

MAXWELL, VIRGINIA. 10.30 PM.

Hannah drove in a daze. He couldn't recall how he got to Cody's apartment.

It was an uncivil time to receive visitors but Felice didn't seem fazed. Not even by the swaying bloodstained figure at her door, clutching a stained paper handkerchief to his lip.

Hannah thrust his badge of office into her hand.

'Special Agent Thomas Hannah, Ms Cody. I've been looking for you for weeks.'

'So I heard,' she said, ushering him into the hall.

'I imagine your sister, Mrs Behr, informed you that I have some questions concerning your recent disappearance.'

'My sister informed me of a hell of a lot – especially about you, Agent Hannah. So you can knock off the Bureau-speak and come and have a drink.'

Hannah followed her meekly into the kitchen. As he registered the silky switch of her hips beneath her kimono he began to perk up.

At her bidding, he took a seat at the table.

'Would brandy and a Band-Aid suit you?' she said. 'At a guess, I'd say you've been snacking on broken glass.'

'Sorry. I must look like shit.'

'What happened?' She splashed cognac into two tumblers and passed one over.

'I . . .' The spirit set his bruised mouth on fire then blazed a trail down his throat – the warm glow that followed, however, was worth it. 'I tripped on the steps of my building as I was coming out. I was in a rush to see you,' he added with a grin.

'Such eagerness – I'm flattered.' She also didn't believe him, he could tell, but that was too bad.

'You know, Ms Cody, you vanishing like that set a few pulses racing at the Bureau. I understand you're involved in some pretty sensitive work.'

'Sure but I've got a life too, you know. I'm owed a ton of vacation time – I just took some that's all.'

'But you didn't tell anyone. You didn't even let your sister know. She was very upset.'

'Since when have the Bureau cared ten cents about people being upset? I arranged to have my cats looked after and I sent Brigitte a card. I meant to call the lab but I had too much on my mind.'

She smiled at him. It was a very attractive smile. There were lots of attractive things about Felice Cody as Hannah well knew from watching her videotapes. It occurred to him that she might have been on the way to bed when he rang the bell. She didn't look like she was wearing a heck of a lot under that kimono.

'Aren't you going to ask me what I've been up to for the last three weeks, Agent Hannah? Or are you happy just to swill my booze and stare at my legs?'

'Actually, Ms Cody—'

'Felice.'

'Felice. I *am* curious what you've been up to.'

She leaned forward to top up his glass, offering a tantalising glimpse into the shadows of her cleavage. He accepted the invitation.

'Guess,' she said.

'I'm sorry?'

'I'd like to hear your theories. Guess what I've been doing – apart from getting laid, of course.'

'Oh – right.'

'Don't go coy on me, Hannah. You've seen my VCR tapes and you've been banging my sister – Brigitte and I had a heart-to-heart this afternoon – so you and I are not exactly strangers. Just tell me how much you know and I'll fill you in.'

Hannah took another drink. The ache in his body had now faded to a gentle throb that could be pain from his wounds or desire for the half-naked beauty beside him. He ignored it and tried to gather his thoughts.

'Well, I know you went on a self-help course in New Mexico a couple of months back, run by a man called Rolf Leonard. As a result – and like a number of other women in similar circumstances to your own – you have been reborn sexually. In fact, you can't get enough. However, you are also a bestselling authority on unexplained phenomena and I suspect that what you've really been doing is researching a new book.'

'Very good, Special Agent. So far. Before you continue, do you mind if I take a look at your chest? I'd say a mule kicked you in the ribs from the way you're holding yourself.'

There wasn't much point in protesting – she was already on her knees beside his chair, sliding his jacket off his shoulders. She opened his shirt and her fingers were warm on his skin as she traced the scarlet swelling on his ribcage where Glen's blows had landed.

'That looks nasty,' she said and fingered him expertly, searching for damage beneath the skin.

He flinched, he couldn't help it, but her other hand was on his neck and her perfume was intoxicating.

'This won't take a moment,' she said. As far as he was concerned, she could take as long as she liked.

'I think it's only a bruise,' she said. 'I'll fix you an ice-pack.' She stood up. 'Tell me more of what you've discovered.'

'Frankly, Felice, it's not much. There's a bunch of respectable women and a guy who turns them into insatiable sex-machines. But we can't lay our hands on him. Bonny Jarvis, my partner, went on his last course but when we returned to talk to Leonard he'd gone.'

'Really?' She was back with the ice wrapped in a towel. He grimaced as she placed it over his ribs.

'Yeah – vanished as if he'd never been there. The whole place had changed too, like it had gone back in time to before his arrival. We're not just dealing with a regular con-man here, that's for sure.'

'What does your partner make of it?'

'She – she and I don't exactly think along the same lines. I can't talk to her about off-the-wall stuff. Like time travel.'

'Why time travel?'

She was kneeling by him once more, holding the ice-pack against his skin. Her face was about two inches from his and her eyes filled his vision.

'You're leading me on, aren't you, Felice? You're aware of what happened in nineteen thirty-four at Lake Musgrave.'

'You know about that?'

'Sure. I got the lead off your e-mail. We looked up the Bureau file.'

Her eyes widened.

'I'd like to read it.'

'Perhaps we could trade. You fill in my gaps, I'll fill in yours.'

'Now you're talking.'

How had his hand found its way onto her breast? He hadn't been aware of reaching for her. Not that it mattered. She was in his arms anyway, ministering to his bruises, it seemed only natural to return the favour.

Her mouth was warm and wet, her nipple hard against his palm. He explored further and found he'd been correct in his assumptions – she wore just a pair of panties beneath her thin robe.

'You have a unique flavour,' she said. 'Your mouth tastes of blood and brandy.'

'I'm sorry.'

'I like it. You don't have any other wounds, do you? Apart from this swelling here.' She laughed as she squeezed his cock through his pants. 'Let's go to the bedroom. The kitchen's no place to fill in gaps.'

Hannah woke in the small hours of the night. The room was almost dark but he could see a faint reflection off the TV screen at the end of the bed – the screen on which he had watched the tapes of Felice fucking and sucking her way to ecstasy. That had been on his first visit to this apartment with Brigitte – who he had then screwed on this very bed. Now Felice lay beside him, the warm kiss of her hip on his, her breathing soft in the silence. The whole situation was damn weird.

Though not as weird as what Cody had told him last night, in between bouts of sex play which had left him as limp as a rag.

He turned towards the sleeping woman and a jolt of pain shot through his chest. A grunt escaped from his bruised lips. Felice stirred.

'Are you still hurting?'

'It's OK.'

'Can't you sleep?'

'I can't get that stuff you told me out of my head.'

She leant over him and kissed his lips – a leisurely caress designed to comfort not arouse. The pliant sphere of her breast pressed against him.

'You know, Hannah, there are two things I look for in a man and I thought you had them both.'

'What are they?'

'The first is an open mind.'

'I'm worried that mine's too open. Your theory is loony tunes, Felice, but you've convinced me that it's true.'

'Really?'

'Well, it fits the facts. So what's your second requirement?'

'A stiff cock.'

'I flunk on that one. You've had the best of me.'

'Give me five minutes.'

It took her less than that. With lips and tongue and a finger eased gently into his anus, she soon had Hannah as stiff as a poker. Then she lay down with her back to him and wiggled her full buttocks into his crotch. Without him moving a muscle, it seemed, his rejuvenated prick was swiftly sheathed to the hilt in her moist and hungry channel.

'This will take your mind off things,' she murmured, rocking backwards on his stem.

'You could be right,' he said, filling his hands with her bountiful breasts and nuzzling into her neck.

But even as his body responded to hers, lighting a fire that burned till dawn, one thought could not be dispelled from his brain.

How the hell was he going to break Cody's theory to Jarvis?

FORTY-THREE

JARVIS'S APARTMENT. OCTOBER 17TH. 11.45 AM.

Jarvis was in a bad way. It was around thirty hours since she had had sex and the fever was upon her in its full fury.

The mist had started to descend during the flight back from New Mexico with Hannah by her side. Maybe that's why she had been so brusque with him. The pressure of maintaining a professional veneer had told on her and she'd shut him out. On reflection that was stupid. God, did she ever need a shoulder to cry on. It wasn't as if she could break this particular addiction by going cold turkey.

She'd rung the Bureau and left a message for Stone saying she was finishing off a report on the New Mexico trip at home. Which only postponed the evil hour when she'd have to face both him and Hannah. She could hardly concentrate right now. She turned from her computer screen and picked up the phone.

'Damnit, Quinn – be there!' she moaned as the ringing tone sounded in her ear. But, as it had done since her return the previous evening, it was only answered by a nasal invitation to leave a message. The snake-hipped blonde with the wicked mouth was obviously not in town.

Jarvis crashed the receiver back into its cradle and flung herself face down on the bed. A large black object mocked her from a few inches away. Such was her condition that even Kate Karlsen's dildo hadn't been able to ease her frustration. She'd cradled it inside her all night but it had only scratched the surface of her desire. She craved more than self-stimulation – she needed the heat of another's passion to satisfy her urges.

The phone rang and Jarvis snatched it up.

'Quinn?' she cried.

'No – it's Hannah.'

'Oh.' There was no way she could hide her disappointment.

'Look, Jarvis, can I come over? We've got to talk.'

She forced herself to take a deep breath. He was right – they did have plenty to discuss.

'All right. I'll meet you in half an hour. In the coffee shop across the street.'

At all costs she knew she couldn't allow him into her apartment the way she felt right now.

'Jesus, what happened to you?' said Jarvis as Hannah sat down opposite her.

He gave her a lop-sided grin as he sugared his espresso. 'I tripped and ran into the sidewalk.'

'Ran into some blonde's boyfriend, more likely.'

'Are you psychic, Jarvis? He was her husband, as a matter of fact.'

'What a sleaze merchant you are.'

'Please, partner, let's drop the holier-than-thou. Your halo has slipped since your night flight with a certain helicopter pilot.'

Jarvis blinked at him. *How did he know?* Not that it mattered. The way things were he was going to find out sooner or later. The cup in her grasp rattled against the saucer.

'You've got it bad, haven't you?' he said, reaching to still her hand. 'The course has changed you like it changed Cody and the others, right?'

She nodded. There wasn't much point in denying it.

'It's Leonard. The stupid thing is, I don't know how or why he's done it.'

'I do.'

She stared at him.

'At least I think I do,' he continued, 'and you're not going to like it.'

'Try me.'

'First off – Cody's back.'

'When?'

'When we were in New Mexico. Brigitte tipped me off. So I went to see her last night. She's spent the last three weeks researching her new book. It's about alien contact.'

She pulled a wry face. '*Close Encounters* – that kind of thing?'

'*Very Close Encounters*. She's researching alien experiments into human behaviour.'

'What?'

'She thinks there's a programme of alien investigation into man's – well, woman's – libido.'

Jarvis began to giggle, she couldn't help it. Especially as Hannah's battered face earnestly implored her to take him seriously.

'Look, just hear me out, Jarvis. Cody's got it documented. Things like this have happened before, she says. There's been a series of experiments by some alien intelligence into the female sex impulse.'

Jarvis's laughter shut off like a tap.

'So what's Leonard then? A sexy spaceman?'

'In a way, I suppose. He's the human face of alien research. I mean, I haven't got it all figured out yet—'

'Knock it off, you dipstick. This is just the kind of flaky, unscientific mumbo-jumbo I'd expect from a sex-crazed moron like you. You'd love to imagine women cavorting round the planet spreading their legs in the cause of alien research. "Give it to me now, Agent Hannah, the sex programme is at stake!" You'll get yourself locked up if you're not careful.'

'That's not what I'm saying!'

'Isn't it? You'd swallow any bunch of bullshit if it wore a see-through brassiere and silk stockings.'

He drained his coffee. 'So how do you explain the fact that since you spent a week with Leonard all you want to do is get laid? Pete the pilot's not the only one, is he? I've been checking. There's a rumour in the Chicago office about a red-headed hooker giving it away for free in a hotel on the

Loop. Didn't you stop over on your return? And who's this Quinn you're so keen to talk to?'

She could have killed him. Smashed the glass sugar bowl on the table and lunged for his throat – except, as she glared at him, she could see only sadness in his eyes.

'I'm sorry, Jarvis. I've made a hash of telling you about this.' He scribbled on a paper napkin. 'Here's Cody's address. Go and talk to her. She'll make more sense than I can.'

Jarvis took the paper from him.

'You look terrible,' she said.

He shrugged.

'I'll see her if you promise me one thing.'

'Which is?'

'You'll go home to bed. Alone.'

FORTY-FOUR

MAXWELL, VIRGINIA. 2.05 PM.

It seemed like Cody was waiting for her. She buzzed Jarvis up at once and was standing at her door when the elevator came to a halt.

The woman was smaller than Jarvis had imagined. Maybe it was the image of her from those VCR tapes – all that opulent white flesh in the arms of those rough men – that had led her to expect a big blowsy tramp. In person, Felice was a couple of inches shorter than Jarvis and stylishly dressed in black slacks and a bronze cashmere sweater. By her side, in her oldest skirt and a sweatshirt, Jarvis felt like a slob.

'Make yourself comfortable,' said Cody as she shoo-ed a fat tabby off the living-room sofa. 'Can I offer you refreshment of some kind? Coffee? Soda?'

Jarvis bristled. She had not rushed over for a ladies' tea-party.

'Nothing thank you, Ms Cody. I'd like to get straight to the point.'

'Which is?'

'I've just heard that garbage you told Hannah. Did you tell him before or after you fucked him?'

Cody seemed amused. 'I can understand why you're angry, Agent Jarvis.'

Jarvis blew a fuse.

'Hey, don't start with that psychotherapy bullshit. I want you to repeat to me everything you told Hannah. If I'm not convinced you believe every word you say I'm going to book you for perverting the course of a Federal investigation.'

'OK.' Cody seemed unmoved by the threat. She studied Jarvis's face intently, concern in her big almond eyes. 'First I'm going to play you a recording I made a couple of days ago. It would be helpful if you could relax. Here.' She scooped the tabby off an armchair and placed it on Jarvis's knees. 'As far as I know, no one ever died of apoplexy stroking a cat.'

Jarvis stiffened. She'd never seen the appeal of furry animals. But the cat settled on her lap like a rug and at once began to purr. As Cody placed a small cassette machine on the low table in front of them Jarvis found her hand automatically fondling the soft pelt of the contented beast. She took a deep breath and tried to clear her head.

FORTY-FIVE

TRANSCRIPT OF FELICE CODY'S INTERVIEW WITH
MARTHA McKEE. FORT MUSGRAVE. OCTOBER 12TH.

MARTHA: You want to talk about what happened at the lake?

FELICE: I'm more interested in what led up to it.

M: That makes a change. All everybody ever wanted to talk about was what they called 'the incident'. And they treated me like I was some crazy whore or something. Well, I wasn't no whore, I swear to God. Though I admit, for a while back then, I *was* a little crazy.

F: Tell me.

M: I know now what it was that set me off. I was seeing this new doctor in town. A handsome fellow, very polite and slick and he was real popular. He had lots of fancy diplomas from out of state and he was supposed to be an expert on the mind as well as doing regular doctoring.

F: What was his name?

M: Dr Leonard.

F: And why did you visit him?

M: Well, as I said, he was reckoned to be some kind of mind doctor and when I started acting funny my Mom sent me to see him.

F: So you were behaving strangely before you even met him?

M: Let me explain. My Dad died when I was little and my Mom brought me up. I was her only child and she was real protective – and strict. So I reckon I was pretty naïve for my age.

F: Which was eighteen?

M: Just turned. Some of my schoolfriends had had two kids by that time and quite a few were proper married ladies. Me, I knew nothing about boys. I had a job in town at the store on the haberdasher counter. I'd blush if a man came by with his wife to look at ribbons or anything. After work I'd go to bible class and stay home with Mom. Believe me, I'm not making this up. I was the original shrinking violet. Then, about six months before I first saw Dr Leonard, Mom started courting. That really shook me. Arthur Brennan was a home-town guy who'd been working out east, where he'd made a lot of money in the clothing business. When his dad died he'd come back to look after his mother and sisters and he opened a ladies store in town. Boy, was it an overnight sensation. People came from miles to gawk at all the big-city fashions. Naturally the women threw themselves at Arthur and it didn't hurt that he looked like Clark Gable. But Arthur liked my mother best. She was a fine-looking woman, book-learned and cultured. They just hit it right off.

F: How did you feel about it?

M: Jealous, of course. It changed everything. You can imagine. What made it worse was that I suddenly discovered I did like men – at least, men like Arthur. Boys my age – forget it! But handsome, sophisticated, good-looking men were another story. The trouble was, there were no others apart from Arthur.

F: What about Leonard?

M: I'm getting to him. At first I didn't want to go see him but my mother insisted. I'd started staying home all day. I'd say I felt ill and I'd moon around the house. I did it so often I lost my job at the store. Of course, Dr Briggs, our regular doctor, couldn't find anything the matter with me. So my Mom got the idea of me seeing Dr Leonard. Him being a student of psychoanalysis, maybe he could help me – that's what she said. I kicked up a storm and refused. This went on until Arthur stepped in. He took me to lunch at the Egmont Towers dining room and treated me like a real lady. And he made me a proposition – if I agreed to have consultations with Dr Leonard, he'd offer me a job in his fashion store. Well, most girls my age would just die for an opportunity like that. So I said yes. The next day I went to see Dr Leonard.

F: How long was this before the picnic at the lake?

M: Two or three months, I guess.

F: What happened?

M: At first he frightened me. His eyes were so big and green and staring. And he wanted to talk about my body and the way I felt as a woman, things I'd never discussed with anyone. But he swore that everything we said was just between us. He got me to talk about Mom and Arthur and the way I felt. And when lots of angry, bitter stuff came tumbling out he didn't blame me. That made me feel much better and I looked forward to our next meeting. On about my third visit he explained how I could give myself pleasure.

F: He showed you how to masturbate?

M: He sure did.

F: That must have been a shock.

M: I trusted him by then. And, boy, was I grateful. Though I was damned angry no one had told me before how much fun I could have with my own body. It was soon after that that he touched me fully.

F: What do you mean by that?

M: I think you know, honey.

F: I'd like you to tell me. It's most important.

M: He said he wanted to hypnotise me and I agreed. It was a hot sunny afternoon, I remember that, and he was sitting opposite me in a big old leather armchair. Then suddenly it was night and I was at a barn dance with music and people whirling around. It was a big stuffy barn with a stage at one end and an area for dancing. Everyone was having a high old time and I was in the thick of it thinking, this isn't really me. I was never much of a dancer, too self-conscious and clumsy-footed. But here I was throwing myself into the arms of the boys and clapping my hands and jigging in time. I didn't recognise anybody but that didn't matter. Everyone was laughing and smiling and the band had a fiddle and I always loved that. Then the boys –

they were all handsome farm lads – began to snatch kisses off me and the other girls. Just little pecks at first then longer, deeper ones. Mmm, were they good! I'd never had a man's tongue in my mouth before and it scared and thrilled me all at once. Then a blond boy squeezed my breast through my dress and, ooh, it was like getting an electric shock. He kept his hand there as he kissed me and I could feel his fingers fiddling with the buttons on my bodice. He got his hand inside and he kind of grunted in his throat when he felt my bare skin. As he pressed against me, I thought of Mom. The boy had this big thing in his pants and it dug into my belly as he held me tight. Was this what Arthur did with Mom? I wondered. I'd bet he did. Well, I thought, if it's all right for her then I want some too. Then I was pulled away by another boy to join the dance with my bodice all undone and the tops of my breasts showing. I didn't care – hell, there were other girls there showing more than me and the guys were all over them too. Soon I was letting the boys put their hands down my dress. It was wild! And I knew it could only get wilder. All the boys had bulging pants and their hands were going just everywhere. There wasn't much proper dancing going on, you understand. Soon there were two or three boys at me. They had my titties in their hands and one of them was scrabbling up under my skirts tugging at my pants. Then they pulled them off and there were fingers in-between my legs and hands all over my body.

F: Weren't you frightened?

M: Some. But it was like I was riding a big fast horse and I was determined to hang on even though it was travelling a damn sight quicker than I'd ever gone before. Then, to my surprise, the boys let go of me and there was someone else there lifting me up. It was Dr Leonard, only he was somehow burlier and more rugged. He had on this Stetson and a check shirt and he looked like a real cowboy. He pushed through the crowd and carried me out the door in his arms as if I was as light as tumbleweed. He walked into the pasture nearby. Nobody followed us, we were quite alone though I could hear the fiddle music and the laughter from inside the barn. The doctor laid me down in the grass and brushed the hair from my face. Then he kissed me and I kissed him back and my heart just burst. Kissing the boys had been a thrill but this was different, it was like he was a powerful animal and he wanted to eat me right up even though he was being so gentle and tender. And, boy, did I want to be eaten! I pushed my naked breasts against him and wrapped my legs around his hips. He grinned at me in the moonlight and then a funny thing happened – his face seemed to blur and suddenly he wasn't Dr Leonard any more, he was Arthur. It was like a miracle. His clothes disappeared too, least I wasn't aware of him undressing. There was just Arthur, naked and strong, holding me in his arms like I'd dreamt of. Except this was a million times better because he was guiding my hands to the golden wand that thrust up from his belly. It was soft like silk to the touch yet hard as timber beneath the skin and I knew I had to have it deep inside my body. He spread my legs and stroked me till I was almost out of my mind. Then he made love to me properly under the big fat yellow moon.

F: And then?

M: I don't remember much after that, except leaving Dr Leonard's house. It was still a sunny afternoon and I couldn't believe it. I went home and slept for a long, long time. And when I woke up I needed a man beside me. I guess I'm the only person around who lost her cherry in a dream. I've never been the same since.

FORTY-SIX

CODY'S APARTMENT. 2.45 PM.

'Don't say anything,' said Cody as the tape-machine clicked off. 'There's a few other things you should know.'

Jarvis watched the author in a daze as she reached for a file on the shelf behind her. The cat on her lap stirred itself from slumber, slipped to the floor and stalked out of the door, its task accomplished. Jarvis was no longer burning up with anger, she was confused and very, very curious.

'I've been researching unexplained phenomena for years,' said Cody. 'At first it was a hobby, then an obsession. Paranormal events, unscientific science, weird behaviour of all sorts – I love it. And there's an entire community of people out there who share my interest. When I started writing books I found I'd tapped into a network of contacts throughout the world. My family and colleagues used to think I was some kind of solitary spinster with no real friends and no romance in my life but that wasn't the true picture.

'I didn't sign on Leonard's course entirely by chance. One of my correspondents put me on to it and told me how it had given a sensual dimension to her life. That interested me, of course, because I was well aware I was missing out, though I'd kind of resigned myself to it. However, some of the things she said tied in with my obsession with weird phenomena. She told me that after meeting Leonard she became so crazy for sex that, on one occasion, she forced a man to make love to her at gunpoint. She went on to say that the madness that came over her must have been like the feelings of the girls in the Lake Musgrave Incident.

'That was the first I'd heard of Lake Musgrave but I began to check it out. It was damn difficult to get anywhere because it had never been officially reported. No charges were filed against the girls and the relatives were so embarrassed they erected a wall of silence around the event. But I had a lucky break. Through my contacts I was able to get in touch with the grandson of the Reverend Andrews, the minister who took Martha and the girls on that church picnic. He sent me his grandfather's journal for nineteen thirty-four and in there I found a fascinating account of what happened.'

'I know,' Jarvis butted in. 'The Reverend believed that the new doctor in town had driven the girls insane by subjecting them to hypnotherapy. I read it in the file.'

Cody smiled, her almond eyes gleaming. 'And the doctor's name was Rolf Leonard. You can imagine how I felt, seeing that name. I knew then I had to sign on for the course.'

'But, Felice, that's got to be pure coincidence. The guy who treated Martha can't be the same man we both met this year – unless he can work his dirty tricks from beyond the grave.'

Cody shrugged. 'Hear me out – there's more.' She opened the yellow file in front of her and pulled out a pile of photocopied press cuttings.

'Nebraska nineteen-eight. A mob runs wild in Sunfish City, springs a man from jail and strings him up outside the courthouse. The man is an animal doctor – a vet – and he's from out of town. To many people, especially the womenfolk, he's a miracle worker. To others he's a fraud, a devil-worshipper and a seducer of women. Guess his name.'

Jarvis stared at Cody. 'Rolf Leonard, I suppose.'

'You got it.'

'That's truly weird.'

'More than that.'

Cody pulled a piece of paper from the pile, a cutting from the *Sunfish Sentinel* of May 1908. A dense article recounted the activities of the lynch mob that had rampaged through the town on Saturday night; it was accompanied by a series of line drawings. Jarvis's eye was drawn to one, larger than the rest, in which a crew of bearded men with blazing eyes were dragging a man in a frock coat and winged collar towards the waiting noose. The victim was clean shaven but for a small moustache and the artist had made much of his luxuriant curly hair. His features, despite the poor quality of the reproduction, were without doubt those of the man who had turned Jarvis's life upside down just a week ago.

'Oh my God,' she muttered softly.

'It's an incredible story,' said Cody. 'He was only being held in jail for his own protection. In the next cell was a farmer who'd shot his wife to death after he'd caught her entertaining a couple of cowpokes in his bed. He claimed that Dr Leonard had done more than treat a sick cow, he'd turned his wife into an adulterous woman. The mob set the farmer free but he gave himself up the next day, stood trial for murder three weeks later and was acquitted.'

'Any other fascinating scraps of information?'

'Just one. They buried Leonard in an unmarked grave but unknown hands turned it into something of a shrine. They say whores from the brothel on Jefferson Street looked after it. I visited it myself and there were fresh flowers on the spot.'

Jarvis looked sour. 'Don't tell me, the gravestone read "Laid in peace".'

Felice laughed. 'So you do have a sense of humour, Agent Jarvis, I was beginning to wonder.'

'To be honest, Ms Cody, I don't find this whole business so all-fired funny.'

'Nor do I, believe me. I could tell you more about my research. For instance there's a nineteenth-century memoir by the legendary courtesan Florence Beauchamp, which begins: "I was first introduced to the pleasures of the flesh at the age of sixteen by a handsome doctor called Leonard" – but I can see you're not in the mood.'

Jarvis sighed heavily. The fever had returned in all its intensity and she found it hard to focus on all this historical stuff. She had to get to the one thing that was bothering her and then leave. Maybe Quinn would be back. The thought concentrated her mind.

'There's some things I'm never in the mood for, Ms Cody. So why don't we get it over with. Tell me about the aliens.'

'You don't believe that there may be other life forms beyond ours, I take it?'

'You take correctly.'

'Your partner is not so cynical, Agent Jarvis.'

'My partner would believe anything if you were pulling his dick at the time.'

Colour blazed in Cody's cheek and she gripped Jarvis's hand. 'Come *on*, Bonny, don't be so cheap. We're in this together.'

Jarvis wrenched her hand away.

'No!' she cried. 'We are *not* together. I have no common ground with a woman who believes in fucking spacemen!'

She began to shake uncontrollably, her teeth chattering as if she were freezing yet she was burning up.

'Listen.' Cody's hand was in hers again and this time she clung on to it. 'You've been touched by Leonard – that's how Martha puts it. All of us who've been touched by him have a bond. I know how you feel. It's new to you and you hate it. But that will change. You'll harness this urge and see it as a gift. In a few weeks you'll be in control again, I promise.'

'Will I?'

Cody hugged her and Jarvis allowed the other woman's embrace to still her quaking.

'What I told Agent Hannah is what I sincerely believe. I believe there are other intelligences in the universe. I believe there are non-human life forms out there taking an interest in us. I believe that Leonard is a manifestation of that and his continued reappearance in our history signals an experiment by whatever he represents.'

'But why the sex? I don't understand.'

'Because this other intelligence wants to examine people like us – intelligent, independent, childless women. What's the link between every life form you can think of? From the flowers in the field to the microbes in the skin to the lichen on the trees – what's the thing they and mankind have in common? We breed. It's the one safe response to the question "what's the purpose of life?" Answer – "to create more life".'

'So?'

'You and I and Kate Karlsen and Stacey Pine and Madeleine Simons and all those other women on Leonard's course have chosen not to procreate. We've pursued careers and cut ourselves off from sex by choice despite the fact that we are ideal mother material. I think – and it's only my theory – that this is the reason why we are the subjects of this particular experiment.'

Jarvis seized on this. 'You mean there have been others?'

'Sure, all the time. I think we are of great interest to other life forms. As a rule, however, their attentions are not so invasive.'

Jarvis shook her head.

'You think I'm mad, don't you?'

Jarvis didn't answer. Felice smiled and took her hand.

'I think the point of Leonard's experiment is to see if the sex impulse can be controlled.'

'So what did the – aliens – do to me?' Jarvis's head was spinning. She couldn't believe she'd even asked the question.

'I think they've examined your most important sex organ – your brain – and readjusted your sex impulse. But they haven't got the adjustment right. It's like the volume's turned up too loud.'

'I still think it's mad, Felice.'

'I'm not saying I'm right but that's my theory. Whatever Leonard is, it's damn clever. I've spoken to quite a few women now who've been touched like we have and each time it's different.'

'What do you mean?'

'Well, with Martha, like you heard, Leonard made love to her at a barn dance and then turned into her mother's lover, Arthur. This had a powerful effect on her. It's not on that tape but she seduced him a week later and then she realised she was quite happy to let her mother keep him. Luckily the mother never found out.

'In my case, I found myself up a mountain at sunrise and there Leonard turned into my ex-fiancé. David was the only lover I'd ever had and he dumped me a week before our wedding when I was twenty-one. Basically it stopped my sex life in its tracks and I used to tell everyone I'd never trust a man again. But on top of that mountain David was the boy I used to know and I loved him just like before. I'd forgotten what it was like.

'After the course was over and I realised that sex was back in my life, I went to see David. I'd always kept track of him – he works in a law office down in Atlanta. I surprised him at the end of the day and made him take me to a bar. He'd gone to seed, lost his hair and put on weight. I didn't care. I had him fuck me in the ladies john and that was the most therapeutic experience of my life. I haven't looked back. He calls me regularly but I've no interest in him now. You could say I've moved on.'

Jarvis was silent.

'You don't have to tell me what happened to you,' said Cody, 'but I bet Leonard became someone else when he was making love to you.'

'Yes.' Jarvis's voice was barely a whisper.

'I suggest you think hard about that person's importance to you. And then, if you've got the chance, honey, go fuck his brains out!'

FORTY-SEVEN

JARVIS'S APARTMENT. 5.50 PM.

Jarvis stood for a moment at her front door, trying to get a grip on her swirling senses. Her hands were shaking so much the key wouldn't go in the lock. The fever raging through her body was worse – far worse – than it had ever been. Returning from Cody's place, it was a miracle she hadn't stopped the car and thrown herself at some guy in the street. *Any* guy – provided he could fuck. The tops of her thighs were slick with sex juice and her panties were soaked through. She didn't know what she was going to do. Not to put too fine a point upon it, she needed cock.

To her amazement the door opened as she stood there quivering.

'Hiya, Special Agent, I've been waiting for you.'

Her heart sank. That Lovelace was inside her locked apartment did not surprise her – in her experience he was always where you didn't want him to be. But even as her lips curled into a snarl and she snapped, 'You've got a damn nerve,' her loins pulsed and a voice in her head whispered: 'Problem solved!'

He pulled her inside with one massive hand. 'My, you're in a state, aren't you? Looks like you've got it *real* bad.'

'I don't know what you mean.' She pushed past him into the small kitchen and pulled a bottle of mineral water from the refrigerator. 'Say what you've got to say and get out.'

'Don't be silly, Bonny. You know it doesn't work like that. Ain't you got any proper booze?'

Jarvis opened a cupboard filled with bottles. She'd

rounded up all the alcohol in the place and stashed it out of sight when she returned from New Mexico.

'Help yourself,' she said ungraciously and walked into the living room, aware of the skin of her thighs slip-sliding together in her wetness. God, she must give off signals like a bitch in heat. Lovelace was not a man to miss a message like that.

He came into the room with glasses in one hand and a bottle in the other.

'Why don't you take your top off?' he said.

'Get lost.'

He sat on the couch and poured two glasses of neat vodka.

'I mean it. It's been a while since I've had the pleasure of surveying the prettiest tits in the Bureau.'

'Not this time. There's nothing you can give me now on this case.'

'That's where you're wrong.'

For a big man he could move quickly. His hand was round her wrist before she was aware of it. He yanked hard and she fell across him, the length of her body pressing into the granite of his bulk. A huge arm trapped her there.

'You're shaking like a leaf, honey, and I know why.' His face loomed over hers, the nose huge and hooked, the eyes like chips of ice. 'You've got the nympho disease, haven't you, Bonny? Just like all those respectable vanishing ladies. Well, it so happens that I found a couple of those girls for you. I put your partner onto Karlsen and Pine. So, if it makes you feel any better, you owe me.'

Her mouth opened but nothing came out. What had gone before in the horse-trading of their relationship was now irrelevant. Up till now she'd never let him touch her and she'd doled out her favours – a hand-job here, a peek at her breasts there – strictly as a trade-off. It was the only way to get information.

It seemed he always had something she wanted and, despite what she'd just said, right now that was as true as ever. She could see the object of her desire bulging obscenely against the black cloth stretched over his crotch.

He chuckled, a sound like gravel rattling in a pan, and ran

his thumb along the fleshy curve of her upper lip. The touch was like fine sandpaper on her jumping nerves. She opened her mouth and lapped at him, kitten-like. She couldn't help herself. She knew there would soon be lots of other things she wouldn't be able to help.

He probed her mouth with his finger and she sucked on it like a baby at the nipple. Then he trailed the wet digit along her jawline and down her throat into the neck of her sweatshirt.

'Off,' he said.

She hesitated for a second then pulled the garment over her head and sat back. Her pouting breasts thrust forward, the cleavage accentuated by the tight clasp of her lacework brassiere.

'That too,' he said, his eyes glistening as her fingers found the catch between her shoulder blades and the halter slipped from her full bosom. Her tits shifted as they were freed, out and down a fraction, their swollen tips a raspberry red.

'My, my,' he murmured. 'Lookit those bells swing.'

Jarvis swallowed, her fingers were on her nipples, pinching hard – maybe the pain would stem the mist of lust that fogged her brain.

A big hand landed on the back of her neck and pulled her to him, crushing her mouth to his.

It was a coarse and brutal embrace – and it was just what she wanted. She'd never allowed him to kiss her before. She'd never allowed him to handle her like this before – and she knew it was just the beginning.

She tore his shirt open and crushed her tits against his slab of a chest. He was very hairy and the coarse mat scraped against her tender flesh, enflaming her more. She pulled his zipper down and reached inside for him. He was hard like bone, his cock so massive she could hardly get her fingers round it. She pulled it clumsily into the open.

'Fuck me, Lovelace,' she whispered. 'I want it in me now.'

He squeezed a tit, almost enclosing it in his huge hand. 'I never imagined you'd be so enthusiastic, Agent Jarvis.'

'Come *on*, Lovelace,' she said, her voice now urgent.

'In a minute maybe. We don't want to rush things, do we?'

She attempted to climb onto his lap and place his big poker between her legs. He laughed and held her off. His resistance infuriated her – she was dying to be filled to the hilt.

'For God's sake, Lovelace – what the hell do you want me to do?'

He grinned. 'What I want is for you to stand up and show me your pussy.'

She climbed unsteadily to her feet and unzipped her skirt. Her white cotton panties were wet through with her juice and clung to every contour of her loins. She stepped close and let him look while he sipped his drink.

'Take them off.'

She did it with shaking hands, peeling the wet material down until her nude and hairless pussy was revealed to his gaze.

He savoured the sight.

'Now jerk off.'

'You bastard!'

'Do it, Bonny.'

She swallowed hard and reached for her untouched glass. The vodka went down in one gulp, masking her inhibitions as she went to work.

She put her foot up on the arm of the couch and used both hands, plunging her fingers into her syrupy depths. As she did so, he gave her obscene instructions – 'Spread your lips', 'Show me your clit', 'Put a finger up your ass' – and she did all he said. Did it moreover with helpless energy, knowing that otherwise she wouldn't get what she really wanted – that great solid thing now jutting up like a club from his loins.

A small thrill gripped her, then another but they didn't touch the deep desire blazing inside. She cried out in frustration and fell to her knees.

He laughed and threw her face down over an armchair. Then his spade-like hand rose in the air and crashed down onto the creamy flesh of her ass. She yelled as the pain shot through her.

Smack! He cracked a hand across her seat again, turning

her buttocks crimson. Her ass was on fire and the pain was turning into something else – an aching void that *had* to be filled . . .

'Please, Lovelace, I beg you!'

'Beg me what?'

'Please fuck me!'

Suddenly a solid baton of flesh was lodged into the upturned cleft of her sex and at last the broad head of his monstrous tool began to stretch her wide.

She moaned in delirium as the vast limb was inserted and his muscular torso pressed down her back, pinning her to the seat like a butterfly to a board.

'Yes, yes!' she cried, the giant prick sinking into the wet mouth of her cunt. Then the words became formless sounds in her throat, drowned in a tide of sensation that flooded her body as he filled her up.

After the first orgasm had died away she muttered, 'God, Lovelace, what took you so long?'

He cackled nastily into her ear. 'Honey, I just wanted to hear you beg.'

Later, at about ten, Jarvis slumped at the kitchen table in her bathrobe and continued her assault on the vodka. She'd showered after Lovelace had left but she felt far from clean. She shifted uneasily in her seat. After he'd thoroughly ploughed her cunt he'd plunged his colossal penis into her anus and she was feeling the effect. He'd been as brutish in bed as she'd always suspected and he'd certainly made the most of his rare opportunity. She swore he'd never get another one.

Jarvis had to face the fact that the sex fever had taken over her life. Felice had warned her it would at first – but how long was that precisely? At least the bout with Lovelace had placed it at bay for the moment.

What she needed in her life right now was a friend. Someone who could satisfy her cravings safely and keep her out of trouble. Felice had urged her to think about her experience with Leonard but she'd resisted it so far. She didn't want to consider the implications of what had happened in her vision on the beach. But . . .

Her hand reached for the phone. There *was* one person she could call.

Before she could pick up the receiver it rang.

'Hello, darling,' said a longed-for voice.

'Quinn,' shrieked Jarvis. 'Where the hell have you been?'

FORTY-EIGHT

BUREAU HEADQUARTERS. OCTOBER 18TH. 10.35 AM.

Stone drummed his fingers impatiently on his empty desk, so hard that Hannah fancied he could see the miniature American flag next to the blotter tremble.

'Damnit,' said Stone, as much surprise as irritation in his voice. 'It's not like Agent Jarvis to be late.'

He stared at Hannah, almost as if he were noticing him for the first time. 'What the hell happened to you? Somebody's boyfriend punch you out?'

Hannah grinned as best he could. His lip was split and the bottom half of his face was as tender as finest sirloin. Shaving had been impossible.

'I slipped down the steps of my building,' he said, half believing it himself by now. 'Why is it everyone jumps to damaging conclusions about me?'

Stone did not respond. He glanced at his watch. Jarvis was now nine minutes late. His face was like thunder.

'OK,' he said, 'we start without her. Give me a sit rep and make it snappy. I can't waste any more time.'

Hannah made it as snappy as he could. Frankly, it helped having to speed along. There were some things he had no wish to elaborate on – like Jarvis's behaviour since returning from New Mexico. Not to mention Cody's research on alien experimentation. But that was hardly a topic he could gloss over.

'Holy shit!' yelled Stone and slammed the desk in front of him with an open palm. This time the flag did tremble, no doubt about it.

'Are you telling me in all seriousness, Agent Hannah, that bug-eyed monsters from outer space have been giving some of the most respectable women in America sex fever?'

'Well, they *have* developed sex fever – we've always known that. Cody has simply found historical precedents and, given her interest in the paranormal, she's come up with a theory that fits the facts.'

Stone stood up violently, sending his chair skittering across the floor behind him.

'Fits the facts!' His tone was contemptuous. 'That woman is a screwball.'

'A very successful screwball, sir. The military think so much of her they say they want her to start back in the laboratory next Monday. And her last book was three months on the *New York Times* bestsellers list. She's a real celebrity in her field.'

Stone's face suddenly relaxed and the deep rumble of his laughter took Hannah by surprise.

'I'm glad you reminded me,' he said. 'Felice Cody is part of the entertainment industry. And you've bought a ticket to the show.'

'Come on, Jeff, I'm not saying I believe every word. But how do you explain the ranch in the Antelope Mountains? The place we saw hadn't been occupied in the last three years let alone last week.'

'Well, you must have seen the wrong fucking place. It's big country down there. The pair of you are hardly experienced mountain types, are you?'

'Not exactly—'

'In any case, Agent Jarvis should never have gone back. She's not well at the moment – which is obviously the reason she's not at this meeting.'

'But how do you explain the book? The inscription in Cody's hand-writing?'

'Are you sure it's Cody's writing? It sounds a hell of a flimsy basis on which to hang a whole theory of alien experiments on the human race. Anyhow' – Stone returned to his seat, looking much less agitated than when he had stood up – 'I've come to a conclusion.'

'Yes?'

'We bury the thing right now. We'll nail this pussy-expert Leonard when he pops up with some new scam. Until then we'll file the investigation away in Jarvis's secret archive and get on with some serious work.'

'But we can't bury it. What about Cody? This entire case is the subject of her next book. It's going to be all over the media. It's bound to be an international sensation.'

Stone laughed again. 'So? It's just a piece of fluff on the paranormal, Hannah. No one with any brains takes that stuff seriously. Steven Spielberg can make a movie out of it for all I care. Remember what I said about Cody's books when we first talked through this business?'

'Remind me again.'

'Should be published as fiction. And that's the truth. Do you get it?'

'Yes. Sir.'

Hannah went back to his desk and called Jarvis. And left another message on her machine – the third that morning. Where the hell was she? He began to feel something he had never thought he would feel for that red-headed ball-breaker.

Concern for her safety.

FORTY-NINE

BALDRY, PENNSYLVANIA. 2.30 PM.

Jarvis was in freefall, cut loose from the constraints of her old life, about to embark on an adventure that would scandalise her former self.

She had a new career. As a whore.

The idea had taken root some time during the night. Maybe at the point when she had opened the second bottle of Stolichnaya. More likely when Quinn had taken her over the edge with a double-ended dildo which curved upwards into her own well-juiced pussy.

At any rate, during a lull between one swooping orgasm and the next, Jarvis had said, 'I want to be a hooker.'

Quinn let Jarvis's swollen left nipple slip from her lips. 'Are you crazy?'

'Probably. But it makes sense. I can't function without sex right now. I have to fuck night and day. How can I do my job like this? I could if my job was hooking.'

Quinn laughed, a sly little chuckle, and shifted her slim hips to send a thrill reverberating through Jarvis's sex as it gorged on the dummy cock that linked their loins.

'I'm serious,' said Jarvis. 'But I need an up-scale operation. No street corners, no pimps, no cheap hotels.'

'You're really not kidding?'

'Quinn, I don't kid. I need a working vacation in a discreet and expensive whorehouse. Actually' – she slipped a finger between the girl's pert buttocks and tickled her rosehole – 'I think I know of one.'

★ ★ ★

Chris Shaw and Kate Karlsen were open to the idea – Stacey Pine was another matter. But Pine was in session, dispensing discipline, when Jarvis arrived and so her attitude was academic.

'She won't mind,' Karlsen had said on the phone, 'not when she knows you're one of us.'

And that was the crux of the matter. Jarvis was no longer keeping tabs on these women, observing their unconventional behaviour like a scientist peering down a microscope. She was one of them.

Karlsen looked younger than she'd expected. In the file shots she had appeared stressed out and weary, far older than her twenty-seven years. Now she was glowing with health and energy.

'It's fucking that does it,' she said as she took Jarvis's hand. 'Chris lines the men up and I knock'em over. There's one upstairs for you right now.'

He was a florid type of guy, a bigshot round the boardroom table. He had neither time nor words to spare. That suited Jarvis just fine.

'Suck my dick,' he said as he unbelted his towelling robe. 'And when it's stiff, get up on top and shake your stuff.'

Jarvis tongued his balls and ate his flaccid joint till it began to grow like a swelling balloon. Then she climbed onto his prone body and began to move.

There was plenty of her to shake and that was what he liked. She placed her palms on either side of his head and titty-whipped him with her swinging breasts until he was drooling with pleasure. And all the time she ground her pubis down on his thick pole, swivelling her hips and screwing her loins into him to extract every nuance of pleasure from the invasion.

He couldn't last long with this treatment. She just had time to take care of herself as he squirted inside her, slipping two fingers into her crotch to strum her clit and catch her thrill before it slipped away, like his deflating cock.

'I can see you love your work,' he grunted as he got dressed. 'If I had more time I'd stick around.'

She was glad he was on a tight schedule, she didn't want to have to wait.

Next up was a little bull of a guy. Younger, forceful – and keen, so he said, on women's asses.

'Bend over and stick it out,' he said to her. 'Yeah, just like that. Wow! It's like a big white peach.'

Then he took her by surprise. He got down on his knees and kissed her buttocks, kneading the resilient mass of flesh in his fingers until her knees trembled. Then he put his mouth to her crack and went to work with his tongue. She heard herself moan as he sucked in the swollen lips of her pussy and probed inside her. By the time he'd spread her moons wide and licked her circlet she was coming like a steam train.

'Jeez, you're a hot one,' he muttered as he got to his feet and bulled the thick stub of his dick into her cunt.

She knew he wouldn't be content with a straightforward doggy-style screw and, after his homage to her rear, neither was she.

'Fuck my ass,' she whispered. 'Do it in my butt until I come.'

He did just as she asked. Really, she thought, as the ragged breaths of orgasm blew through her body, she ought to be paying him.

After that she took a breather but she knew she wasn't done. Her hands shook with the fever in the shower when she adjusted the spray and, as she dried herself afterwards, even the soft towel abraded her skin like the touch of a lover. Her senses were on fire and she could only think of appeasing them. Jarvis had never taken drugs but she knew, as her fumbling fingers drew on a flimsy silk kimono, that she was high. High on fucking. And she craved more.

In the lounge downstairs she was introduced to a man and a woman. He was older, mid-sixties maybe, but tall with a head of silver hair. The woman looked young enough to be his daughter. Jarvis knew at a glance she was his current wife.

They were having tea, him in an armchair and her

opposite on a deep upholstered sofa. Jarvis sat next to the woman, as was expected, and the man poured her a cup. She killed it in one gulp and accepted a refill. She never usually drank the stuff but she was damn thirsty. She took three little bitty sandwiches and compressed them into one bite. She was hungry too.

The woman was looking at her chest. So was the guy – not surprisingly since the kimono gaped as she bent to fill her mouth. She straightened her back and the silk cut into her big tits, outlining their pouting curves and the raised buttons of her nipples.

'You're lovely,' said the woman, a slim bobbed blonde with cornflower blue eyes. Mia. 'I wish I had breasts like yours.'

Jarvis laughed and grabbed a wedge of cake. 'I've spent most of my life wishing I had a pair like yours.' She eyed Mia's small bosom encased in a tight pastel-pink sweater.

The man, Adam, chuckled. 'Why don't you ladies compare?' he said.

You smug bastard, thought Jarvis and immediately suppressed the thought. He was paying the piper and he got to play the tune.

'Oh yes,' sighed Mia. 'That is – if you wouldn't mind, Joanne?'

Jarvis licked a cake crumb off her upper lip. 'Be my guest,' she said. She was enjoying this. Being Joanne Martin again was like coming home.

Mia's hand snaked out and pulled open the kimono. Jarvis's full breasts spilled out.

'Jesus H. Christ,' said Adam, leaning forward.

Jarvis bathed in their lascivious looks. This little tea-time farce was amusing – though she hoped the action would hot up soon.

'Come on, baby, get yours out,' the man snapped and Mia quickly pulled her sweater over her head. Jarvis appraised her high-slung bowls with little pink nipples – a neat pair. It was true what she'd said earlier. She'd have swapped them for her own lush jugs at almost any point in her life. Until now.

Mia slipped an arm round Jarvis's shoulder and bent to kiss her lips. As she did so, Jarvis felt the woman's fingers close on the globe of her left breast. She opened her mouth and let Mia make all the moves. It was a bit like a hesitant teenage embrace. But, despite the clumsiness, Mia's touch excited her. She opened her mouth wider and pushed her chest into Mia's. The fusion of skin, bare tit on bare tit, enflamed her and she kissed Mia back hard.

The blue eyes flashed open wide as Jarvis's tongue thrust into her mouth. There was a message there but Jarvis couldn't read it.

'What shall we do, Mia?' she said. 'Do you want me to lick your pussy?'

The woman shook her head but the man cut in.

'Yes! Put your tongue up her snatch. It might loosen the silly bitch up.'

Mia looked less than thrilled as she allowed Jarvis to pull off her skirt and panties but Jarvis wasn't worried about that. The pair of them could play what games they liked, she was too interested in the honey-furred mystery between the woman's slim white thighs. She explored with her fingers, tracing the in-folding mouth of Mia's cunt. The lips were barely moist. By now Jarvis had worked it out – this was the husband's turn-on and the wife was play-acting. Surprise, surprise.

Jarvis shrugged off the kimono and heard Adam grunt in appreciation. But she didn't care about him, she wanted to light those cornflower blue eyes of Mia's with more than reluctance.

She put her arms round the woman and kissed her mouth gently.

'Forget about him,' she whispered. 'This is just for us.'

Small frown lines creased Mia's smooth forehead but Jarvis ignored them. The feel of the slim soft body in her arms had fired her up anew. After the men she had had earlier, satin-smooth woman flesh was just what she craved. She sank to her knees and spread Mia's alabaster thighs.

The woman quivered and tried to resist the pressure of Jarvis's hands.

'No!' she squealed as her pubis thrust forward, the

thatched triangle now pouting and prominent, just inches from Jarvis's face. 'Please, Adam,' she cried, 'don't let her.'

'Knock it off,' the man growled. 'Go ahead, sweetheart, she loves it really.'

But Jarvis needed no urging. The golden purse in front of her, with its shy, in-rolling groove was a sweetmeat she could not resist. She licked the feather-soft flesh of the woman's inner thigh, then blew a gentle breath across the wet skin. Mia squirmed and Jarvis did it to her again, on the other side, right up next to her concealed and pretty cunt.

'Oh no,' muttered Mia but there was resignation in her voice. She knew what was coming.

Jarvis blew on the blonde hairs and saw them stir. This time Mia's whole pelvis flinched in reaction, the pussy mouth jerking forward, the petals of her lips now beginning to unfurl. Jarvis detected the first faint must of the woman's excitement in her nostrils. She had the little bitch now, she had no doubt, and yet she'd hardly touched her.

She pressed a kiss on Mia's gently domed belly, then another further down. With her tongue she began to skirt the woman's pubic curls when she felt a hand pressing down on the nape of her neck.

'If you're going to do it,' breathed Mia, 'then please . . . please . . .'

'Please what, baby?' That was Adam's voice, hoarse and breathy. 'Tell the whore what you want her to do.'

'Please kiss me! Kiss my cunt!'

Mia's voice was firm now and so was the pressure on Jarvis's neck

Jarvis kissed, opening the shy pink lips of Mia's pussy and exploring the quivering petals of flesh with her lips and tongue.

The woman was no longer reluctant. Her cunt was as sweet as honey and dripping with desire. She sprawled back on the couch and Jarvis slipped her hands beneath her ass to cup and spread the cheeks while she tongued the length of the now fully-exposed crack.

As she did so, Jarvis thrust her bare buttocks backwards, acutely conscious of the empty cleft between. She hoped the old guy would take a hint and that he could give her what she needed.

She was in luck. As Mia approached a squealing, full-pitched climax, strong hands gripped Jarvis's waist. A hard baton of flesh was fed into her gaping hole and at once set up a steady beat. Jarvis savoured the pump of Adam's cock. The man knew how to fuck, she could tell from the surprisingly tender touch of his hands on her body as he traced the curves of her trembling flesh.

Stretched between husband and wife, her mouth glued to the woman's sex while the man's penis drove into her from the rear, Jarvis gave herself entirely to the pair of them.

Afterwards, the man made his wife lick Jarvis's cunt clean of spunk while the red-headed agent took his spent cock between her ever-eager lips.

'Sorry, sweetheart,' he growled. 'It won't stand up again even for you.'

A pity, thought Jarvis, though she didn't say so. She just smiled. She might be new at the hooking trade but she was catching on fast.

FIFTY

HANNAH'S APARTMENT. 6.00 PM.

Hannah was worried – as in seriously freaked out. He'd been calling Jarvis on the hour since leaving Stone's office that morning and only got her damned answering machine. In mid-afternoon he'd gone round to her apartment and failed to raise her. The super had said he'd seen her leave around eleven and her car was gone from its spot. Where the hell could she be?

In the normal course of events Jarvis's non-appearance would not have bothered Hannah. But events were not normal. Jarvis was behaving just like the other women who'd fallen under Leonard's spell. First they'd played the field at home – then they'd vanished. True, Jarvis had only been gone for half a day, but she'd no-showed Stone's meeting and switched off her cellphone. This was uncharacteristic of such a meticulous Bureau operative. On the other hand, it was entirely characteristic of a Leonard disciple with one thing on her agenda – to disappear and fuck her brains out.

The phone rang and Hannah snatched it up before it was halfway through the first tone.

'Jarvis?'

'Hey, you're quick off the mark. You're worried about her, right?'

The Brooklyn voice was unfamiliar.

'Who is this?'

'Quinn Duncan. I'm a friend of Bonny's.'

The name rang a bell. Dale Kennedy's girlfriend – the

designer punk with a stud in her nose. Jarvis's description had stuck in his mind.

'Do you know where she is?'

'Maybe.'

'So?'

'I can't say on the phone.'

'Why the hell not?'

'You know L'Escalier? I could meet you.'

Hannah had to think for a moment. It was the hot new French restaurant in town but the way she mangled the name it could have been in China.

'We'll never get a reservation.'

'I can. Meet me in half an hour. Ask for Miss Kennedy's table.'

'Couldn't we do something less elaborate?'

'Not if you wanna hear what I got to say. Wear something smart. This ain't the kind of low-class joint you Bureau guys are used to.'

She was right. L'Escalier was ritzy and pompous. A winding chrome-and-glass staircase led up to a dining room with a fountain and acres of starched white tablecloth. Hannah wore his grey-flecked designer suit without a tie. Quinn wore not much – yellow satin hotpants and a tight black vest. It was funny what women could get away with, he thought.

'Pleased to meetya, Special Agent,' said Quinn, holding out a small hand. 'Bonny never told me you were such a hunk. You bin in a fight or somethin'?'

Hannah gave her a perfunctory grin as he took his seat. 'Where is she?'

'Not so fast. Let's order.'

'I'm not hungry. I'd just like to find Agent Jarvis as soon as possible.'

'My, you are concerned.'

'I'm in a hurry.'

'Well, Mr Special Agent, here's the deal. I *am* hungry. I need to build up my protein level. When I'm done, I'll try to help you out.'

'What are you? A cheap dyke whore?'

'Close. Expensive would be more accurate. In case you haven't noticed this joint is stratospheric price-wise. And you're paying.'

Hannah watched with appalled fascination as Quinn ate her way through seared tuna with quail's eggs and olives followed by calves' liver on a bed of caramelised onions. He picked at a house salad.

She talked as she ate and her conversation was loud and salacious. If he were less anxious he would have enjoyed the experience more. He was ashamed to admit he found her damned sexy.

'You're wondering,' she said as she filled her glass from a hundred-dollar bottle of Burgundy, 'how come I've got into her pants and you've flunked out.'

'Have you got into her pants?'

'And how. She's one red-hot redhead between the sheets, believe me.'

'I'm not sure that I do. I didn't think Agent Jarvis was sexually interested in women.'

Quinn smirked and waved at a flunky attending at a discreet distance. 'We're ready for dessert, Pierre. I'll have the strawberry millefeuille. Wanna join me, Special Agent?'

'Coffee,' Hannah grunted.

'Great idea. And bring me some of that sweet wine I had last time.'

'The Muenchberg Riesling, madam?'

'Yeah, that sounds like it. Great stuff, Hannah, you should try some.'

'No, thank you.' He itched to tan her plump little backside. He'd give her strawberry millefeuille – she'd have a strawberry-coloured ass by the time he finished with it.

'Suit yourself. Now, where were we? Bonny's sexual preferences, is that right?'

'Yes.'

'Well, I think she *prefers* it all night long from a wild but sensitive lover like me. But I ain't so stupid as not to realise that, right now, she'll fuck anything that moves. Even you.'

Hannah had studied yogic breath control. It was useful in

situations where you had to keep your temper in check. Like this one.

Pierre returned with dessert. Quinn took a mouthful of her pink-iced concoction and carried on.

'So, when you catch up with her, if you wanna verify my credentials just check out her pussy. You'll find it as smooth as a baby's ass.'

'She shaves it?'

'Uh-uh. *I* shave it. Gave it a little trim last night, as a matter of fact. Sweet as a peach on the tongue. And twice as juicy. Just like mine.'

'You're some piece of work, Miss Duncan.' Hannah had a quick flash of what he'd like to do this dirty-mouthed blonde slut. Bend her over with her pants down and lather that creamy confection on her plate up her snatch. And then lick it off – he couldn't deny it.

Her big brown eyes were laughing – it was plain she could read him like a book.

'So, you wanna know where she is?'

'Tell me.'

'There's a guy called Chris Shaw who's set a couple of women up in a house in Baldry. They're friends of Dale's and they got the bug too – you know, for sex. So they've teamed up with Shaw and they offer exclusive services, if you know what I mean.'

Hannah knew exactly, though he wasn't going to say so.

'What's this got to do with Agent Jarvis?'

'She's gone to join them. Says it's the ideal career for a woman in her position.'

'I don't understand.' But he did. Light was dawning even as she replied.

'Face it, Special Agent, your partner's run off to become a hooker.'

FIFTY-ONE

BALDRY, PENNSYLVANIA. 11.25 PM.

For the first time in this whole adventure, Jarvis was scared. It wasn't the chains she wore or the instruments of punishment that surrounded her or even the hooded figure with the whip who barred the door. It was the look in the eyes of the woman who confronted her. The blonde in the black leather basque whose bare breasts quivered with excitement. Judge Stacey Pine.

Bewitched though she was, her nerves pulsing and her abused sex still crying out for more, Jarvis could spot a crazy when she saw one. And this Pine woman fitted the bill. Her grey irises were rimmed with red and she stared at Jarvis's exposed flesh like a wolf about to feed. Jarvis was not entirely comfortable.

Her anxiety was caused by the fetish costume in which she was held captive. But for locked leather cuffs at her wrists, ankles and round her throat, she was entirely naked. The cuffs were linked by chains, from ankle to ankle and wrist to wrist, with the two strands joined by a single vertical length which ran up to her collar. She had laughed when Kate had helped her into the outfit upstairs. It had given her a thrill to look at herself in the mirror tied up like a chainlink parcel.

'You look fabulous,' said Kate. 'Stacey will go insane.'

And that, now Jarvis looked into Pine's swirling madwoman's eyes, was precisely the problem.

'Let me go,' she heard herself say.

'Silence, you little fool!' cried Pine and slapped her across the face.

'Look, I've changed my mind,' said Jarvis, trying to stay calm. This was her own fault, she'd put herself into this situation and now she had to talk her way out. She pointed – with difficulty – to the man with the whip. 'Give him his money back. I'll pay. Just let me out of here.'

Pine smiled. 'The court hears your plea and rejects it out of hand. For your impertinence in raising commercial matters within these proceedings your sentence is increased to twenty lashes.'

'Look, Pine, cut it out. This farce is over. If you don't set me free in ten seconds I'm going to bust you on a string of vice charges so long—'

'Gag her!' Pine shouted and the man with the hood grabbed Jarvis from behind.

There wasn't much she could do, naked and chained as she was. A rubber bung was thrust between her teeth and tied in position with a black cloth. She could breathe but only a strangled gargle issued from her lips.

'String the bitch up,' said Pine and Jarvis heard an ominous *snap!* as of metal locking on metal, followed by the whirr of a motor.

Suddenly her feet were jerked from beneath her and she was sprawling face down on the floor inches from Pine's glistening black leather boots. She felt herself being pulled, back and up, as her feet left the floor. The cuffs bit into her ankles and then she was hanging upside down, twirling slowly in space.

She looked up, along the chain which ran from her throat, and saw that she was attached by her ankles to the cage that hung from the ceiling. She was suspended, chained and gagged – and utterly, utterly helpless.

Fingers explored her displayed flesh.

'Interesting, isn't it?' said Pine to her hooded customer. 'This position has so many intriguing possibilities.'

Jarvis tried to hit out with her arms but succeeded only in setting her body spinning – and providing additional entertainment.

'Would you look at that?' said Pine. 'Her tits look like jelly on a plate.'

Jarvis forced herself to let her limbs hang loose. Her head felt like a ton weight and the loadbearing strain on her ankles was already shooting tendrils of pain down her legs.

Big hands closed on her hanging breasts, lifting and squeezing, then letting them fall back into their unnatural upside-down position. Obviously the sight amused the man. He did it again.

The guy was huge, his body cloaked from head to foot in glistening black leather – apart from the crotch, which was cut away to reveal his cock and balls. Jarvis found herself staring at a distended penis of breathtaking proportions. It was thick and gnarled and wet. And familiar. Few men could possibly have a weapon of this awesome nature. Jarvis now knew with terrible certainty who her second tormentor was. Lovelace.

She looked into the masked face. Only the eyes and mouth were unconcealed. She implored him with her mute gaze – *Have pity – let me go!*

The eyes in the hood were as implacable as shards of ice. But the mouth smiled. He picked up the whip.

'Yes,' said Pine with glee. 'Let the punishment begin!'

Jarvis saw her executioner raise his arm. Then a snake of fire wrapped itself around her body, across her back and stomach, its tail cutting like a blade into the soft flesh of her ass. She screamed in silence into the rubber gag.

The snake bit her again and her whole body spun. She tried to ride the agony and embrace its flesh-searing, bone-jarring assault on her system. A voice from the past sounded in her head. 'In a torture situation, pain is your friend,' that's what some Bureau instructor had once told her. Asshole.

Crack! The whip spoke once more.

Oh God, oh God, how could she have been so stupid as to put herself in this situation?

'Stripe her tits,' that was Pine's voice, followed by a lance of pain across her chest.

'Now do her ass.'

Jesus!

'Whip her on the other cheek. I love a pretty pattern.'

Jarvis stared at the floor beneath her head, at the spots of crimson that had blossomed on the varnished wood. Her blood. For the first time in her life she believed she was going to die.

When she heard the gunshot, she knew it for sure.

She didn't want to wake up because that meant leaving her dream of the beach and the man making love to her on horseback. It also meant waking to the pain. But there was light and a voice and she couldn't block them out any longer.

'Jarvis. Hey, Jarvis. It's Hannah. Speak to me.'

But she couldn't speak. She looked at his bruised and half-shaved face and the hurt in his warm brown eyes. She had no need of dreams now. Not when the man in her dreams was right by her side

FIFTY-TWO

BAHAMAS. OCTOBER 24TH. 3.30 PM.

Hannah checked his fishing line over the stern of the yacht. You didn't hire a boat because of its name but he'd bet generations of tourists had enjoyed a special time aboard the *Rum Punch*. Just like he was doing.

'Hey,' he shouted down into the cabin. 'Fancy a drink?'

'Mineral water,' was the reply.

'Aw, come on, you gotta help me get through this booze. We can't go back to work till it's all drunk. Stone said so.'

'Like hell he did.'

Hannah shrugged and fixed himself a long one in the galley. He snagged a bowl of ice and a Perrier for her and went through into the cabin.

Jarvis was sprawled on the bed, nude. An open book lay face up beside her. She was still on chapter one.

'My brain's not working yet,' she said as she reached for her glass. She winced as she moved. Hannah's eyes followed the shifting of her breasts. The wine-coloured weal that ran across both globes was mesmerising. He gently cupped her left one and watched the nipple harden under his touch.

'Perhaps we'll sail to one of the tourist islands and find some shops,' he said. 'I could buy some paints and you could be my model.'

'You're kidding, right?'

Her skin was satin soft and warm beneath his palm.

'I'd do you in abstract. Carmine on Cream. Magenta Ripple Number Ten. You'd be my inspiration.'

'I suppose you think that's funny.'

'Don't you?'

His hand slid down her body, tenderly skimming her luscious contours.

She sipped her drink.

'What I think is – thank God I don't have a personal relationship with you.'

'Strictly professional, huh?'

'You said it. From the moment we get back to DC.'

He bent his head and kissed her navel, flicking his tongue into the hollow. She squirmed her ass against the sheet.

'Maybe I should have left you in that chain suit,' he said. 'Could have put us on a regular master-slave footing.'

Her thighs shifted apart. He placed his lips below the livid whorl on her belly, just above the hill of her pubis.

'I thought it was Karlsen who unlocked me,' she murmured, opening her legs further.

'Well, she was keen to show she was on the side of the angels. A bit late if you ask me.'

He licked downwards to the shaved and fascinating junction of her pussy. He could feel the heat rising against his cheek.

'Why didn't you kill the fucker who was beating me? You should have plugged that judge bitch too.'

He opened her with a finger, licked the coral-pink interior with the tip of his tongue.

'To be honest, Jarvis, I missed. I'm not much good with guns.'

He pushed the finger deep inside her.

'About as good as you are with computers?'

'Pretty much.'

He added another finger, moved them stickily in and out.

'Hannah, you're hopeless.'

'Right.'

He placed his mouth over her clit and sucked. She came at once.

They lay in silence for a moment. There was the sound of water lapping gently against the hull and her breathing, short and fast.

'How long did Cody say before I got this sex fever under control?'

'A couple of weeks.'

'Oh God.'

He slid up the bed and put his arms round her. Her hand burrowed into his shorts and found his cock. It was big and stiff.

'Don't worry, partner, I'm going to take good care of you.'

'That,' she said as she positioned his dick at the mouth of her cunt, 'is exactly what I'm worried about.'

A Message from the Publisher

Headline Delta is a unique list of erotic fiction, covering many different styles and periods and appealing to a broad readership. As such, we would be most interested to hear from you.

Did you enjoy this book? Did it turn you on – or off? Did you like the story, the characters, the setting? What did you think of the cover presentation? How did this novel compare with others you have read? In short, what's your opinion? If you care to offer it, please write to:

> The Editor
> Headline Delta
> 338 Euston Road
> London NW1 3BH

Or maybe you think you could write a better erotic novel yourself. We are always looking for new authors. If you'd like to try your hand at writing a book for possible inclusion in the Delta list, here are our basic guidelines: we are looking for novels of approximately 75,000 words whose purpose is to inspire the sexual imagination of the reader. The erotic content should not describe illegal sexual activity (pedophilia, for example). The novel should contain sympathetic and interesting characters, pace, atmosphere and an intriguing storyline.

If you would like to have a go, please submit to the Editor a sample of at least 10,000 words, clearly typed in double-lined spacing on one side of the paper only, together with a short outline of the plot. Should you wish your material returned to you, please include a stamped addressed envelope. If we like it sufficiently, we will offer you a contract for publication.